MW00442674

*To Ben /*
*Harvard's best ///*
*More on Jpro !*
*With admiration,*
*Judi*
*2020*

# RICH WHITE TRASH

*Judi Taylor Cantor*

*Rich White Trash* is a book of fiction.

All events are products of the author's imagination, and are used fictitiously, unless noted.

Any resemblance to actual events is coincidental.

© 2019

ISBN (Print Edition): 978-1-54398-467-5

ISBN (eBook Edition): 978-1-54398-468-2

*Cover art by Tony Maples.*

*I am nobody*

*Who are you?*

*Are you nobody, too?*

*-Emily Dickinson*

# TABLE OF CONTENTS

# Introduction

They were a big, insular Texas family. Some people called them the Crazy Eight or the Landry Clan. The former was a play on VF Landry's real name, Krejci. Pronounced "Cray-chee." He used to tell his kids that his co-pilot in the war called him "Captain Crazy."

What few people knew is that it took a lifetime for Colonel Landry to get used to this Americanized name. After a perilous WWII mission into Czechoslovakia, Bill Casey, his commanding officer, said, "No one knows how to pronounce that Commie name anyway. We're changing it to Landry." Krejci meant "tailor" in English, but somehow his superiors confused the translation, thinking that it meant "landowners." The switch to Landry seemed innocuous to them.

There were eight kids—five girls, three boys. Enough, plus Mom and Dad, to fill the front pew at St. Ignatius' Sunday Mass. So many children that their mom would summon most of them as a run-on sentence, "Vicki-Hap-Bits-Jillian-Iris…." and then forget the rest. Five born in six years—from '43-'49, then Mrs. Landry took a break for five years and had three more in six years.

Here's an org chart:

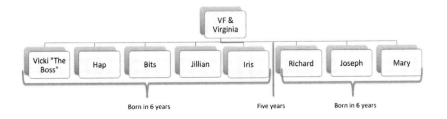

People called them the crazy Landry tribe because there was always something exciting or totally nutty going on at their house: screaming, fighting, yelling, singing, trying the latest dance step with the music blaring, with two of the five beautiful girls tearing each other's hair out because one of them stole either the other's hair rollers or the latest issue of *Seventeen* magazine, or sneaking out of the "girls dorm" to make out with a handsome football star.

Usually it was the mother, Virginia, beating on the kids or verbally abusing them. She was prone to extreme highs and lows in her behavior. She had too many children too soon in her marriage during WWII. "I didn't count 'em," she'd say, "I just had 'em." Her anger management issues before the marriage acerbated all the hormonal changes from the pregnancies and drove her to do things she never acknowledged.

By the time their father would arrive home from his law firm, the kids had calmed down, done their chores, made the dinner, and were ready to succumb to his demands for hearty discourse at the supper table, usually about Texas politics. "Take what you can eat, but eat what you take," he would demand, and then he would take out a large piece of white cardboard covered in his "Top 10" questions for discussion.

This wild little tribe fit snugly in a city that now brags to "Keep Austin Weird."

Today, the area of Austin, Texas where they were raised is chic, selling itself as SoCo, for South of the Colorado. In the go-go years of the 50s and 60s, it was Travis Heights, where families like the Landrys were "rich white trash."

"Rich" because VF was a successful attorney who was able to pay cash for a new home on Alta Vista with its view of both the UT Tower and the Capitol dome of Austin, new cars, and a *ranch*. Unlike a *farm* (which he also owned) where crops are raised, a ranch runs cattle and the owner must have a working knowledge of animal husbandry and veterinary practices.

Spring-fed by Barton Creek and equipped with a veritable zoo of ranch animals, including armadillos, scorpions and deadly snakes, this desirable piece of property was purchased via just one major personal injury case, which eventually put Braniff Airlines out of business. Named Silvercreek Ranch because it had an abandoned silver mine beside the creek, it served as a weekend work camp for the kids. Hauling rocks, battling rattlesnakes, rounding up cattle, and shearing sheep were just a few of the tasks for these part-time cowgirls and cowboys. The teenagers would bop till they dropped at the Friday night "Y", and then trade their bobby sox and loafers for boots come Saturday at six a.m. while the youngest of the Landry tribe stayed in the city with Virginia, their mother.

"White" because, well, they're white.

"Trash" because anyone living south of the Colorado River, separating Austin between north and south, was trash. That's how divided the city was during the 50's through the 70's, and the Landrys lived in south Austin. The south Austin high school, William B. Travis High, was so proud of its southern heritage that their school flag was the confederate flag. Cheerleaders for the school wore uniforms emblazoned with the flag across their chests.

Of course, VF, whose given names were Vincent Frank, didn't think of himself as "trash." He was of the greatest generation, a rags-to-riches marvel who was going places. He wasn't one to brand another person for where they lived.

The Landrys thought they were hot shit. VF had ambition and a good friend in the PR business, so his daughters saw their photo in the *Austin American Statesman* every year or two—going to Girl Scout and the YWCA Teen Camp, glorifying their cheerleading trophies, displaying their first place swim meet ribbons, showing off the two generations of loyal American Legion auxiliary members, and announcing that they were Daughters of the American Revolution through Virginia's genealogy with Roger G. Williams of Rhode Island.

There were secrets buried within the seemingly well-behaved, well-groomed family. Secrets that everyone preferred to keep from the outside world.   Most of the kids went to college, got good jobs, and began raising their families. Oh, no, no, no! I know what you're thinking—*they have an education, they can't be trash.* Well, trash they were. Put their footsteps in the wet cement in their south Austin home. Virginia couldn't be in the Jr. League—that was the sophisticated north Austin, not south Austin. But not just white trash. Rich white trash.

Then mortality hit.

# PART I

CHAPTER ONE:

# *The Mongoose*

## 1994

"I feel like I have a mongoose in my head." VF muttered these words to his favorite daughters as he was wheeled to surgery. He had complained about searing headaches for months—headaches that worried him as no other ailment. In fact, he never had ailments, save a broken toe when he was six. At 75, he did his calisthenics and eye exercises in the morning, drank his coffee black, ate his steak burnt, never smoked, drank sparingly and always rose with an erection.

When the headaches began, he willed them away. For a while. Then they returned with a vengeance, causing him confusion and exhaustion. He broke down and went to see his primary care physician who examined his eyes and sent him to an eye specialist, Dr. Wang. He was misdiagnosed with a retinal disorder. "Dr. Wang's a quack," he announced. "I can see perfectly." He had 20/10 vision, considered to be rare for his age, and didn't even need reading glasses.

After far too many months of muddling through the maze of health care in Austin he consulted a neurologist at Brooke Army Medical Center in San Antonio. "I am so lucky to live in a country that cares for its veterans," he told his family. The neurologist gave him the usual physical tests of touching his nose with one hand while holding out another, holding his arms straight ahead while trying to keep them parallel, etc., and then ordered an MRI.

The tumor was quite remarkable in size and position in the brain.

"Colonel Landry," the neurologist announced, "we need to see what this tumor is. Could be benign. We don't know. We'll get in there, take a sample, test it while you're still under anesthesia, and if we need to remove it, we will. You'll be in good hands, sir."

VF was so dumbstruck he couldn't think of questions to ask the doctor. He had never had surgery. For anything. The only time he had been in a hospital was to pick up his wife after babies were born.

The word "benign" stuck in VF's mind. *Yes, it's benign. Of course it is. There is nothing else it could be.* No one in his family died of cancer. *Damn that word.* His father lived to be 95. His mother died at 101. He was going to beat this beast.

"Colonel," the doctor said, interrupting VF's daydream, "we'll schedule this right away. You'll be prepped for surgery the evening before, so you just need to arrive late afternoon, probably 1600 hours. I'll be your surgeon and I prefer early morning surgery. I'll have you out of the OR by oh-eight-hundred I should think….."

The doctor's rapid-fire monologue stung like shot pellets hitting him in the chest. As he continued, VF heard the words "bed rest" and "recovery" and felt nauseous.

*Dear Lord. This is not what we bargained for. I'm supposed to live forever and that woman I married is supposed to die of a heart attack from all the sugar she eats. She cannot get the land. She'll sell it, or give it away.*

Benign. It's gotta be benign. Not cancer. That six-letter word rolled around and around in his mouth and his mind. Then he put his big boy pants on and walked out of Brooks Medical and into the bright sunshine of another hot-as-hell day in San Antonio.

*    *    *

The evening before his surgery, he lay tucked into the crisp white covers of a military bed, looking so much smaller than the strong, virile man he was. He took to orders like the soldier he was, and although lying in a hospital bed had never been his MO, he assumed the role of patient.

His daughter Iris sat at his bedside, trying a little too hard to be optimistic. The bed faced a long line of tall, sun-drenched windows looking out at the live oaks and livelier squirrels on the grounds of the hospital. It was early June and even at 8 pm the sun was blinding.

"I wonder if squirrels get brain tumors," VF mused.

"Well, if Hap was here he would say, 'naw, they just lose their nuts!'" Iris countered. She got a smile out of her dad. Hap, the oldest son, was the jokester, and probably he would have said that. It helped break the tension in the room.

Then VF reached under the hospital mattress, pulled out $2,000 in crisp hundred dollar bills and handed it to Iris. "I brought this just in case."

Iris was surprised and amused. "Dad, you won't need this," she said, "they'll bill you for anything that's not already covered under your insurance."

"You never know, darlin.'"

"Yes, Dad, I do know," Iris said kindly. "This is how it works. Your expenses are paid for. Anyway, no hospital takes cash anymore. I'll be happy to put this back in your bank account."

"You do what is right."

The surgery began at oh-six hundred the next day. Seven and a half hours later VF's daughters Mary and Iris sat facing the neurosurgeon who had just drilled into their father's skull.

"Your father's tumor was right here," the surgeon said as he pointed to the blurry image on the X-ray. "We got *most* of it. It was larger than predicted."

He grabbed another X-ray, turned on the adjoining light box, and pushed the film into its clasps to compare. "You can see the difference. This is after our work today." The second X-ray had a ghostly spirit about it.

Mary, VF's very favorite daughter, and Iris, the most organized in the family, sat side-by-side in the surgeon's messy office in matching Ann Taylor outfits, sticky pantyhose, and smart pumps. A faulty ceiling fan wafted the warm, humid air around their heads. Although eleven years apart, people mistook them for twins with their thin 5'6" frames, long legs, dark hair, and dark eyes framed with long thick eyelashes. They were the family members closest to the patient, and the only family there at that time. The trauma of VF's sudden illness had sent Virginia, his wife, into a tailspin, and Vicki, the oldest, was by her side back at the ranch to calm her. Vicki lived in Colorado but drove all the way to the outskirts of Austin to help her father. The last thing the family needed was Virginia at the hospital, alternating between rage and inappropriate humor.

Mary, a prosecuting attorney, and Iris strained to see the difference between the fuzzy films. They looked suspiciously at each other when they heard the words "most of it."

"What are you talking about?" Mary demanded. "Why *most*? Why not *all*?" Mary knew from her work with the cancer foundation that in order for someone to be cancer free, the whole tumor must be removed.

"This is a stage four GBM. Glioblastoma multiforme. It's not just one separate tumor. It was entangled in your father's brain. If I were to try to get more of the tumor, I may paralyze him…or worse. At this point of the game, he'll need chemo and radiation, if he chooses."

Mary began taking notes. Iris was stupefied, trying to grasp the acronym GBM.

There was a long pause. The surgeon stood and walked around the desk, folded his arms and lowered his voice, "I'd say he has three to five months. If it were up to me, I'd take a fishing pole and head to the nearest tank."

The sisters were speechless. Our father? ***Three to five months***? How could this be? Here was a man who had the energy of ten people half his age. A handsome, chiseled-featured former college wrestler, VF was mid-seventies and looked 60 tops. He barely had any gray hair. Well, before the surgery. Chemo would definitely change that. Iris felt nauseous. Memories began swirling. She heard "three to five months" over and over and over. She pushed herself to focus.

Mary needed more information.

"How are you going to tell him about this death sentence?" she asked.

"Well, I thought I'd tell your mother first so that she could soften the blow to VF...."

The sisters exchanged glances.

"We don't think that's a good idea. *She's* a bit of a hysteric," Mary noted, downplaying Virginia's neuroses.

"Your father confided in me that, depending on what we found, Virginia may need more medication than him," he said with a slight smile. That opened up some air in the room. Iris and Mary sighed at the same time, knowing what an understatement that was.

Virginia's meltdowns had been a topic among the kids for years. Many of them wondered if she was bipolar. Vicki had been a nurse and came across the diagnosis of dissociative identity disorder. This was an explanation for people who were associated with being possessed of the devil. It fit Virginia's behavior perfectly. She was convinced her mother needed an exorcism.

As children they were terrified of their mother's rages. For the slightest indiscretion, she would tear into a child—usually Hap—with one eye twitching and her body pounding the child into submission. Iris remembered a time her mom told a ten-year-old Hap to find a switch so she could whip him. He brought back a tiny twig.

"Are you stupid or just plain dumb?" she screamed. "Get me a strong stick."

Hap's MO was first to run into his bedroom and put on two pairs of Levi's and then find the most bendable switch imaginable, but neither the jeans nor the bendable switch prevented the terror the children felt when Virginia was mad.

Over the years, Vicki had become her mother's handler. Virginia refused to see a psychiatrist, although she had to know something was wrong with her when she flew into rages and her eye twitched so badly she could hardly see. She even told her girlfriends once that she "would never let anyone put me in a loony bin," when they talked of a mutual friend who went to a sanitarium. Vicki thought that homeopathic remedies she researched and then used on Virginia helped calm her.

After her nursing career, Vicki became a massage therapist and could read Virginia's moods. When she saw it was time for what Virginia called a "rub down," they would make plans for an appointment, using aromatherapy along with the deep tissue massage.

Mary and Iris decided to break the news to Vicki so that she could run interference with Virginia and prepare her to meet with the surgeon.

"Perhaps you should talk with Mom and Dad in the same room," Mary suggested to the neurosurgeon. "Mom is coming to San Antonio in a couple of days. We'll tell her that the surgery went well and that he will need a lot of medical care in the following months. That way at least she'll be prepared to hear about the additional treatments."

The surgeon agreed with them. They listened (Mary took notes again) as he laid out the treatment protocol for the next several months—radiation in Austin, chemo by mouth, pain medication, and then palliative care.

"You'll be able to see him in a couple of hours. He is still in the ICU. Go grab an early dinner and come back."

The daughters pulled themselves off the stiff chairs and headed out to Mary's favorite restaurant, Cappy's, on Broadway.

They were seated at a tile-inlaid table next to the wall of wine in the cool, comfortable restaurant. Both ordered ice cold Chablis. They were somber. "I was too dumbstruck to ask about the side effects of all of this medical care," Iris admitted. "I just kept thinking about the last time I drove out to the ranch to feed the cattle with Dad in the back pasture." Mary held Iris' hand as she went on.

"It was only a few months ago. I had had a sixth sense all day at work that I needed to see Dad, so at five I changed into my jeans, t-shirt and tennis shoes…" Iris never wore boots. She claimed they were too hot.

Nestled in the Texas hill country outside of Austin, defined by its deep Barton Creek spring fed stream, the 700-acre ranch of their childhood had a fortress of a house designed by esteemed architect O'Neil Ford with all the green certified accouterments long before solar panels were fashionably sustainable. It stood at the top of the hill from the entrance to the ranch.

"Dad was in the pick up beside the front cattle guard as I drove up.

"I was so glad to catch him before he started his rounds. I told him I thought he might need some company."

"Yeah, he probably already knew you were coming," Mary said. "He's always had extrasensory perception—especially when we need him." Mary began tearing up.

"Yes, he did. He said 'perfect timing' and he smiled sweetly and opened the door for me to jump in. I parked my car and got out and walked around to the truck and hopped in.

"He was playing his favorite cassette tape—'Moon River'—as we rolled over the berms in the pasture."

Iris was quiet, remembering the moments with her father.

It was near sundown when he stopped the burnt orange Ford truck with the "Silvercreek Ranch" logo on the driver's door, and honked the horn as was his custom.

The horn is never enough for cattle ranchers. Most have unique ways to sing "come-and-get-it." VF's was "Sue....Sue....Sue...weeee.... Sue...Sue... Sue...weeee..." at the top of his lungs.

Together they watched the cattle jostle over, random clicks from the hooves striking the flat limestone rocks in the pasture.

VF and Iris simultaneously opened their doors and jumped from the truck.

Iris grabbed bags of large chunky pellets from the bed. She carefully pulled the strings just so, the way VF showed her when she was a child, and the bags opened cleanly.

She stood and inhaled. The smell of hay mixed with cow dung, the open bags of pellets with their rich aroma of corn, grains, molasses, phosphorous, the baying of the calves, the anxious heifers' breath and saliva on her hand as she offered them more pellets—all of this was comforting. She breathlessly watched a giant ball of orange rest over the hills in the distance as the sky melted into multiple shades of grape, melon, and pumpkin. She felt like a kid again, a welcome breeze in the air and big plans ahead for her future. She would finally be going to New York City to work. Getting her PhD in paleontology together with all of her hard work at UT had paid off. Her dream job in an exciting city was waiting at the American Museum of Natural History.

Iris returned to telling her story to Mary.

"Something wasn't right that afternoon. Dad usually joked with the cattle—you know, he was always naming them and talking to them. 'OK, now Trigger, go easy on those new gals, ya hear?' he would say to the bull. But that day, no jokes. He watched the cattle wistfully. He kept putting his hand to his head and rubbing it.

"I asked if he was OK.

"'A headache. That's all,' he said.

"I thought it odd. He never had a headache. Not even a cold. He never was sick. Ever."

"So true," Mary said. "He is a rock."

"Before we drove back to the ranch house, Dad detoured to Inspiration Point…"

Inspiration Point was VF's favorite spot on the ranch. It was a high cliff overlooking the canyon where the creek burbled below, where they used to hunt fossils and arrowheads. In fact, it was in these creek beds that Iris found her passion. There lay the Buda limestone with its millions of years of Cretaceous era remnants.

"Did you know, Mary, that below Inspiration Point lay my inspiration for a career in paleontology?"

"No."

"You were just a twinkle in Dad's eye at that point. I was ten years old. It was a summer of drought and I was enthralled at finding traces of tetrapods on the dry creek bottom as I searched for fossils. I did this for hours and hours for days. On my knees. Climbing the cliffs. Pocket knife and pail in hand. I found all kinds of fossils and imagined the unusual creatures that had come before us. That was my first romance with paleontology…."

"But back to my last day feeding cattle with Dad… Dad stopped the engine and turned to me and said that he had had, and kept having this strange experience of seeing depositions from his law practice of forty years ago. Forty years ago. Can you imagine? He said he saw them word-for-word as if they were in front of him, while he was driving. And he actually complained about headaches. He said he was about to see a neurologist, finally.

"I didn't know what to think. What in the world could it be? How would your brain start bringing up details that vivid from so long ago?

"Then he said he hit a car in the parking lot at his office complex. 'No big deal, little scratch—but for the life of me I never saw that car' he said. I told him that things like that just happened.

"I said, 'Dad, one minute you think no one is in back of you and the next thing you're backing into them. It's happened to me before.'

"Then he said that the other day he couldn't find his way home after the American Legion meeting. He said he drove down one unfamiliar looking street after another. He didn't know how he finally got back. It took three hours! Mare, can you imagine? Driving what used to be familiar roads and then all of a sudden everything is strange—foreign."

Mary nodded, "A nightmare. A living nightmare."

"Truly, **then** he finally gets home and said Mom was livid. She accused him of having an affair. 'Oh! She went on and on,' he said. He just needed to lie down. It was after midnight!'

"His voice carried a whiff of vulnerability. It really frightened me.

"'Whatever happens,' he said, 'you'll keep this land together? You and the others. Land and family. That's what matters in life.'"

"What did you say?" Mary asked.

"Well, of course, I promised."

Iris always understood how important the land was to her dad. The land more so than almost anything else. It was his mistress. Many times her mother, Virginia, accused her father of affairs, but the only affair he had was with his land. It was in his DNA. His father and his father's father were farmers. His grandfather gave up a life in Prague to farm a piece of hot, dry dirt in Texas. And he succeeded. Both his grandfather and his father, Czech through-and-through, imbued a sense of purpose and awe of the great American farmland in their sons. Land was to be owned, not sold. Good, arable land could always produce, no matter what your circumstances. With that kind of land, there was no poverty. That was their credo.

"I watched him grab that sweaty Stetson and pull his thick black hair back with one hand while placing his hat above it, then saw him wince in pain.

"On the way back to the fortress, he drove around the ranch as if to take it all in before it was all gone. Before he was gone. I didn't realize it then, but I think he knew he was dancing with death.

"He pointed to the remains of that old stone cabin on the rocky plain by the creek. He said, 'I'm told Indians killed everyone in there.' I've heard this story many times and it just becomes more horrid by the telling. That evening's story had the wife captured and enslaved by the Tejas Indians. In a previous story, the children were enslaved."

Mary and Iris laughed. "Dad loves storytelling, doesn't he?"

"Yep. So we continued the journey in the pick up around hundreds of acres to the old silver mine. Dad inched the truck along the rim of the mine as he always does to scare the shit out of us. That enormous, bomb-sized crater always makes me cringe, thinking that the truck might fall in. I asked him if he ever found out if the mine produced any silver of any value."

"And…."

"He said it made a small fortune for one character."

"Yeah, that's what I've heard. But it's full of rattlers now," Mary said.

Iris' tone grew breathless. "Mare, while we were sitting beside the mine, there was this magnificent sunset. Swathes of orange and crimson were painted in the wide-open sky. I felt the essence of the land. It was a fall on your knees experience."

"I know what you mean, Iris. It's priceless…being present at the ranch with nothing between you and the sky but acres and acres of land and critters and color. The air feels clean. It smells sweet."

"Will you keep your land? I know I am not getting any of the ranch," Iris said.

"It's too early to talk about that," Mary said with a whiff of denial. Deep down, though, Mary was her father's daughter—his pet name for her was "Little Buck" because she learned how to hunt deer as a toddler—and she would never part with that which felt part of him.

*   *   *

VF's next ride in a vehicle together with Iris was after the diagnosis, the surgery and the terminal prognosis. It was Iris' turn taking him to radiation. The family, with their oldest (read "the Boss") sister's coaxing, had created a very specific chart of activities to drive VF back and forth to radiation, doctor's appointments, meetings at the American Legion, meetings at his law office, etc. Iris' task was radiation. He was very appreciative and felt as never before that he needed to communicate with his family—especially those he felt he had hurt.

"Want to hear about my dream last night?" VF asked.

"Sure," Iris answered, eyes on the road while driving.

"I walked into the waiting room at the Radiation Center and all the people had their heads screwed on backwards."

"Whew!" Iris laughed. "Getting ready for Halloween?"

"That's not all. Suddenly, they see me. Their eyes pop out and their heads pop up and swirl around."

Iris and VF chuckled together.

"Yeah," she said, "it all seems so absurd, doesn't it?"

VF then stopped the narration and turned serious.

"The big C. I don't have that."

He continued to deny his disease. The big C clearly brought dishonor to this immortal.

"Bad headaches, yes, but I'm a survivor. WE are survivors."

Iris nodded.

"Fred called and asked if I had cancer. Can you believe that? Cancer?"

Fred was his best friend. Fred had been in the Great War with him, one of the members of the Greatest Generation. Fred had fought in the Pacific. VF had written a book about it—*Cabanatuan Japanese Death Camp*.

What was Iris to say? Should she have told him that yes, indeed, he had survived a childhood of poverty, a crappy marriage, the worst possible case of espionage behind the lines in the worst War in history, and crushing career disappointments only to die of one of the most horrible forms of cancer? She and other members of the family just hoped the doctors were wrong. Maybe he could beat this.

So she said, "Yes, we are survivors."

"I need to tell you something, Iris. Remember when you wrote and asked me for $800 for your toddler's surgery?"

They had just pulled into the Austin Radiology parking lot. Iris stopped the engine, unbuckled the seatbelt and turned to face him. That incident was decades ago, when she worked full time, went to college and had two small children and an alcoholic husband. That $800 was real money then. She thought of the desperation she had felt.

"Yes, I remember."

"I've always felt bad about that. I should have given it to you."

She gently touched his hand.

"Oh, Dad, that helped me grow up. I had to get a loan for the first time in my life." Inside, though, she felt a great burden escape. *Now we can put his anger over my shotgun marriage behind me...finally.* VF had disowned her when she got pregnant as a teenager. He had expected great things of her, but her behavior felt like a betrayal to him. He decided that if she wanted to get married so badly then her worthless husband would have to provide for her and the family. He washed his hands of her, her education, and her little family during that time. Despite his lack of help, she got her college degree, a good job, raised her kids, divorced that husband, got her doctorate, and now had a good life with her second husband and third son.

She exhaled as she held back tears, escorted him into the facility and watched as the technician scolded him not to adjust his mask during the radiation.

"What?" VF said, incredulously, "it's my Halloween costume. I'd never do that!"

After the radiation treatment and before VF dozed on the ride back to the ranch, he looked at Iris plaintively. "Iris, you think you could get everyone to the ranch next month? The last Sunday?"

"I can try, Dad. What are you thinking?"

"I'm thinking there's something I want to do before I get too tired and addled to do it."

*   *   *

Three months post op for VF and counting, the last Sunday dinner together with most of the family did not go as planned. It was fall, 1994. VF had invited everyone, as he did monthly, for a feast. Iris had written the invitations and mailed them promptly as she promised she would do.

He was finished with the radiation, and although some of his functions were beginning to fail, he still had the spirited, wry mind they all admired. He knew he couldn't keep up these family dinners much longer, and Virginia would never get the family together.

"These big family gatherings are too haphazard," she confided in Bits. "I'm glad Daddy puts them together because it makes him happy, but they exhaust me. They're really for him. He likes to be the center of attention."

This fall, though, felt like a much more symbolic fall than just a season. It felt as if everything was falling apart—the Democratic Party, his family, his health, and his land, which he could not maintain under these circumstances. Most of the family was there.

Bits lived in Toronto, but made the trip because Virginia begged her to be there to be with her.

Vicki and her two daughters, Jessica and Jennifer, aged twenty and twenty-seven, had driven over from Colorado.

Iris and her ten-year-old son, Thad, were making a last supper appearance before moving to New York to her new job and to join her husband, Miles, who was already there. Iris' oldest son, Will, was away serving in the Navy and her middle son, Jason, was away at college.

Mary, who was noticeably pregnant with her second child, was there with her dentist husband, Todd, and her four-year-old son Luke.

Joseph arrived wearing his collar since he raced from helping say Mass in downtown Austin.

Hap and his wife Karen brought special dishes to devour.

Even Richard came, looking anxious because of his status as a persona non-gratis in his dad's eyes.

And of course there was an empty place setting for Jillian. There would always be an empty place setting for little Jillian.

Everyone saw this as his or her last chance to be together. VF was determined to make this a final grand performance.

The stage was set with Virginia's family's heirloom china and silver in the wide swath of the high-ceiling, sunlit dining room, its twelve-foot maple expandable table covered with Bits' French La Mer blue table linens and napkins.

"I brought these just for you, Mom," Bits said as she pecked her mother's cheek and handed her the package of goods from Canada, tied with a cornflower blue grosgrain ribbon.

"Merci!" Virginia said with a flourish.

Bits was always ingratiating herself to Virginia, and cleverly keeping things from her all at the same time. Their relationship was equally narcissistic.

Maple captains' chairs attended each place setting. The granite floor absorbed the giggles of the two grandchildren jostling for places at the kids' table. Ice melted in tall glasses filled with tea.

Everyone had brought a favorite dish. The table was laden with sausage, venison, turnip greens, tossed salad, cornbread, chili, rice, and raisin pie on the sideboard. VF walked unsteadily down the stairs into the open dining room, carrying his usual "top 10" poster with nine topics. His "I'm Having a No Hair Day" baseball cap covered his bald head.

"Here's Dad's teaching opportunity," Hap said to no one in particular. He whispered to Vicki, "doan cha think he could at least finish the topics and make it a real top 10?"

"That's his little joke," Vicki shot back as she nudged Hap, "you know that!"

VF sat the poster against a tall chair, looking pleased. The poster read in big red letters:

1. Governor Ann Richards' hair

2. W Bush

3. Molly Ivins

4. Should electric chairs be banned?

5. Silver Spoons

6. Fireside Chats

7. Karl Rove

8. What's the matter with the Cowboys?

9. Clinton's stupid Health Care

"Something to chew on." He smiled, thinking how much he loved absurd, crazy Texas and DC politics.

"First thing, kids....everyone...." VF's voice grew strong.

Everyone stopped talking.

"Can I please have you all in the living room now before dinner?"

Sons, daughters, son-in-law and daughter-in-law were joined by the grandchildren and Virginia, and sat on the leather couches and chairs.

"I've been thinking about this," VF began as he removed his hat, "for a long time now. I know it's not the Easter holy days. But I don't know how much longer I will be able to do what I feel I must."

Most of the adults looked puzzled; the grandkids were amused.

There on the coffee table was a large basin with warm water and a stack of hand towels. Beside it was a stack of spiral bound books.

"I've written something for each of you," he said, clearing his throat. "I've been thinking a lot about things we've done together. How we've worked the land together, and celebrated holidays and holy days together, and how we have cheered each other when the candles were blown in one fell swoop. I seem to be a little forgetful lately, so I don't want to forget to tell you how important each of you are to me." He then handed each of his daughters a spiral bound book called "When My Daughters Come Home." He stepped back and coughed, as if to disguise his emotion.

"And Hap, Joe, and Richard—I have something personal for each of you." He then walked to a cabinet and pulled out three large photo albums. "I wanted to write a book for each of you, but time is of the essence so I gathered all the photos of you we had from the time you were infants, and I've written something about each part of your life that I think was significant."

He stopped, put down two of the albums and opened one. "See, Hap," he said, turning to a page in the latter part of the book, "here we are with old man Stoggeheim with that new fence we built." The photo was a black and white with two rugged men wearing hearty gloves and a teenage boy dressed in sleeveless, sweat-soaked t-shirt and jeans standing ramrod straight next to a newly made barbed wire fence. The teenager's arm pushed against one thick cedar post as his bicep spoke of the hard work.

"Remember, we had to blow dynamite holes through the granite in those fields to get the posts to set?" Hap smiled, remembering the pain of the grueling hot days and the way the barbs in the fence wire tore his skin to shreds.

VF handed the album to Hap. He noticed that Hap opened it to the personal letter he had typed, and he noted the expression of sadness on Hap's face. He turned to Richard and forced himself to smile.

"Richard," he said as he opened the album he was about to give, "here's one of my favorite pictures of you." He turned the album to show everyone. A little boy stood in a field with cowboy hat, cowboy vest, jeans, boots, and toy guns strapped to his waist. "Here you are, five years old and king of the ranch. This is the day we bought this ranch and you demanded to wear your cowboy outfit. You said you were gonna kill some snakes and rustle up some cattle." Richard took the album as if it was the first meal after a long fast. He knew whatever was in it was going to be delicious.

VF paused and wiped his eyes. "Gosh, I must have allergies today. Never bothered me before. Joseph, the last is not the least. I've really enjoyed finding this treasure trove of photos of you." He held up the album, again for everyone to see, "Just look at this little tot!" The photo was a close-up of a drooling baby, one tooth visible, finger in his mouth, with a wide, precious smile and a big head of fine chick hair. His other hand offered a rounded arrowhead. "You loved teething on arrowheads. Drove your mother crazy. I'll bet you still have a collection." Joe nodded. Indeed, he did. VF handed him the album, and then stepped back to take command of his family. He sighed.

"Could you remove your shoes and socks…those who have socks… please?" Everyone took off his and her shoes and socks, except Virginia. She gave them all a disgusted look and left the room.

They ignored her behavior because they knew she could always be counted on to be unpredictable.

VF began. "Remember that Jesus washed the feet of his disciples? I am going to wash your feet. I am doing so because this is a sign of my respect for each of you, and…."

As he said this he took the basin and two hand towels, stood first in front of Vicki, and dropped to his knees, unsteadily at first. Vicki grabbed his arm. He gently dabbed the towel into the water, washed her feet, noticing her toe ring, and dried them.

"and…" he continued…"I want each of you to know how much I care for you."

Bits glanced warily at Hap with an all-knowing look. VF rarely verbalized his affection for his children. Saying that he wanted them to know how much he *cared* for them was earth shattering.

Vicki stood up and orchestrated the parade of sisters and brothers, making them move down one at a time to sit in front of their father, so that he would not have to continue to scoot on his knees.

As he washed Joe's feet, VF felt the power of humility in the holy oil and water. Joseph was the only family member who knew that VF was going to do this. Earlier that week, he had taken time off from his parish duties in West, Texas, and had driven VF to St. Martin's in Dripping Springs to collect the blessed water, and the holy oil. The parish priest there knew both of them well. Father David and Joe had studied together at the same seminary.

"Son," VF said as he dried Joe's feet, "I ask forgiveness for any and all wrongs committed against you." Joe touched his father's head, gulping back his emotion.

Each of the Landry clan was speechless as their father washed their feet and repeated his repentance. They understood the symbolism of this brave act. They had grown up Catholic, and each knew that Christ washed the feet of his apostles before He died as a symbol of respect for them and to infer that all must do things in life that may be unpleasant.

The last to get his feet washed was Thad, Iris' five-year-old son. "Granddad?" Thad asked.

"Yes, son?"

"Granddad, where's your crucifix?"

VF smiled. *Always a question from that one.* "Thad, it's on the wall in my bedroom," he answered.

Everyone filed back into the dining room, and soon began talking softly.

"Dad loves pageantry," Vicki whispered to Iris.

"You've got to hand it to him. He is full of surprises," Iris said.

"He still has some clown in him," Vicki said, smiling. "He tweaked my little toe when he was washing my feet—just like he used to do when I was a child."

VF sat at the head of the table. The adults and grandchildren took their respective seats.

Father Joe, the youngest son and a Jesuit priest, stood to offer grace. No matter how old they were they still said grace, and made the sign of the cross before and after.

"In the name of the F...f...f...ather, and of the S..s...son, and of the Holy Spirit." Joe stuttered in front of the family.

"Dear L..l..l...ord, we humbly ask your b..b....b..blessing—for us..... especially for Colonel Landry [he always called his dad Colonel Landry]...on our en...en...endeavors n..n...near and far...and that this food may nourish us...with your eternal grace."

Everyone breathed heavily, eyes closed.

"Ahhh…men"

There was a stillness bathed in sadness, then an eruption of energy as food was requested and passed back-and-forth along the long table.

Hap, the son named for the war hero Hap Arnold, started the conversation in his usual manner. "What do you call a nun who sleepwalks?"

Bits took the bait. "What?"

"A roamin' Catholic."

A collective groan.

"Pass the deer, dear," Hap sang.

Vicki sat at the opposite end of the table next to Virginia. Vicki was the tallest of all the children. At nearly six feet, she took after her Grandfather Krejci. She wore large dark eyes, accented with remarkably full lashes. When she was born, the story goes, she was as "hairy as an ape," her daddy said. Within a year, the hair on her back was gone, but her long black hair, bountiful lashes, and arm hair remained. When she was a teenager, she would exfoliate her lip hair, her arms and legs and even her pubic hair. She said it made her feel "clean and neat."

She helped pass the food, and managed the children's table. "Look, kids, we have a quiz," she said as she motioned to the head of the table.

VF stood and wiped his mouth. He wasn't going to eat much anyway. "Time for Texas goober-nay-torial politics! A very important year this is," he announced, gesturing toward his poster. "I beseech each of you to vote."

Hap couldn't help himself, "And vote often!" he joked.

"Are you asking our opinions about Ann Richards versus Bush's machine led by Karl Rove?" Hap questioned.

"Are the damned Republicans going to drive the agenda for the next hundred years?" VF answered.

Mary bristled a bit, knowing Todd, her Republican husband, might feel uncomfortable. Todd sat rigid and whispered, "They know I'm not a tax and spend liberal, don't they?"

"Here in Texas," VF continued, "we've got a recovering alcoholic with nice hair, a mama's boy, a skinny rich bigot, and a lot of land to pump. What do you think? Are our vets ever going to get their due process?" VF asked.

"Dad, you know Texas is going Republican. You can't fight it," Mary argued, winking at her husband.

"To hell I can't. This is a Democratic family. I have always fought for Democratic values. I will continue to fight for Democratic justice."

Vicki jumped in, "You've gotta love Molly Ivins. Did you see that last piece she wrote about George Bush? She said, 'it appears that he doesn't know much, doesn't do much, and doesn't care much about governing.' She was assuming that if he does become governor, others will do his job."

"That's the problem," Iris said, "others like Karl Rove. Then we'll have a puppet dictatorship in Texas."

VF watched his daughters, then picked up a letter, grabbed his reading glasses from the top of his head, and waved it for everyone to see. Reading glasses were his new accessory—compliments of surgery and radiation. The letterhead was emblazoned with an officious blue banner: United States Senate. And centered below that in all caps: WASHINGTON DC 20510.

The table conversation came to a halt. He bored them with a recitation of "our esteemed Republican Senator Kay Bailey Hutchison's" letter of October 15, which took the party line of support for Senator Dole's plan of healthcare for small business insurance pools, freedom of choice, and market, malpractice and administrative reforms.

"Now do you really think those Republicans can pass this damned healthcare bill?"

Bits yelled at him, "Dad, just call Jake and find out." Jake was Jake Pickle, former UT roommate, friend and long-term Congressman from Texas.

"Awwww….Jake's just a Congressman. It's the Senate I'm worried about."

Everyone began talking at once. Richard, usually a quiet attendee (as to not call attention to his past incarceration, his addiction, or his gun running), spoke up, "Health care reform? Hell, if they'd just think about *prison* reform…"

Mary wanted to re-focus on VF. "Dad, when you get to be Judge, you'll change this gerrymandering nonsense and then we'll have our State back."

"My darlin' girl, the only person in this room who is going to be a judge someday is you," he shot back.

VF thought about the three things in life he wanted before he slipped his mortal coil: *a Texas judgeship, the Coors distributorship, and promotion to Brigadier General in the Air Force.* He briefly frowned as he felt the sorrow that all were unobtainable, and then smiled, telling himself, *crybabies are losers.*

He sat down, as if to pause to catch a wave of energy, and then picked up a leather bound file, cradling it with both large hands, and announced in his booming, court-enhanced voice, "There's one more thing I need to discuss with all of you here."

The room grew silent as all eyes were fixed on the thick portfolio he held with a vise grip.

"Your mother and I have worked on this for the past several weeks and now, together with Trudell, our lawyer in Drippin', now we have our last will and testament. Now kids, when I tell you what we are leaving to you I want you to remember this day. Remember the sweet smell of this family meal, and the light from the beautiful Texas sky. Remember how it felt to drive the dusty road over the cattle guard and to see the cattle out in the field. Recall the sound of the wind and nothing else. Hold these memories close. Hold this land close. Do not let this land go. It is part of all of our hard work. It will pay dividends to you and yours forever."

Then he stood, mustering all of his strength, and watching the anticipation in the eyes of his children and grandchildren, he opened the portfolio, handing seven legal-sized slim packets to Mary. "Please pass to the kids, Mary." As she got up and handed each of her siblings their packet, he continued: "Mother gets all of the assets we hold together. If she chooses to give anything except the land away, that is her choice. She will then have a life estate for Silvercreek Ranch. When she passes, each of you—except Iris—will receive equal shares of this land. DO NOT SELL IT. Keep it in the family. It is valuable land. Now, Iris," he paused and looked at Iris, "I am still working on what you will receive."

VF sat again. "Shall we have some of that good looking raisin pie? Do we have some ice cream to go with it? I'll bet Thad would like some ice cream."

After the dessert and more discussion about politics, Democrats vs those evil Republicans, Iris asked if everyone could talk about VF's care. VF looked at her with resignation. His energy was waning.

"I'm afraid I need to retire to my reading room." He shuffled from the dining table to the back library.

Thad, Iris' youngest, got up to run outside to play. "Hey, kiddo— go grab some rattlesnakes for me, would cha?" Hap called after him, "but remember what I told ya about coral snakes."

"Yeah, Uncle Hap…red and yeller kill a feller," Thad chimed back, mimicking his uncle's accent. He giggled as he ran outside to the broad fieldstone patio with its kids' climbing range and the rock fort inlaid with trilobites. Jennifer, Vicki's older daughter, followed him to supervise.

People began to clear the table and take dishes to the kitchen until Vicki nearly screamed in her unpleasant voice, "Please, everyone, could you just sit down and let's talk?"

The activity ceased. Everyone took their places.

"Yes, your sister Iris has *something to say*," their mother Virginia said, mocking Iris even before she started.

Oh, boy! That tone meant trouble, and everyone knew it. Every time Virginia was about to blow a gasket she took that tone. Iris looked hard at her, trying to detect the twitch in her eye.

"Gosh, Mom," Iris felt her heart racing, "I had hoped we could talk calmly about this."

"Calmly? Just spit it out, Miss Priss." Virginia sat staring angrily.

Even though she had discussed this with Virginia and some of her sisters prior to dinner, Iris had hoped for less vitriol.

"It's important for us to talk about care for Dad. Just last month, I had to ask Dad for his keys because he is beginning to have minor accidents. He can no longer drive—not even his tractor. As his disease progresses, his faculties will fail him. The doctors say he'll have some cognitive issues—memory losses, then motor difficulties that just get worse with time until he is confined to a bed. Right now, that doesn't seem possible but this disease is hateful. You just don't know how it will respond to the various treatments he's getting. He's going to need some *serious* help in the next several months."

There was a collective sigh.

Iris continued calmly, "Hospice professionals could come care for him here, so that he would be home. We'll need a hospital bed. We have to face this. We need to prepare. I have some brochures," Iris finished, watching the denial in everyone's faces, and hearing the neighbor's lamb bleating in the distance in a moment of silence.

As Virginia listened to her daughter she grew more and more impatient. She felt feverish. Finally, she reached the boiling point.

Before Iris knew what was happening, Virginia rocketed up from her seat and knocked the brochures from Iris' hands.

"I don't need strangers in my house. If you want to get me hospice, they'll wash…my…. windows."

"Mom, you can't take care of Dad by yourself."

"I'll have no god dammed strangers in my house," Virginia yelled.

Father Joe gulped. Others sat cemented to their chairs and looked down as if a solution was to be found on the table. Iris quickly glanced at Hap, knowingly. As Hap paid tribute to her look of terror, she soon felt emboldened.

Vicki gently took her mother's arm and brought her back to sit down.

Usually Iris was extremely respectful and never argued. She always tried to let anger wash over and away from her. This situation was different. She wouldn't/couldn't be there to help her beloved father. She had a new job waiting for her half a country away. Miles, her professor husband, had already relocated to Manhattan, reveling in the joy of joining a group of academics at NYU who believed in his new discoveries of artificial intelligence algorithms that defined new theories in social psychological health. She understood he had to leave her and their son to work through VF's disease. She had promised that within six months she would join him. She so wanted to be sure that her dad had the care he needed before she left.

She chose her words carefully.

"Mom, you'll need professional help—to manage his pain, to move him around, this is a serious prognosis—he will grow weaker and unable to care for himself. It will happen pretty fast. He'll be in great pain."

Virginia mocked her as her face became an angry mask. "Oh, he'll be in great *pain. Pain? Pain?*" Her voice grew more sarcastic, higher and louder, "You know what I told him the other night when he fell out of bed trying to get up to pee? I told him 'Death Doth Have Its Sting.' And that's what I have to say. NO HOSPICE IN MY HOUSE."

Iris was steaming—not only at her mother's complete lack of empathy but that she told her dad this weird quote. Where in the world did she get

*Death Doth Have Its Sting*? From her stupid Roger Williams family bible??? And he had fallen out of bed?

"He fell out of bed?" Iris asked.

"Yes. And I left him there. Not man enough to get up and get himself to the pot."

Iris was incredulous. "What? You left him on the floor?"

Virginia's past cruelties—to VF and her siblings--surfaced in Iris' memory. It was time to speak up.

"That's criminal, Mom. How could you say and do such things? How can you deny him comfort and care?" As her anger grew, Iris was shaking. She was about to say something she had felt many times but was so disrespectful she had never articulated it. In the moment, to drive home her point, she yelled, "How can you be SUCH...A...BITCH?"

There was a complete one second silence as everyone froze and then....

Virginia jumped up again and ran towards Iris, knocking a chair out of her way. "Get the HELL out of my house!" She pulled Iris out of her chair by her hair and began throwing her out of the room.

"What are you doing?" Iris asked, frightened as Virginia pushed her harder and harder, Iris turning, stumbling.

"You'll never set foot in this house again. I'll make sure of that. You'll never see your 'precious' father again. Period. You disrespectful little brat."

Iris gained her footing and stood strong at the door, ready for the onslaught. "And YOU will die a lonely old woman."

VF had entered the room by that time, startled by the ruckus. "Dad, don't believe her—I will be back." Her face was burning, her arm outstretched. If ever she could wield a steak knife into her mother's cold, hard heart it would be now.    Instead, she turned, walked out the door, grabbed her son who was playing with his cousin, got into her Lexus and drove over the cattle guard in a cloud of dust back to Austin, pounding the steering wheel and weeping uncontrollably.

VF turned to Virginia. "Honey, what happened?"

"What happened? That little brat thinks she rules the world. Well, she doesn't. That's what happened. Case closed. Asked and answered."

VF could not have felt more helpless. A daughter he loved deeply was wounded, the gathering he hoped would engender love and tenderness had been torn apart, and he was so weak he could hardly stand.

He went to bed that night pondering what to do about the dysfunction in the family. He married Virginia thinking he could change her behavior. Yes, he had had previews of her rages, but never the kind of rages she exhibited after the birth of the first three children.

Fifty years ago, she was so beautiful. That curvaceous body, her long silky black hair, dramatic doe eyes, and full lips! And from the moment they first held hands and kissed he felt that she was the one. She was wildly exciting, sexy, reckless, and creative.

His memory turned to their first sexual encounter. She seemed so experienced for a 17-year old! She was the city girl, he the country bumpkin. He was so surprised when she removed her bra from under her blouse, held it up and giggled. They necked with abandon, him caressing and then kissing her nipples and her nibbling his ear in the back seat of his car.

He controlled his passion. He had just graduated from law school, and he knew if he went further with her this constituted statutory rape. "Hold back, Krejci, hold back," he told himself, barely able to control the growing need within.

*But she was so delicious!* Every moment for the rest of his life he knew he would carry those memories with him. Even if his mind left him befuddled. He just wondered, "What happened to that woman?"

CHAPTER TWO:

# *The Queen of Red Lobster*

## Two months later

*The sun is up, the sky is blue, the day is beautiful and so are you.*

Virginia accompanied the Beatles in her squeaky voice as she drove jauntily to South Austin from the ranch to meet up with her Wild Women friends. Two years ago, she had become the president of the Palette Club, twenty-five seniors who loved to paint Georgia O'Keefe knockoffs while downing Chardonnay. These five members became best friends and met at Virginia's favorite eatery every few months just to gossip and gab. All of them loved hearing of Virginia's exploits with her many children and what she said was her horny husband. She was always clever and made them laugh.

Virginia was dressed in her white linen suit with her black velvet hair in a French twist and red nails to accent the look. She loved looking good when the occasion called for it.

As she neared her destination she quickly turned the dial to the top 1940's hits.

*Kiss me once, then kiss me twice, then kiss me once again....*"Ah, Bing! If only I could."

She was in her element.

*You'll never know how many dreams I've dreamed about you. Or just how empty they all seemed without you. So kiss me once, then kiss me twice. Then kiss me once again...*

Her new gold Caddy pulled up to the front of Red Lobster and parked in the first spot. Still carrying on a conversation with herself, Virginia turned off the engine. "It helps to say your Hail Mary's—Hail Mary full of grace, help me find a parking place! Works every time," she continued.

She slid from the air-cooled buttercream leather seat into the stifling heat, closed the door, and strolled around the car, past the Longhorn plates.

The doors of Red Lobster swung open and the hostess greeted her with an appropriate Texas drawl, "Aw, Miz Landry, the Wild Women are here waitin' for yew."

Virginia giggled, "Aren't you sweet...awwww..I see 'em!" She nearly sprinted to the back table, arms extended, hands waving, where four 60-something friends were waiting.

Her friends turned simultaneously and squealed like teenagers, "Ginny!" "Gin!"

"Vir...gin..yuh!"

"Queen of Red Lobster!"

Virginia laughed heartily, "Gimme sum shugah!" She always fell into an exaggerated southern accent around her girlfriends. She hugged each like a long lost lover.

Max, the waiter, inquired, "Miz Landry, the usual?"

"Piña colada!"

"Coming right up."

Dottie, the most vivacious gossiper, was dressed in blue with her Hermes cobalt blue and gold scarf around her neck, her black hair in a bun.

Her accentuated eyebrows were reminiscent of Joan Collins. Dottie was French, which gave her the upper hand in all conversations. She loved braiding her English with a touch of sophistication. "Mon ami...tell us...Where's VF? What's happening?"

"Well, after his poor performance....first time EVER...." Virginia held up her hand and with an emphatic pout, crooked her little finger for all to see.

"And that was after doing it twice in the morning..."

Everyone laughed uproariously at the nasty anecdote and added feigned shock. "Oh, no!" several ladies added.

"Then he took off."

Dottie was on it. "His shirt?"

Laughter from all.

Max arrived with Virginia's drink. She sipped.

"Ya know, when I was younger, guys I met would ask my name. I'd say 'Virginia.' Then they'd say, 'Ah, Virgin for short, but not for long.'"

Her friends laughed heartily.

"That's a good one," Dottie tittered. "But tell us about VF. What's up?"

Virginia replied a bit too seriously, with hidden anger, "On a cruise... to Australia....he is completing his bucket list."

Patsy, the youngest at 65, couldn't help herself. "Oh....a cruise to down under? I'm not gonna touch that one." She shook her head, grimaced, and placed her palms toward Virginia. Dressed like a cowgirl in stylish boots, jeans, and western shirt, Patsy always kept her sorority charm bracelet dangling from her right wrist with her nails shined natural and cut to the quick. Her thick red hair was gently streaked with grey, and flowed around her pretty freckled, clean face.

They laughed again, but saw that Virginia was not enjoying the moment. "Australia" she deadpanned, "with Happy—the hapless son of mine." The reference to Hap was a favorite saying of Virginia's and her friends laughed nervously. Virginia grimaced momentarily.

"Why the sad face?" Patsy asked.

"Well, VF will be gone soon enough."

PJ, dressed like her name in flowing flowery pants and a comfy flowery blouse, wore her dishwater blonde hair in a ponytail. "So it's true," she said, almost in a whisper.

The Wild Women leaned in, all eyes on Virginia.

"Brain cancer." Virginia took two more sips.

Everyone at once began: "Aw, honey!"

"Terrible."

"What a way to go."

"Didn't Ethel Merman die of a brain tumor?"

"I think it was Susan Hayward."

"Nightmare."

Virginia looked up from her drink. "Nightmare is right. He had the surgery five months ago, then the radiation, and now it's just chemo. Glioblastoma they call it. Everyone holds out hope that with proper diet… or some new miracle drug or procedure… But really, practically, my doctor says a stage 4 brain tumor is an incurable cancer." Her voice trailed off.

There was a beat.

Virginia perked up, "I suppose it's separate beds for us…finally."

Her friends laughed as girlfriends do, the all-knowing kind of laugh about sex, especially since Virginia was so forthcoming about what a "bull in a china shop" VF was with her.

"I'll drink to that!" someone said.

"How're the kids?" PJ asked.

Virginia nearly dropped her drink. "Kids?"

Patsy asked, "Doan cha have seven?"

Immediately, Dottie raised eight fingers.

"I just had 'em, I didn't count 'em," Virginia winked and laughed, trying to add wry humor.

Everyone joined in the giggles, snorts and chortles…and then Virginia couldn't help herself, "I love every one of 'em….Bless their hearts. But they are no longer children. Well, except Jillian."

"You've never talked about Jillian," Betty said.

"Let's not. Sad story. This is supposed to be a fun lunch." Virginia smiled, keeping that secret to herself.

The waiter deposited a large order of appetizers--popcorn shrimp, Cheddar Bay biscuits. Then he refreshed the drinks.

Dottie felt the need to emphasize Virginia's statement about the kids. "Mais oui! Vraiment! They are all ad-ults. What are they doing these days?"

"Well, let's see. Vicki, my oldest, has a massage therapy practice in Colorado. Then Hap thinks he's a musician. I think he never got Viet Nam out of his system. Bits is the only really successful child of mine. She's in Toronto with her fragrance business…"

"Ahhh…oui, oui, oui—she ees very successful," Dottie exclaimed, "but all of your children are successful."

Virginia rolled her eyes.

Betty, the baker, was kind of plump and very Austin-au-naturel stylish, her grey hair pulled back with a hand-decorated clip in a grey seersucker pantsuit. "Mais oui!" she said, smiling.

Virginia laughed, "why yes, that's the name of Bits' brand. Then there's Iris. She grew up too fast. She's in New York. And Richard. He's away at camp. Joe you know is a priest. And then there's little Mary the attorney."

Virginia took another sip of her cocktail. "Good Catholic. Five in six years. Waited a few, then my Joseph and Mary. All my little chicks."

"I think you forgot one," Dottie noted.

"Well, yes—as I said before—*Richard*….and Joseph and Mary."

"And today you're the pretty white hen," Dottie said, smiling.

Virginia's tone turned sour. "Oh, yes, they're just waiting for *the land*. But they'll have to free it from my cold, dead hands."

"Ginny, you HATE that land. Won't you just sell it?" PJ asked.

"Oh, the damned *land*. I know I said I hate it. Once I **loathed** it. The land. The ugly cattle. The horses. The smell. Somehow, I guess I've grown fond of the land. You know, VF used to tell me that the Navajos would take the umbilical cord of an infant and bury it in the earth close to its birthplace so that the child would grow up tethered to the land. He said he felt that way—that he was part of the land."

Virginia grew silent. Her friends stared wide-eyed at her. They had never seen this contemplative side of her.

"Maybe it's growing on me. What would you do?" she finally asked.

"Oh, Ginny, you have so many options," Patsy, an award winning realtor, opined. "That area is going to be the next bedroom community of Austin. The value will just skyrocket. It's not my territory, but I have friends in the business who are beginning to sell ranchettes in the hillcountry for a pretty penny. There's a fortune to be made there in the next twenty years, Ginny."

"I'd give my left foot for all that property, Gin. You have it free and clear, right?" PJ, the former teacher and community newspaper writer, asked.

"Yes. I never thought it was worth that much," Virginia said.

"Oh, you can do so much with it—it has water, part of Barton Springs! You could dam up that creek and create a lovely little lake and we could come out there and boat up and down the lake and sip mimosas all day long!" PJ was daydreaming.

The Wild Women had been to the ranch for little afternoon teas when no one else was around. It had been memorable.

PJ had more ideas. "You could have big barbeques and music out there, Gin. Just think of the headlines: 'The Hillcountry Meets Austin at Silvercreek Country Club.' Create a golf club and offer exclusive rights for a certain level of membership who could attend special musical evenings. Like with Willie Nelson. Doesn't he live nearby?"

"That pothead? Willie Nelson? Who would want to hear him sing?" Virginia was ashamed that Willie Nelson owned nearby property, and could hardly bear to hear his name. That was not her kind of music.

"These are good ideas! Mangeon!" Dottie said.

Virginia was satisfied with the ideas, although uncomfortable thinking of all the responsibility of that land, her grown children, and her husband's demise. The waiter brought lunch orders while the chatter of husbands, kids, grandkids, and holiday plans commenced.

*   *   *

Hap was VF's designated driver to and from his law office and the American Legion meetings, and on several occasions VF had talked about Australia.

"So, you want to see kangaroos and koalas?" Hap mused.

"Well, I'd like to see the outback. I want to get a feel for the land of opals and gold. During the War, I had a sojourn at Cairns Air Base, where MacArthur built up forces to recapture New Guinea. I've always wanted to return."

Hap was intrigued. He never heard VF talk about any of his exploits during the war, and decided this might be a way to heal old wounds.

"I'll go with you," Hap declared, and he enlisted the help of his wife's friend, a travel agent, to make the plans.

While Virginia chatted with her Wild Women, VF was fulfilling the last wish on his bucket list. Virginia refused to travel with him to Australia, and VF would not have normally chosen Hap, since he abhorred smoking and heavy drinking. The idea of traveling with Hap grew on him, though, because he really wanted Hap to forgive him.

A James Dean look-alike, Hap was the oldest son, a Vietnam vet. He had a way with women, a thirst for Jack Daniels, and played a guitar like Willie Nelson.

"Yew look mawvelous." Hap was at the bar of the luxury liner, speaking to an attractive older woman with rhinestone cat glasses. Her hand, large diamond rings around long fingers, rested on Hap's arm. Even though he was happily married, he loved pouring that phrase on any woman he met just to hear her response. It never hurt to sprinkle a little fun on a woman with rhinestone glasses.

"Is that your daddy over there or your sugar daddy?" the cat lady asked, pointing to a man in a *New York Times* baseball cap.

"Oh, the reporter?"

"Is he really a *New York Times* reporter?"

"Why? Doesn't he seem like a *New York Times* reporter?"

"Well, his accent is odd, and he's asking strange questions. He wanted to know if I ever smoked marijuana, and then he asked if I knew what Texas gold was."

Hap cocked his eyebrow and smiled broadly "Well, have you?... Do you?"

The woman just smiled wryly.

Hap continued. "Listen dawlin' I wonder if you've heard this one: On a really hot day, a penguin takes his car to a mechanic. The penguin asks, 'How long will it be?' The mechanic says, 'Just a few minutes.' So the penguin decides to get ice cream across the street. When the penguin gets there, he climbs inside the big freezer door and starts to eat ice cream. Three hours go by and the penguin jumps out of the freezer and races back to the mechanic with ice cream all over his face and stomach and he asks the mechanic, 'So how's my car?' The mechanic comes walkin' out wipin' his hands on a rag and says, 'Looks like you blew a seal.' The penguin says, 'Naw, I was just eatin' ice cream.'"

The older woman pealed over in laughter. Hap gave a little grin and sipped his Jack on the rocks.

"Why don't you sing one of your other songs?" she asked. "It's open mike. I heard you sing that Patsy Cline song *Crazy* last night."

"You do know Willie wrote that?"

"Well, you know how to sing it—don't care who wrote it."

"Just for yew…because…yew look mawvelous." Hap walked to the mike, picked up his guitar, and in his deep, exaggerated Texan accent said, "This is for all of yew Eddie Chiles fans. Eddie and me toured Texas with this little song uh mine:

It was early in the morning, I was

going for my work…

I turned on my AM ra-dee—oh…

I heard a man who was

Fightin' mad

Tell a lot a people where to go…

He said now I love my country

And I don't under-stand why so

Many people put it down….

Now I'm mad, too, Eddie,

I'm with you….

I love A..mare..ica..too"

The room burst into applause and whistles.

"My silver-tongued crooner!" the older lady-turned-groupie yelled.

VF watched the adoration, and then walked out to the open deck, intent on finding the North Star. Hap soon followed. The night sky was expansive, inviting, and a slight sea breeze ruffled their jackets.

Neither Hap or VF wore dinner jackets in real life, but the cruise required so they complied. Hap was attired in a light blue jacket with white lapels, light blue shirt that matched his eyes, dark slacks and shiny dark shoes. VF wore a white jacket, white tuxedo shirt, dark slacks and his Sunday boots. They stood looking out to the great beyond, arms outstretched on the railing.

"Can you believe that flight from Austin to San Fran?" Hap asked. "One female and two male flight attendants. World's going crazy. They used to wear the prettiest little outfits. But no more. Baggy shirts and pants. Nothing tight fitting. I told them they didn't have to dress up for me."

"Hap, I had the strangest dream," VF said, changing the subject.

Hap was not surprised at anything VF said anymore. He chalked it up to the brain tumor. He was quiet.

"Your grandmother and grandfather Krejci were there."

"You mean *dead* granma and granpa Krejci?"

Hap looked away, then lit a despised English *Rothmans* cigarette. His favorite was Winston, but alas none to be acquired on this boat.

VF observed coolly but dreamily and continued. "On the farm. The O-Bar. When I was five I wanted a tricycle so badly. The one in the Moulton hardware store. It was $3.00. They couldn't afford it…."

"They were standing there in the dream, beside the tricycle."

"Did they talk to you?" Hap asked.

"No, they just stood next to the tricycle, looking regal and pleased with themselves. And then it began to rain. That beautiful, hard rain that was about the only thing I liked so much about the farm. Pop. Pop. Pop. Big droplets against that dusty earth. I could feel it. But the tricycle stayed dry. I felt joyous."

Hap inhaled and blew the smoke downwind. He wondered if this was a premonition. This was getting pretty heavy. VF never ever told anyone how he felt. That was a little too squishy. Hap needed to give a little lift to the narration.

"But you got your tricycle, didn't you?"

"I did in that dream. That tricycle was my heart's desire. In my community anyone could work, even the five year olds."

Hap had heard this story before, but he never tired of it. "So you took on a summer job?" Both men smiled at each other as VF continued.

"It was healthy outdoor work if you could survive an aching back and the burning Texas sun. Boy, did that scorching soil burn your bare feet. Just getting your feet into the shade of a cotton stalk was a reward in itself, but then you'd have to move on down the row with additional shade never guaranteed. Big white clouds would drift across the blue sky and play Russian roulette with the sun. You'd bend down for hours and then fall on your knees in that hot dirt for more hours."

"But you got paid, right?" Hap asked.

"You were paid what you were worth. Usually one dollar per hundred pounds of cotton. If the scales read '27 pounds' you earned 27 cents. Sometimes I picked cotton for as low as 50 cents per hundred.

"At the end of the first season, when I was five years old, I had two silver dollars and a fifty-cent piece. We went to Moulton to get my tricycle. I was so excited.

"When we got there, I was crushed to find that the price tag was $3.00. The cotton picking season was over. I couldn't borrow a couple of quarters."

Hap flicked his cigarette into the vast ocean.

"You had a hard life, Dad. Maybe your dream is a reflection of what your parents wanted to do for you—give you your tricycle and some soothing rain." Hap said this while thinking *Wow! They're coming to get him.* He felt it was time to change the subject.

"Dad, I've had at least two women stare at me so far. I don't think it's because they find me attractive, but because they've never seen anyone wearing boots before. Too bad. They were a couple of the younger ones. Somewhere around 65 or so."

Both of them laughed.

"What the heck, at least they could stand up without the help of a cane! When I felt those seniors staring at me for too long, I skipped lunch and ran as fast as I could to the bar to drink my lunch."

VF was determined to make a confession.

"Hap, I just want to square things with you. I want you to know I know that I was pretty much a failure as a father. I was rough on you. And I should have stood up for you when Mom hurt you."

"You knew about Mom?" Hap would rather not revisit those days.

"I probably don't know…everything Mom did to you. Your sisters told me at times, and I should have done something. I thought maybe they exaggerated about the 'torture.' And that business with all your model planes—I just thought maybe you threw some of them away."

"Dad, you did the best you could."

VF was not convinced. He remembered what he wrote Virginia when she had taken one of her long travel vacations to New York, when the children were quite young.

*My Dearest Virginia,*

*The children are fine. They miss you and I've enclosed some of their letters to you.*

*Today Hap gave me a picture of a cowboy on a horse that he drew and then inked. It's very good. He has real talent. I think he could be a professional artist some day.*

*Honey, I don't want you to get upset when I say that I think it's very important to be supportive of Hap and to praise him for his artwork. If we don't make him feel good about himself, he will not be able to be successful. Please think about this and don't get all mad because I've brought it up.*

VF knew that Virginia had rages, for heavens' sakes, he bore the brunt of many. But he never knew the extent of them with the children. By the time he arrived home every day after working in his downtown office, or after days of long travel on the road, the children were always complacent and cooperative.

Side-by-side the two men spoke calmly. The decades of competition and anger subsided. Tonight they were adversaries no longer. Tonight they were father and son and the moments were tender.

"I know I can't change the past, but maybe I can do something for your future. I've got to save the land. When I'm gone, she'll sell it you know."

"Oh, Dad. What will be will be. Isn't that what she always says—*que sera sera*. You're a good lawyer. You'll make it work." Although he did not have the same attraction to the land, Hap felt that the hard times between them were starting to melt away and both of them were beginning to relax.

The next day was Hap's wife's birthday. Hap and VF started the day at 6:30 am doing laundry, and then Hap went to the cruise ship's driving range to hit balls with his golf buddy Doug.

"How about a good laugh?" Hap said to Doug. "Dad and me doing laundry! We worked out in the gym and then decided to do some laundry. Too much soap—we had to rinse the clothes half dozen times. They took forever to dry. A real Abbot and Costello scene. But then the machines are a little different than what I'm used to. You wash in one—spin in another—it's crazy. I needed a drink after that."

"What about the roses for Karen?" Karen was Hap's wife.

"You talking about the love of my life?" Hap felt comfortable around Doug. "I sent a dozen, but should have sent her a truckload. My dad sent my mom some roses, the copycat. He said he wanted her to know he missed her. I doubt that, but it will keep her from screaming at him….I don't know what it is about flowers, they sit there a day or two and then wilt. But it's not really the flowers that women get excited about; it's the mush that goes with it. Well, that's OK because I like the mush."

Doug was surprised. "You like the mush?"

"OK, now, I know you're Crocodile Dundee, and there's no mush in your orbit."

The rest of the trip around and in Australia was uneventful. VF felt as if he got what he wanted. He had some semblance of closure with Hap, he enjoyed seeing the Australian backcountry and talking to a diverse group of people. And he got a great new sign for the ranch. Mission accomplished.

CHAPTER THREE:

# *Ranch. Landry Here.*

## Thanksgiving 1994

"Ranch. Landry here." That's how VF answered the phone: He said that's what he wanted on his tombstone in the family cemetery. It was a joke. Kind of.

While VF's health continued to decline after he returned from Australia, he came to the realization that he did not have enough time or energy to write his life's story and agreed to sit for a video memoir. Mary would ask the questions and he promised to answer truthfully. It was nearly Thanksgiving, but still quite warm at the ranch.

VF had fulfilled his bucket list: his cruise to Australia with Hap, a quick trip to the Rockies with Bits to visit Vicki, a rollicking canoe trip down the Guadalupe River with Fred, a pre-paid funeral just in case he was mortal, and the ranch tied up neatly in a living trust with most of the kids as the remaindermen. Translation: Virginia got the ranch and when she died, the kids were to get equal portions. He thought he had made it clear that she could not sell because of their shares that bound the parties to the land. "Keep it together," he kept telling her.

The O-Bar's 300 acres, a farm located close to Houston, in the deepest Czech community where VF was raised, was to be given to Iris. This was to ameliorate the fact that Iris would not receive any of the acreage of Silvercreek Ranch. Iris had been written out of the family trust when her untimely pregnancy forced her to marry her high school sweetheart. Now, though, VF forgave her indiscretions by making sure she was given the O-Bar. "Iris will never sell the O-Bar," he told his attorney. He was sure of that. He wasn't so sure about his other children and their intended acreage on Silvercreek Ranch. He knew this because he had watched them grow up as weekend warriors on the land. The south Austin city house was their refuge, but the ranch was their religion, or lack thereof.

VF knew instinctively which of his children would and would not hold on to the land, but he hoped that all of them cared as deeply about its monetary value not to discard it.

Earlier in the week, VF thought he had prepared Virginia for taking over the assets. He sat at his massive desk in the library, Virginia facing him. He opened a large, legal-size brown leather portfolio and pulled from it three major files clearly marked. "Virginia, see this file? This is our stock portfolio. It's worth $2 million right now."

Virginia tried to understand what he was talking about, but he had never mentioned a stock portfolio before. She wasn't sure what that meant. The closest she came to complicated financial matters was keeping her bank account in the black. She did not know "net worth."

She nodded, faking comprehension. "And this file marked PENSION AND SOCIAL SECURITY. That's my Texas State pension information and the information about my social security that will benefit you. There are names and addresses and phone number here for you if you need them."

He handed both the files to her. Virginia looked at them, a bit dumbfounded. *He thinks he's dying*, she realized, and now her denial was being challenged.

VF continued as he opened the last file, pointing to the title page, "This third file holds our will. Please don't tamper with this. We've both signed it. It gives equal shares of the ranch to the kids after your life estate. We've already ceded land to Will, Iris' son, because of his veteran status. All the kids except Iris get Silvercreek acreage. She gets the O-Bar after your life estate. Remember?"

Virginia nodded.

VF closed the file, and held out his hand, summoning the other files. Virginia held them close to her chest, and then handed them to him.

"So all the debts are taken care of, everything is paid off, you'll collect on my life insurance policy and there's cash in the savings account—you have the savings books?"

"Yes."

"OK then." He pushed the files back into the portfolio and slid the leather bundle into the top desk drawer. "Here is everything you need." He stood, knocked twice on the desk, walked over to her as if to hug her. She did not get up.

Everything was so well organized. There were no debts. Virginia should have been thrilled. She did not embrace him.

This arrangement about money, land, and valuables always made Virginia uncomfortable. It was beyond her comprehension. *He's going to die,* she realized. *How will I manage without someone to help me with all of this?*

VF didn't understand how confused Virginia was, just that she was more and more distant. He was going to do everything he could to keep the family together—*maybe a video would help.*

\* \* \*

"So, how does this work?" VF asked as he sat in his favorite UT-emblazoned Captain's chair, holding his UT baseball cap.

Mary was off-camera where she could ask the questions so that VF would be the center of attention. Father Joe was the director. VF was in the screened-in porch, with the wide expanse of land in the background as cattle moo-ed in the distance.

"Can I wear my hat?"

"We'll ask you the questions you have in your hand and you just answer as many as you like, any way you like. If the hat feels right, wear it," Mary answered with a smile.

"Like a deposition?" VF asked.

"No…not like a deposition. Natural," Mary replied

"Like a documentary?" he asked, trying to warm up to being on camera. "I saw that movie Forest Gump recently. You think this will be like a box of chocolates?"

The remark had its intended effect. Mary and Joe laughed.

VF put the hat on. "Proceed."

"So we'll ask you about your career in law…your marriage…your children…your advice….your religion…your gardening and ranching…. Can we start with this letter to Mom?"

VF grabbed his glasses, "A letter to Virginia??? Where in the world??? 1938? Ah, between law school semesters…after that wrestling championship."

VF embraced the letter like an old friend, carefully turning the page over.

He pursed his lips and read: "*Let me assure you sweet Virginia, not a moment has passed that I have not thought about you. When your letters arrive, I get them and read while I'm riding. When you come to the O-Bar you may ride Snip and I'll ride Fanny Crocket. Snip is not afraid of cars…*"

VF grew silent ….. "But she was **never** going to ride. She hated horses. Gosh! I was struck by her. Her beauty. Her youth. She was six years younger than I. She wanted to go places, do things. She played the violin! She was going to nursing school. And I felt sorry for her. She had such a screwed up family." He talked about his wife, his first real love, as if she was gone.

"Her father was a successful, functioning alcoholic. An engineer. The director of city planning for Christ sakes! But he divorced her kleptomaniac mother and took off with his secretary…and that sister of hers in the looney bin, and the oldest sister who died under odd circumstances..Gosh, I was worried about her education."

Mary was surprised by the candor of his answer. The surgeon had warned her that a brain tumor changes the patient's behavior. "They say things you thought you'd never hear," he cautioned. She decided to move on.

"Can you tell us what have been the greatest cases in your career?"

"Texas/New Mexico versus Colorado. It was the Rio Grande Compact case. Water rights, together with the fresh water, claimed by Texas/New Mexico were not coming through Colorado because they were being dammed and El Paso was about to dry up. Went to US Supreme Court. My first and only argument in that auspicious room. Won it hands down. Texas/New Mexico been getting water ever since. Set me on the path to specializing in environmental law. Well, that case and the Braniff case, of course." VF smiled and took off his glasses, staring straight into the camera.

"What happened in the Braniff case?"

"Well, that's for the records. It's very complicated."

"We want to know as much as you can remember," Mary said.

"OK then. I was working for a private law firm at that time, specializing in PI."

"Personal injury?" Mary asked.

"Correct. In 1954 Braniff founder Thomas Elmer Braniff died when a flying boat crashed on the shore of Wallace Lake, 15 miles outside of Shreveport, Louisiana, due to icing…"

"What's a flying boat?" Mary interrupted.

"A flying boat is a plane that tries to land in the water, darlin'. May I proceed?"

"Please."

"So… Mr. Braniff was returning from Lake Charles on a hunting expedition with friends from Louisiana. The wings iced up on approach to landing in Shreveport, and the plane lost altitude. One of the wings hit cypress stumps and the plane crashed against the shore. It caught fire and all 12 lives aboard were lost.

"We had to prove there was neglect in that accident. Took several years and many hours of depositions, court fights. We won. That was a big win.

"After that, Braniff's brother took over the management of the airlines, then died of cancer, and then his daughter died in childbirth. This airline and many more were out of business by 1978 due to deregulation. Goes to show you that the Republicans aren't right about dereg."

"Was there another case that stands out?"

"Oh, dear, yes—the Ben Ramsey insurance case."

"Wasn't he Railroad Commissioner?"

VF's voice rose as his admiration showed. "Why yes, darlin', Railroad Commissioner, Lieutenant Governor, Secretary of State, State Senator. But when this case came forward he was Railroad Commissioner and trying to clean up the insurance fraud taking place in the state.

"There was a particular criminal who fleeced farmers, stealing their hard earned money under the guise of selling crop insurance. I worked two years on that case. It was truly satisfying. Turns out the scoundrel buried a lot of the money across the farmlands of east Texas. A couple of Texas Rangers and I saddled up and tracked down some of the cash. We literally dug up suitcases full of cash! Oh, that was a case for the books." VF smiled, remembering the adventure and thrill of finding the buried money.

"You've mentioned that the O-Bar farm probably has treasure hidden on it. Can you give us hints of where you think we'll find it some day?"

VF adjusted himself in his seat, straightening his back and his shoulders. His eyes brightened.

"It goes all the way back to Kanuna Nate Hortus. Kanuna means bull frog in Comanche. Nate was captured by the Comanches…"

"Wait," Mary interrupted. "Mr. Hortus who owns the farm next to the O-Bar?"

"Yes, darlin', Mr. Hortus, now age 90, was captured by the Comanche Indians when he was just six years old. They held on to him for 5 years, then gave him back to his family because they were being forced off their land. They renamed him Kanuna, meaning bull frog, because he would talk to the frogs in the wild.

"It was Nate who saw three men on horseback come up to Rustler's Hill in the middle of the night with a large saddlebag and shovels."

"You mean Rustler's Hill on the O-Bar? On your farm?" Mary asked.

"Yes, dear."

"When was this?"

"This would have been around 1911, before I was born. The week he was captured. He said the Comanches camped close to our farm that week, and he couldn't sleep, so he was walking in the woods. His memory was vivid. He said he could see the three men at the top of the hill, outlined by the moonlight. They tied up their horses, took shovels from the saddles and dug several holes close to an old oak up on that hill. Then they took off their shirts, poured something from the saddlebag into their shirts, tied them and put them individually into the holes."

"So, you think gold is buried up in that hill?" Mary asked.

"Somewhere up there. I've never been able to find it. But there is buried treasure. Hortus is convinced he saw what he saw, and during that time there were several train and bank robberies around Texas. Folks thought it might be Ben Kilpatrick from Butch Cassidy's Wild Bunch. Someone saw him in town. This was about a year before the Sanderson Train Robbery when he was killed trying to rob that train."

Mary made a mental note to talk with Mr. Hortus.

"And what advice do you have for your grandchildren and great grandchildren?"

"Hmmmm…" VF sighed, and breathed heavily, as if the world was listening.

Then, as if speaking to Mary when she was a child he said:

"Words matter. Words make worlds. When I was a child, I felt so alone out there in the middle of nowhere on that farm…no library…no book-stores… I'd tell that little child, 'read, girl, read.' I'd tell her, 'be true to yourself and truthful to others. Do not let others bully you.' I'd say, 'go to church for Christ sakes. Keep your religion and if you can't keep your religion, then be kind and love one another.' I'd say, 'don't go to law school. Being a lawyer is being a liar.' Look, darlin'.…" VF brightened on a wave of new energy and talked directly to his only child who was a lawyer. "Being a banker gives you the license to steal; being a lawyer gives you the vocabulary to lie.

"And then I'd tell all of 'em how to make Mustang grape wine."

VF looked very tired. He slumped in his chair. All was still. Mary and Father Joe glanced at each other. They had the same puzzled reaction to his 'being a lawyer is being a liar' advice.

VF perked up, "Oh! And tell 'em there is still buried treasure on the O-Bar and someday one of you will find it."

"Buried treasure on the O-Bar," Mary repeated," Got it,".

"Yes. Now I think that's all the advice I have today." VF talked slowly and appeared to doze.

"Think we got enough?" Father Joe whispered to Mary.

"It could never be enough, but it appears Dad is done."

"Stick a f-f-f-fork in it!" Father Joe tried to inject humor.

Mary walked over and hugged VF, took the letter he still had in his hand, and helped him to his favorite reclining chair so he could rest.

When Mary arrived home that evening, there was a letter in her mailbox. It was from her dad. It had been sent to all the daughters from his law office.

Mary sat and read:

*Dear Vicki, Bits, Iris and Mary:*

*I hope you never have regrets in life. I hope you each live long, productive, full lives and that you and your children prosper.*

*I have regrets, though. I should have told you more often how much I love each of you. I know that you think Mary is my favorite and you are probably right. I always wanted a lawyer in the family. I also always wanted each of you to marry a Catholic. But we don't always get what we want, as Bits has sung to me many times. I always thought Bits that you got whatever you wanted because you have such a no nonsense way about you and you ASK for what you want. And Vicki, you've always been the Boss. Will you stay that way and keep the family together? Iris, I am proud of you and I forgive you for your divorce, and I know that your first husband was an asshole and that you got married way too early. And I even know how that happened, even if you didn't want to tell me.*

*I love you. I will always love you, in this life and the next.*

*Forever,*
*Dad*

Mary cried uncontrollably, picked up the phone and dialed Iris's number in New York.

"Mare?" Iris thought maybe Mary was in labor—it was nearly midnight. She never called this late, and she was eight months pregnant.

"Did you get the letter?" Mary asked.

"The letter? That sounds ominous.... Have you been crying?" Iris heard sobs.

"Dad wrote us all—all the girls--the most beautiful letter. He's going to die soon, isn't he?"

"Wow! Actually wrote all of us a letter? Was it anything like that book he wrote, 'When My Girls Come Home' and he tells about all the dirtbags we married?" Iris could be sarcastic at times, and it was clear to Mary that even Iris was mad that their father was dying. Mary thought she understood her sister's sarcasm. She knew Iris had seen a lot of ugliness in the family dynamics. She had witnessed her mother's abuse of her brothers and her father, and she had harbored a deep secret about their sister, Jillian, whom Mary never knew.

"Seriously, Iris. He wrote this beautiful letter about how much he loves us. Why are you always so sarcastic?"

"Loves YOU. OK, we all know you're his favorite. Sorry. That horse has been beaten to death..Ooops... Wasn't talking about your horse, Malka, and what Mom did...."

Mary blew her nose and nearly laughed. "Thanks for the gallows humor, Iris. Let's not bring up Mom poisoning Malka."

"I haven't gotten that letter yet. Now I'll be surprised to read it," Iris deadpanned. "Tell me more."

"Joe and I did the video today and when I got home there was this lovely letter."

"Well, Mare, Dad always did like to write us rather than hug us. So, maybe this is his last embrace."

"Good one, Iris…his last embrace. What do you think—you think he'll hang on for a few more months?"

Iris got up from her bed, wrapped her naked self in a blanket and took the phone to the living room with its floor-to-ceiling windows. It was a large room by NY standards in a beaux-arts building overlooking Riverside Park. The darkness outside enhanced the beauty of the New Jersey lights across the Hudson with the George Washington Bridge twinkling in the distance, and the streetlights below. She stood cloaked in the dark looking at those lights, waking up, trying to think of something to comfort her little sister.

"Mare, do you remember—naw…you were too young. Well, let me tell you this story about Dad when we were kids and he had just bought the ranch."

"I was a newborn, you were eleven, so of course I wouldn't remember," Mary interjected.

"And let me make this clear—I'm talking about Silvercreek Ranch, not the O-Bar farm, which Dad bought from Grandpa Krejci. Am I making it clear?"

"As a bell," Mary said.

"Right. Time is so strange. Anyway, Dad bought all the cattle, the pigs, the goats, and horses for each of us except you, of course, and he wanted us to be so thrilled that we'd get to drive from Austin to the ranch in the hillcountry every evening and every weekend and haul rock around the back forty and drive the stupid tractor, and learn how to shoot the damned guns to kill the damned rattlesnakes and how to burn the ticks off and how delighted he was to open those cans of Vienna sausages to eat with crackers for lunch on the banks of the creek…"

"Your point?" Mary was getting impatient.

"Hang in there. Are you in labor yet? How's the family?"

Mary patted her belly as if Iris could see. "All's well. Continue."

"Well, did you ever know that Bits was attacked by a water moccasin?

"What????? NO!!! I've never heard this." Mary was cringing. She sat down on the couch in her media room.

Iris knew she had Mary's attention.

"Yes. Vicki, Bits and I went skinny dippin' in the creek—sort of—with our underwear—it was overflowing its banks because of a huge storm the night before. Remember that huge boulder straight down from Inspiration Point?"

"Yeah."

"Well, Vicki and I were lying on the boulder and she was tickling the fuzz under my arm, kidding me about becoming a woman, and we didn't see the water moccasins. Bits was swimming and all of a sudden she screamed and we jumped up and pulled her out onto the boulder. Then, sure enough we saw the snake swim away—ewww I get chills remembering it slithering in the mucky water—and we realized she was bitten.

"Vicki got on Rebel, Bits' horse, and rode up to the house to get help. Bits became apoplectic—yelling, jumping up and down until she started crying. I kept telling Bits, 'hang in there, hang in there.' Meanwhile her leg started swelling. I wasn't sure if I should take her pocketknife and cut and suck, like we were taught about rattlesnakes, or what.

"Then I remembered something Dad said to Mom when I was really, really sick in the hospital when I was a toddler. He said 'let go, let God.' So, I said that to Bits. I said, 'let go, let God.' She calmed down. I was able to soothe the bite by putting a flat, hot rock I found beside the boulder we were sitting on, on her leg. I think the heat helped pull out the venom. Then Dad arrived in the truck and they took her to the hospital. They got her to the emergency room just in time, the doctor said. After a day or so on anti-venom drugs, she was fine.

"So I say to you, let go, let God…or just breathe."

Mary held the phone tighter. "I can't believe this is happening."

"It's a nightmare. I agree. I think we all thought Mom would die before Dad. She never exercised. Her diet was for shit. She was always so mean."

Iris was finally opening up. Mary needed to hear this.

"I heard Dad could be pretty brutal sometimes, too," Mary said, more as a question than a statement.

"Well, you are the youngest so you didn't see what happened. I think by the time you showed up in their lives, they began to mellow.

"It was awful when Hap and Richard were growing up. I think Dad felt he needed to discipline the boys the same way he was disciplined as a kid. He didn't know better. He would take out the belt for bad grades, for acting out. In fact, our neighbors on Alta Vista wanted to adopt Hap. They thought he was being abused." Iris felt the time had come to set the record straight.

"Well, didn't Mom abuse Hap more than anyone?"

"Oh, what an understatement. She did all kinds of horrible things to him. And to Jillian before her accident. Things I just can't talk about."

"Why can't you talk about them?"

"Because they make me sick to even think about them. And then the memories keep roiling in my mind. I'd like to forget those horrible days when I hid from the anger—the abuse. I literally hid. From the time I was about three or four, I can remember hiding in the dirty clothes basket just to be invisible while the beatings and torture were going on. Let's talk about something else."

"Dad is so afraid we won't stay together as a family," Mary began to sob.

"Did he say that?"

"Yes, after we shot the video he looked at me, straight into my eyes and said, 'how can we keep the family together?'"

Iris thought about the scene and how hard her father always tried to keep the family together, how hard he tried to keep his marriage together. He said the family that prayed together stayed together, so prayer was a ritual. Attending Mass was an ultimatum.

"Well, we probably won't Mare. Why would we? By the way, who is helping with his care right now?"

"Vicki told me she and Richard are going to care for him as it gets worse."

Iris was alarmed. "Richard???? Are you kidding me? He'll steal them blind."

"No, Vicki said Mom is paying Richard to help, thinking he'll stay off the heroin while he's around Dad."

"Well, good luck with that. Is Vicki moving back from Colorado? What about her daughters?"

"Yes, she's going to move in with Mom and Dad. Her partner will stay in Colorado with her daughters. You should talk with her."

"She wrote me. I need to call her. That's going to be hard for her to do— to care for Dad while Mom rants and raves and then while Richard shoots up."

"Hmmmm…I really don't think he'll be shooting up at the ranch."

"Mare, I love you. You are so naïve. Of course he'll be shooting up— both heroin and his guns. Last time I saw Richard before I was summarily kicked off the ranch, he asked for $3,000. He said he needed it for 'the horse.' He was reading a gun magazine at the time….but Vicki will need a partner to help move Dad around as he gets weaker. If they can't have hospice, then Vicki and Richard will have to do."

Iris could hear Mary quietly snoring.

"Mare?" Iris loudly asked.

"Oh, sorry…I'm so…tired."

"When are you due?"

"Around Christmas."

"Please get some sleep and take care of that child within. I love you. G'night."

\* \* \*

Iris made arrangements with Vicki to see VF and try to say goodbye before he died. Vicki gave her explicit instructions for the timing of when their mother Virginia would be gone from the house and when Iris could safely be there with VF.

"Wednesdays from 10 am-2 pm. That is when Mom leaves religiously to meet with her Wild Women friends….. He can barely talk anymore," Vicki said, trying to prepare Iris for what she would see. "We have him in the hospital bed, he can't walk, he's not eating much. And…" she stopped to add emphasis. "We have a hospice nurse every day."

"Really? A hospice nurse? How did that miracle happen?"

"Well, Mom finally was convinced because of Dad's frailty that he needed a nurse for palliative care. We just kept the word 'hospice' out of the title."

Iris was pleasantly surprised, visualizing her dad being appropriately cared for.

"Do you think he'll recognize me?"

"He will," Vicki was sure of that. As if to emphasize that his mind was still clear, but that time was of the essence, she said, "It's critical that you come **now**. A couple of days ago he whispered that he saw all these people behind me as I was massaging his face. He told me their names." Her voice dropped to a near whisper, "Iris, they are people who have all died."

"I'll be there Wednesday at noon."

Iris bought a direct flight from JFK to Austin Bergstrom Airport. She had recorded her last letter to play for him because she knew she probably could not read it aloud. When strong emotions welled up inside her, she could not hold back the tears. She had always been this way. As a child, she imagined being a movie star would be so easy for her. The director would just shout "cry," she would think of any mildly sad story, and the tears would flow. On the day she would say goodbye to her father she wanted to be strong for him, and she wanted him to hear her message. If she was saying it, she would surely choke and not finish.

Wednesday morning December 7 the flight arrived on time. 10:59 am. She had no luggage. It was a same day round trip flight. She would be back in NY by midnight, only losing a day of work. She raced directly to the Gold Members board at the Hertz rental station, noted her stall number, inspected her rental car, and pushed the ignition button.

As she drove from the airport she marveled that what was once the Air Force Officer's Club was now a Hilton Hotel. Bergstrom AFB. VF's old stomping grounds. The family went to brunch there on Sundays on a monthly basis. Colonel Landry loved showing off his family as he and his buddies re-told old war stories. The kids enjoyed the array of food, the respect they and their father were shown, and the special formality of the club. Remembering those times helped her shake off the anticipation of confronting Virginia. She turned on the radio and listened to her favorite PBS station, KUT. Austin music accompanied the forty-five-minute trip.

Vicki was ready for her when she arrived at the ranch. No other cars were there. "You're safe for another hour," Vicki said. Iris hugged and kissed her sister.

"Thank you."

They walked to the back bedroom, Iris handed Vicki the cassette tape to play. It had been taped at a studio and under dubbed with "Moon River" as background music.

VF was dozing. An IV drip was in one arm, various sponges, ice water, tissues and lotions beside him. As Iris approached the bed, he opened his eyes, but couldn't speak. He was so shrunken from his starvation, his skin so terribly irradiated. He rubbed his head, then pulled on his left hand which lay useless by his side. Iris felt his scalp—it was rough and radiation-burned. She took lotion from the bed stand and gently rubbed his head. Then she changed his pillowcase and sat close to him, holding his "good" hand. As the tape played, she looked closely at his hands with their long, unlined fingers, perfectly manicured nails and marveled that she had never noticed how magnificently sculpted his hands were.

"Daddy," the tape said, "I love you. I am so sorry I have not been with you physically these past weeks, but I have been with you in my heart and will always be with you. You are my all. Look what a wonderful life you have had. You went to Texas' finest law school. You survived World War II. You commanded the Texas American Legion. You've achieved your greatest dream—to have *this land and the O-Bar*. You have beautiful, strong children and grandchildren, and loving friends.

"You will be carried on eagle's wings to see your mother. Will you tell her hello from me? I love you, Daddy."

Iris cried softly as VF continued to squeeze her hand at certain words— "the land" "your mother" "I love you."

VF then fell into a deep slumber.

Iris kissed her father. She stood and savored the privilege of being with him for several minutes. Then she tiptoed out of the bedroom, gently closing the door. She and Vicki talked quietly about his care. Vicki had, after all, convinced Virginia they had to have a nurse. His name was Roman and he came every day to adjust the morphine level. Richard helped with the diapering and bathing, and moving VF from lying to sitting up in the bed.

"God bless you, Vicki," Iris said, as she hugged her sister.

"I don't think it will be more than a week or two." Vicki looked exhausted.

They hugged again, holding each other for a long time as Iris wept.

"Travel safe," Vicki said, tears welling in her eyes.

"Vicki, I will remember this forever. Thank you so much. I'll call tomorrow to let you know I'm safe and sound. We'll talk."

CHAPTER FOUR:

# *See you at Sunset, Roommate*

## December 23, 1994

Friday, December 23, 1994 was a crystal clear day in Austin, Texas with a mild breeze and sixty-nine degrees. A perfect day for a funeral. VF never thought he really "made it" but you wouldn't know it to see the luminaries lined up at St. Mary's Cathedral in downtown Austin. Some thought VF had held out just long enough so that he could have his funeral in his favorite Catholic church when it was elaborately decorated for Christmas. Kill two birds with one stone. The profusion of poinsettias of all colors filled the deep, illuminated womb of the cathedral—lipstick red at the altar, pink at the entrance, and white in the alcoves that held the remembrance candles.

It was standing room only. People of all ages and walks of life sat in the pews and stood at the back. Velvet aisle toppers indicated dignitaries' seats. The Wild Women sat together, just behind the family. VF's casket was parked at the altar and topped with a cascade of white roses tied with burnt-orange velvet ribbons, symbolizing his devotion to the University of Texas.

Father Joe stood at the pulpit. "All stand. Please feel free to sing as the music moves you. You will find the words to *On Eagle's Wings* in your program."

Mysteriously, Father Joe did not stutter when he was officiating.

Music swelled, paper rustled as people caught up, and the cathedral was alive with voices and incense in the final verse:

*And He will raise you up on eagle's wings*

*Bear you on the breath of dawn*

*Make you to shine like the sun*

*And hold you in the palm of His hand...*

The American Legionnaires, dressed in their respective military uniforms, filed down the middle aisle and were seated at their reserved pews. They were followed by a color guard that marched ceremoniously down the same aisle, parted at the altar, and continued to stand on each side of the casket, staring straight ahead.

As people took their seats, Father Joe began the service. "I, together with my family, are overcome with joy today because we celebrate the life of Colonel Vincent Frank Landry with YOU. We are grateful for your expressions of kindness and your stories about him which many of you shared last night at the wake, and your delicious gifts of food that have nourished us during our sadness...

"Thank you. May God's light shine upon each of you.

"This morning, we will not have a traditional Mass, but we will have a communion of sympathy and coming together to celebrate Colonel VF Landry's life, and to appreciate the gifts he bestowed. After the service, the burial will be at the family cemetery at Silvercreek Ranch. You are invited and welcomed this evening at 5:30 pm to the dining hall for a covered dish dinner with family and friends.

"You, our dear friends, help fill the sudden emptiness we have felt these past few days. Thank you again for sharing your day with us."

The organist began "How Great Thou Art," while the soloist sang.

A pretty Texan whispered to her friend, "This may take a while."

"Didn't you think they were Eye-tal-yun?" her friend asked.

"No, Jewish."

"Even worse!"

The music ended and people shifted in their seats. Father Joe introduced Congressman J. J. "Jake" Pickle, a short, officious though friendly looking politician, dressed in a serious blue serge suit, who walked earnestly up to the lectern above the friends and parishioners.

"You know," Jake began, "it was just today I realized I've done VF a terrible disservice. I've always thought he was a member of the VFW, and now I need to set the record straight for my law school buddy." The audience laughed. "Vince, I stand corrected as I see comrades of yours from the American Legion where you were the Texas Commander-in-Chief. Probably your greatest legacy was the creation of Boys State." Jake went on to explain how VF and he had stayed in touch year after year, VF campaigning for him, writing him consistently about this or that political issue, and always showing up on Memorial Day with his kids to plant flags on vets' graves.

The next speaker was the distinguished tall, thin, handsomely attired Vincent Waggoner Carr, the former Democratic Speaker of the Texas House and Texas Attorney General. This was a man in control. His beautiful thick, wavy hair with a wisp of grey in front, and his suit and shoes said, "I've made it."

"I believe I'm the only non-Longhorn here today…" All smiled, some silently raised their "Hook 'em" fingers, everyone relaxed. His charisma was infectious. "Apologies to all… Like my good friend, we shared a dislike of our first names. But we did love Jesse James, that famous outlaw. In fact, VF had the revolver that shot Jesse and I was very jealous. I remember us talking about which smoking gun was more important. As someone very close to the Warren Commission, I wondered if it was the one that shot JFK or the revolver that assassinated Jesse James….” Speaker Carr continued telling about some of the cases that his office had and VF, an Assistant Attorney General at the time, won for the “Great State of Texas.” People nearly applauded as he left the pulpit.

Father Joe led the assembled in the Prayer of St. Francis, while the organ accompanied. “Please stand.”

> *Lord, make me an instrument of Thy peace;*
>
> *where there is hatred, let me sow love;*
>
> *where there is injury, pardon;*
>
> *where there is doubt, faith;*
>
> *where there is despair, hope;*
>
> *where there is darkness, light;*
>
> *and where there is sadness, joy.*
>
> *O Divine Master,*
>
> *grant that I may not so much seek to be consoled as to console;*
>
> *to be understood, as to understand;*
>
> *to be loved, as to love;*
>
> *for it is in giving that we receive,*
>
> *it is in pardoning that we are pardoned,*
>
> *and it is in dying that we are born to eternal life.*

Virginia did not join in the prayer. She was still in denial. *Why would I pray for someone who has not died?* Various members of the family cried softly as they read the prayer.

Father Joe asked all to sit. He announced the last two speakers—VF’s dearest friends--rancher Verlin Callabasos and lifelong buddy Fred Wiseman.

Verlin was dressed in his Sunday cowboy boots, bolo tie, starched white dress shirt and pressed jeans. Verlin spoke about VF's love of the land, and how he knew VF must be happy in heaven with its magnificent view of the Earth. "I don't know if I'd say that VF was a great rancher. He was a successful rancher. But I wouldn't douse my shorthorns in DDT without slickers and gloves…"

People in the know sighed gently at this suggestion that VF had brought on the brain tumor with his careless behavior.

"He was a man of conviction and ACTION. Years ago, we worked together to save St. Ignatius. When that man had a goal he was on it like ticks on a mule. And he cared deeply for his close and devoted family. They loved each other," Verlin punctuated each word and punched the air.

Betty, one of the Wild Women, gave Dottie an amused look and whispered, "Really? He's never been around **that** family!"

Then Fred Wiseman spoke. He was 6'3" and looked the role of a JAG with close-cropped, parted blonde hair and handsomeness resonant of a 40's movie star, with a sideways smile and crisp blue eyes.

"Whether you talk about VF's serving five great Attorneys General, or being father to seven beautiful kids, or rounding up.."

"Wait," PJ said to Betty "seven kids? What's going on?"

"Shush," Betty murmured, "I'll tell you later."

"…his shorthorns, or making mustang grape jelly, or that terrible potion he called 'wine,' or his writing biographies of heroes, or his great law cases where he saved the Colorado…there's more. Whether you knew about the students at UT Law who loved him so much they gave him a Winchester with all their names engraved on it—whether you knew any of these…"

At this point, Fred's voice faltered. He put aside his notes, wiped his eyes and looked squarely at the assembled.

"What he TRULY was, was a member of a band of brothers. No one knew about his secret mission behind the lines in Czechoslovakia in the Great War, when seven out of nine were killed and Bill Casey made him change his name to 'Landry.'

"Yes. Landry. It had been Krejci, but his commanding officer thought he needed a name that sounded American. Landry fit so well. He was a man of the soil. Born to parents who spoke Czech, and raised on a land grant farm, he became a tough prosecutor, and a no nonsense defender of the environment... more than anything else he was the truest, and the best friend a comrade in arms could count on. He and I grew up in the same small Czech community and we came to UT together. Him in bib overalls because that's all he had. We flipped burgers at Al's on the drag. VF said if we had a job in food service we'd never go hungry!

"We sold bibles in the summers, mainly so that we could steal some long distance time by shimmying up the telephone poles and tapping the lines to call our girlfriends and family."

The assembly laughed.

Fred continued. "We picked cotton on break. We did everything we could to get through college, then graduate school. Then we did all we could to get through the War. He had big dreams. He wanted to marry the most beautiful girl he ever met—Virginia, and raise a family in his Catholic faith, and someday get a nice piece of land. Mission accomplished, my best friend. You're the greatest guy I'll ever know. See you at sundown, Roommate. " Fred saluted.

When Virginia heard her name she looked up and for the first time, her eyes welled with tears. Vicki handed her a tissue.

All was very quiet except for Fred's footsteps that echoed off the oak steps from the lectern to the marble altar where he stopped below the giant crucifix, bowed, and crossed himself, then made his way to his seat.

Father Joe asked all to stand to sing *Amazing Grace*. "The words are in your program. We will sing all three stanzas."

After the first stanza, the pallbearers escorted the coffin to the front of the cathedral, followed by the color guard, then the family, then the Legionnaires.

People who followed out of the church continued singing:

*I have already come;*

*'Tis Grace that brought me safe thus far*

*and Grace will lead me home.*

The State Troopers escorted the hearse and accompanying limos for the family to the Landry cemetery.

The Landry Family Cemetery stood on a hill about a tenth of a mile from the Silvercreek Ranch welcome sign, past the "no trespassing" and "shut the bloody gate" (VF's souvenir from Australia) signs. It was a modest cemetery. An acre fenced with wrought iron, a strong interlocking gate and an old-fashioned molded iron half-circle sign with the Landry name. An ancient, massive oak stood inside the grounds to the right, bringing welcome shade to much of the entire acre, depending on the sun's trajectory. VF and Virginia's dual granite headstone lay grandly in the middle of the graveyard, with ample room for eight children and their spouses and children. A lovely, long grey granite bench sat proudly at the left, nestled in a grove of short cottonwood trees. Manicured boxwoods framed statues of the Virgin Mary, Joseph and baby Jesus in an alcove along the far side of the plot.

The funeral home had set up the green carpet, 100 folding chairs, a speaker system, the lectern, and the carefully carved and draped grave.

Family and friends stood inside the cemetery as the funeral director passed out holy cards with the final prayer, a responsorial hymn. The flag-laden coffin was taken from the hearse by the pallbearers and placed on the transit elevator.

Father Joe walked to the lectern with a rosary laced in one hand. "Please be seated if possible. In the name of the Father, and of the Son, and the Holy Spirit. Amen…."

He paused to gather his strength. He had chosen this version of the 23rd Psalm from the Vatican's psalm book. Everyone began in unison:

*The Lord is my shepherd;*

*there is nothing I shall want.*

*Fresh and green are the pasture*

*Where he gives me repose.*

*Near restful waters he leads me…..*

*Surely goodness and kindness shall follow me*

*All the days of my life.*

*In the Lord's own house shall I dwell*

*For ever and ever.*

All said "Ah….men" as if one voice.

"Please stand," Father Joe said.

Seven soldiers stood at attention and fired three volleys in unison, the 21-gun salute. Taps rang out.

"Damned fire ants," Iris said under her breath. "They're stinging me! It's frickin' December!"

Vicki chimed in, "I told the funeral company to spray for the ants before they put down the covering."

The color guard stood on each side of the coffin, carefully removed the flag, folded it ceremoniously, handed it to Virginia, and saluted. Virginia nodded, and handed it to Vicki.

"If you have a prayer card, please respond where noted," Father Joe asked. The casket was lowered.

Father Joe: "Eternal rest grant unto them, O Lord."

All: "And let perpetual light shine upon them."

Father Joe: "May they rest in peace."

All: "Amen."

Father Joe: "In the name of the Father, and of the Son, and of the Holy Spirit." He took the rosary and placed it on the coffin. He handed a crucifix to Virginia. Family members took handfuls of dirt and tossed them onto the coffin. Richard cried quietly.

People filed out of the cemetery and stood by their cars. "I feel I need to say something," PJ, one of Virginia's Wild Women friends said to Mary. "He was bigger than life." Fred, VF's best friend, remarked, as he overheard her, "It's hard to just let him rest."

"You're Fred, right?" PJ asked.

"Yes."

"Your remembrance of VF was so moving. So you grew up together?"

"Yes, my mother and father were his teachers at our two-room school, Scott's School, in Flatonia, until we both went to high school. My family lived at the school."

"What was it like, growing up in that area?"

"Well, my life was very different than VF's…. My family taught, and my dad was very mechanical. He not only was the smartest person I've ever known, he could fix anything. VF's family farmed for a living. Farming was rough work, and VF was a tough guy. He broke horses, rode his pony to school. He was a skinny guy, but he could really stand up for himself. I remember once we were playing football—very different than today's football. We had no equipment and we played barefoot in the sticker burrs, those thorny burrs so prevalent in the grass in Texas. Anyway, VF was our kicker and he would just ball up his toes and kick that damned ball as hard as he could. Once it was overinflated, and he broke his big toe! He did not let anyone know how much it hurt. He just tied a bandana around his foot and kept playing."

A mysterious lady walked up to Vicki, looking as if she was a model for a senior citizen Lancôme ad.

"Vicki, I know how much you loved your father," the Lancôme lady said.

"Yes, more than everything."

"I loved him too, like a brother. We grew up in the same community. I'm Faye."

"Faye?" Vicki was thrilled. "Aren't you Fred's sister?"

Faye nodded.

"I've heard so much about you. Dad always talked about you. Why have I never met you?"

"Probably because I just had a hard time being around Virginia. It always hurt to know what she did."

Vicki was shocked.

"You mean before his brain tumor? Are you talking about how Mom accused him of sleeping around?"

"I don't know anything about that….. It's about a far more serious secret." Faye was very matter-of-fact.

Vicki took Faye by the arm. "Please don't be so mysterious. Tell me more."

"I live in Dallas. I'd be happy to see you," Faye said. She handed Vicki a personalized, embossed card with her name and phone number.

"OK. I'll call you. It's so good to meet you, finally." Vicki was curious. *A far more serious secret*…hmmm.

Iris asked the family if they could gather together and take a photo outside the cemetery. "It's too bad Mary's having a baby today," Richard said, "she won't be in the picture."

"Mary gave me remarks to make at the dinner reception," Joe said. "She knew the baby was coming about this time. We'll have to have a toast to the new little guy."

"Guy?" Bits asked with an arched eyebrow.

"I'm assuming it's a boy so Mary can name it after VF," Joe answered.

As he jostled for a space among his siblings, Hap noticed the critters crawling all over people's shoes. "Good night, nurse! Look at all the fire ants."

Virginia stood talking with her Wild Women friends, and waited for the limo. "No. No picture for me," she motioned with her hand.

\* \* \*

Both Vicki and Iris had otherworldly experiences of "seeing" their father after his death—either as himself or through reincarnation. When they were children, VF would take everyone who could keep up with him on hikes. "Our family adventures," he called them. Usually they were campouts in pup tents in the Davis mountains, at Big Bend National Park, or hikes in the state parks in the east Texas piney woods. As they hiked he would tell stories of the history of Texas, from the age of dinosaurs to the American Indians.

Often they would find arrowheads. "This one is nearly perfect, just a tiny flaw in the notch here at the bottom. It's flint. See the markings?" He would hold up the five inch sculpted piece of quartz with its scallops along the edge of the pointed arrow as if it was the finest 10-carat diamond. All of the children would gather around, ewwwing and ahhhing and wishing they had found this valuable weapon. "Now, keep looking. You never know when you'll find the perfect one."

He gave all the children an appreciation for the parklands, and especially the hiking trails. His expertise was finding just the right walking stick. It had to be about 4 ½ ft tall and have a notch about 3/4 of the way up on it so a person could hold it just so as she hiked. He would de-nude the walking stick with his pocketknife as they talked in the evening, whittling the bark to make way for a smooth, compliant surface. "This will keep you from having blisters," he would say.

Less than a year after his death, Vicki was living in Colorado, often hiking up Pike's Peak. One beautiful morning hiking alone, she saw a man about 100 feet above her with a sweat-rimmed Stetson and a hiking stick. As she hiked faster, and came within fifty yards of the apparition, he turned to her, took off his hat, bowed his head and smiled. Then he disappeared. She nearly sprinted to where he had stood, and looked around. At her feet stood the most perfect arrowhead. As she told her sisters, "I had chills, and at the same time I felt Dad's calming presence. I picked up the arrowhead and held it, just knowing it was from him, telling me all is well."

At the same time, Iris was hiking alone in Acadia National Park in Maine. It was a beautiful, crisp September morning. Unlike Vicki, she never used a hiking stick. She thought it slowed her down. She was on her favorite hiking trail called Precipice. The hazardous climb up the iron rungs brought her to the top of the small mountain. She sat down, assumed a meditative pose, and felt the ocean breeze. As she gazed across the Atlantic an eagle soared above and then gracefully landed next to her. He was a magnificent creature. "You're beautiful," she told him. He looked at her for a full ten seconds, as if he understood. Iris took his picture. Then he flew a wide circle below her, leaving a feather. She felt comforted.

Later, when Iris returned from her vacation, she had the photo enlarged, framed it tastefully together with the feather and hung it in her home office, a constant reminder of her dad's deep affection for the outdoors. A calming reminder of the great beyond.

# PART II

CHAPTER FIVE:
# El Rancho Diablo

## 1995-1996

"How generous of you, Ginny," Patsy said, using her pet name for Virginia.

Virginia smiled, thinking of how very generous she was. Indeed. Paying for a little déjeuner was nothing.

It was mid-day June 17, 1995 and she and Patsy were sitting at a charming Parisian café sipping café au lait with croissants. The air was thick with French chatter. Bouquets of late springtime flowers blessed every corner of the 1st arrondissement. Virginia had convinced Patsy to accompany her to Paris by paying for first class tickets and accommodations. They were on a mission.

The large box sitting beside Patsy held Dottie, their mutual Wild Woman friend. Or rather Dottie's ashes. Dottie, whom they both loved for her crazy French ways, had died in a car crash in March. Dottie's will instructed Virginia to spread her ashes in the Tuileries Garden, near the Jeu de Paume museum.

Virginia trusted Patsy's judgment and she was glad to share a quiet moment with her. "Ya know, Patsy, I've had time to think about what I want to do at Silvercreek. Lots of things are going to change around the homestead.

I'm gonna auction the horses and Black Angus cattle, unless you want the pick of the litter."

"Oh, I think I'll pass on the Black Angus. I have some suggestions for a better breed. But I'd like to take a look at Thelma, your mare. She's a beauty."

"Sure. When we get back you should take her out for a ride."

Virginia took a deep breath. "I've already sold the damned tractor. It was a mess anyway. I deeded VF's truck to Richard, assuming he gets out of prison soon."

"Ginny, you didn't mention he's in prison." Patsy was surprised.

"Oh, it's some trumped up charge. I really don't understand how he keeps getting himself caught all the time. This time it was for DUI. Two years! Isn't that just a little bit excessive? Last time it was for some kind of trafficking. I don't even know what that means. He tells me he likes the attorney I got him. At the rates I pay he better be helpin' Richard. It's hard to help him when he's cooped up all the time. I send him writing materials, books and magazines. I send him money for his commissary. Helter skelter, it's probably better in there than out here! He gets to read and write."

Patsy laughed nervously, knowing from friends' accounts of the Texas prison system that it was definitely not a vacation in those non-air conditioned cells.

"Now I'm awaiting my request from Drippin's town fathers to re-name the road to the ranch Landry Avenue. I appealed to Governor Ann Richards to come christen the opening of the road when it is re-named. I also bought a custom made golf cart to drive around the ranch."

"That's a lot to do in less than a year," Patsy said, impressed that she had the temerity to contact the governor's office. "Do you know Governor Richards?"

"Oh, she used to be the social studies teacher at Fulmore Junior High, where some of the kids went to school. I met her several times. Once at the school for a disciplinary meeting involving Hap and spitballs, and then other times during Jake Pickle's many campaigns. She's a hot ticket."

Patsy absorbed the information, thinking how mysterious Virginia was.

"You're right, Patsy, I have been busy," Virginia said, "I decided the oldest, Vicki, should leave Colorado and come live in the smaller, redecorated house here at the ranch. I gave her an offer she couldn't refuse. She can have her spa and all."

As Virginia reminisced about all she had accomplished, Patsy re-focused on their final caper before leaving Paris.

"Ginny, I've mapped out the Tuileries and it's a big place. I think we need to find an icon of some sort and leave the ashes there."

"We're gonna spread Dottie's ashes, Patsy. We don't leave the box there."

"No, of course not. I didn't mean that."

"Well, sure you didn't. How about the Arc de Triomphe? I love that monument."

And so it was settled. Stealthily, at five a.m. on June 19, 1995, two older ladies took turns spreading Dottie's ashes around the Arc de Triomphe, then spent the rest of their two-week vacation in sidewalk cafés imbibing bubbly and gossiping.

*  *  *

Ten months later, Virginia smiled and said aloud, "Oh, Dottie! Every time I see this beautiful pen, I think of you and Pair-ee!" She gracefully picked up the slim Mont Blanc pen, and considered what the future held.

She sat at her inlaid teak desk with its cubbies for papers and classically appointed drawers with separators for pens, stationery of various sizes, paperclips, and stamps. *I'm a letter writer and I need my special desk* she had thought when she purchased it, justifying its five-figure price tag.

It was early afternoon on a beautiful March day, 1996. The bluebonnets, the Texas state flower, were abundant this year. A large crystal vase full of the lupines graced her desk. She could look out past the furniture, through the floor to ceiling windows, across to the fields smothered in them, her new herd grazing on golden sorghum within the carpet of wild blue.

It had been a year and a half since she laid VF in his grave.

*Today was a day to bury the past and make plans for the future.* Her friends said she needed a clean slate and she listened. She had just attended a weeklong bereavement session at Cedarbrake, a Catholic retreat center.

"I am closing another chapter of my life," she said coyly to Father O'Keefe and the rest of the participants, as the retreat wrapped up. Ten adults were sitting outside in a circle, offering their gratitude for what they had learned about themselves. She continued, "for the first time in my life my decisions will be entirely my own, with the help of a stronger force that we call God. I will do my best to make my family and friends, both here and in heaven, proud of me for being able to be there for them in time of need." She was saying what she felt people wanted to hear.

"Thank you, Father, and your staff for making everyone feel so special. When my husband died I was thinking only of myself. It was like I had no feelings. I couldn't cry. I just saw the relief for my spouse. Here at Cedarbrake people's stories have brought tears to my eyes, and I feel human again. Now, I can put this part of my life to rest and begin again as a widow until I come to rest someday in the family cemetery at Silvercreek Ranch."

Old Father O'Keefe was her confessor. He had known her since her conversion to Catholicism when she was only nineteen and anxious to marry that handsome attorney, VF. He was unconvinced that she would be anywhere near her family in their time of need. But he had to hand it to her. Her gift of gratitude sounded genuine.

She was determined to do something with a package of letters she had kept for more than fifty years.

However, there was one in particular that she could not part with. The postmark was October 13, 1941, Abilene, Texas. It was written in pencil.

When she saw the swirly handwriting pangs of guilt gnawed at her.

*"Dear Virginia,*

*I received your letter and sure was glad to hear from you and am sure glad you will get me for Thanksgiving. So I will be home for Thanksgiving and yes, we will have a big time for Thanksgiving and Christmas. I have been feeling pretty good, but was a little sick and became sicker but stayed only one day. I don't need any stationery, but need my mother more than anything. And I can't help but worry and get discouraged and anxious. And I want to be home for Halloween and before cold weather. So I wish you would buy me some Halloween candy and put away so I will have it. And I wish you would bring a camera so I can take some pictures. I will let you know if I need anything. And we've sure got a great day today. I miss you, too. Well, I've written all I can think of. So good night and take care of yourself. I hope to hear from you soon.*

*With love,*
*Evelyn*

*P.S. I say a prayer for you all. It's a pretty day."*

Evelyn. Her precious little sister Evie. The letter was written from the Texas State Hospital in Abilene, aka the loony bin. Evie was just 13, five years younger than Virginia. A year earlier she had an epileptic seizure, then another and another until she could not attend school. She was taken to the hospital, examined, tested and told she was untreatable. The doctors suggested the care of the State Hospital since her mother was unequipped to keep her at home and had no resources for a private sanitarium.

Over the next twenty years, Evie endured shock treatments, experimental pharmaceuticals, sexual abuse from her doctor, surgery, teeth extractions, a transfer to the Austin State Hospital and God knows what else.

A hand-coloured photograph accompanied the letter. Virginia remembered the picture. It was taken just days before Evie started first grade. Evie was six, and stood with her arms wrapped around Virginia, smiling with abandon. Her curly blonde hair in ringlets was accented with a satin ribbon, and her million-dollar smile, so loving and tender, was framed with dimples. Virginia held it carefully, looking closely. *She's so beautiful--like a little movie star.* She wore an adorable blue sweater with a velvet collar. She was a carbon copy of Jillian!

Two years after Virginia received that letter, VF and Virginia married. It was the beginning of World War II. Virginia begged to have Evie stay with them.

"Remember what we agreed?" VF asked Virginia. "We agreed that our home was our home, no relatives will ever live with us."

"Yes, Daddy...but," she said, deferring to his judgment. She called him Daddy even before they were married. She fell into a little girl mode with him, perhaps because she felt he had the good sense to be a daddy.

"But what?" he asked.

"Yes, but they are killing her. She now looks like a zombie, with no teeth, her hair shaved, a string bean of a thing. Daddy, when I pick her up for an hour or two every month she just looks at me with those soulful green eyes and says 'I just want to be put in the right place in Austin.' She can't even eat solid food."

Her entreaties fell on deaf ears. "Honey, our lives have enough drama, with the war beginning, and my not knowing where the Air Force will ship me or even if I'll survive..." VF was adamant that their household held enough upheaval without a lunatic living with them. Of course Evie was no lunatic. She was an abused, drugged up epileptic.

Virginia hugged the letter, thinking of the times she would braid Evie's beautiful long, blonde hair when they were children, and how she lulled baby Evie to sleep in their mahogany rocking chair. They were a pair.

"Oh, Evie, Evie, Evie," she said aloud. She did not cry.

She thought about the nights Evie endured the loneliness and sheer terror of being in that horrible place. Now, all these years later, at least she was at peace in the south Austin cemetery with their mother.

Another letter from the package stood out for its distinctive penmanship. Written in blue ink pen with crisp, clear small cursive, it was from her father, dated December 28, 1961. His pet name for her was Gingo.

*"Dear Gingo,*

*I assume your mother left a will and hope you girls will equally share. I recall putting $1500 into remodeling the place shortly before your mother and I broke up. Do you suppose there ought to be any chance of my getting that back when the final settlement is made? Understand, dear, it would be entirely voluntary on the part of you girls as you know I have no claim whatsoever. Just recalled that I am getting older all the time and I don't have as much income...."*

*Of all the gall,* she thought anew. Her mother had died of a brain aneurism and her father never even sent a condolence note. It was he, a city manager and engineer, who had left the family penniless when he divorced her mother, moved to Ohio with his secretary, and remarried.

She wondered why she ever loved her father. True, she had been his favorite. She was so proud of him teaching her to drive when she was twelve. He told her "no one will know you're underage because you look eighteen, and you carry yourself like a lady."

She smiled, thinking of that happy memory. Then she recalled how things at home turned ugly when his alcoholism became apparent, with his risk-taking, his cussing, and with Evie's sickness. He was always working on a scheme. "Big oil," he would boast, "it's going to come through." All the money he earned was gambled away. He was cheating on her mother for years. He never helped the family after the divorce except to bring Virginia to Ohio for visits, which were probably paid for by her stepmother.

He died of colon cancer soon after the letter was written. *Good riddance.*

It was time for her to focus on *this* estate. This land and her inheritance.

She drew up a list in her perfect penmanship with the treasured Mont Blanc pen from Dottie.

1. Meet with attorney to subdivide

2. Art and music lessons

3. Re-do the kitchen

4. Alaska, Hawaii, Yellowstone Park

5. Ranch hand

The jingle of the phone broke her concentration. It was Bits calling from Canada. "Mom! How are you? How's the new herd? I'm coming to Austin next week to see you. Will you be around?"

"Bits! I'm happy to hear your voice." Bits was Virginia's favorite daughter. They resembled each other and bonded like none of the rest of the siblings. If Virginia had had her way, Bits would have been named Virginia, too. The only reason she named her Elizabeth Taylor Landry was because VF had nearly swooned when he saw *National Velvet* starring the young Elizabeth Taylor. When he first held his little infant girl in his arms he said, "Her eyes look violet, and she has the deepest, darkest black hair—like that little Elizabeth Taylor. Let's name her Elizabeth Taylor." Virginia did not protest. She adored movie stars. Elizabeth Taylor Landry sounded regal.

But as soon as Elizabeth was old enough to write her name she stuck to the nickname Bits, which was given to her by Jillian when they were ages three and two, respectively.

Jillian's lisp picked up the Beth in Elizabeth's name and turned it into Bits. Bits enjoyed the abbreviated name. She disliked the formality of the name Elizabeth and felt that Bits was a "jolly good fun name" as her friend Larry always said.

"Well, the Black Angus are gone and the Maine-Anjou/Angus cross-breeds are here. I'll need a wrangler for them. Some of them are ready to drop their babies," Virginia continued.

"Why did you decide to buy more cattle?"

"We've got the grass, and Patsy..."

"One of your Wild Women friends? The cowgirl?"

"Yeah, Patsy says they are the best grassfed cattle alive. Right now, Patsy's ranch hand is helping me out."

That was an understatement. Bits knew that Virginia would not step foot off the paved and caliche ranch roads that crisscrossed the ranch. Virginia was not a ranch gal as she explained years ago to Bits. "There are city girls and country girls, and I will never be a country girl. Neither will you."

"So, will you be in town next week? I have something for you" Bits said.

Thus began Bits' strategy to divide and conquer. Bits was the daughter who always got what she wanted and she wanted the ranch. Ever since VF wrote that "Bits can ride a horse all the way to the barn!" in one of his short stories about his girls, she was convinced she was entitled.

'All the way to the barn' was an extraordinary compliment from VF, who once broke horses on the O-Bar farm. It meant that you could control a FAST horse, you were an expert rider. It was her claim to fame in the Landry family.

She was more than willing to leave her fragrance business in Toronto to prove that she could come home again. She had a plan.

"What in the world could you give me that I don't already have, honey?" Virginia asked.

"Only the finest for you, Mom. It's a surprise."

Virginia smiled proudly that at least one of her chicks loved her enough to come see her, hung up the phone and gazed at the rest of the letters, dated 1938-42. VF's faded love. All his hopes and dreams tied up in those shreds of paper. She divided them: those that could be seen by family and those that could not. She threw away the "could nots" in the trash, never to be found.

The others were bound with the satin ribbon she found in a faded envelope that said "For your 50th: If I was a carpenter, and you were a lady, I would make you a palace." *What a romantic!* Then she placed them in VF's ammo trunk in the basement.

She mysteriously kept one special letter where she thought no one would find it.

*   *   *

A February light rain was falling when Bits drove up to the main house in her rented Mercedes SUV. She honked, cut the engine and grabbed the gigantic box she brought all the way from Canada.

Virginia had had her morning coffee and was in her element.

"Bits! Gimme me sum shugah," she sang as she opened the front door, and escorted Bits into the grand atrium. "What in the world is that? I don't need another car!" They both laughed as Bits put the box on the living room table.

"Mom, welcome to your new life," Bits grinned.

"Coffee?" Virginia offered.

"Nothing stronger?"

"Gin and tonic?"

"That'll do."

Virginia prepared a strong drink for Bits, handed it to her, settled into the large leather couch, and began to open the present.

"It's not my birthday....yet."

"An early birthday present, Mama," Bits smiled.

Once the top was off, Virginia waded through oceans of the finest tissue paper tied with satin ribbons and a beautiful wax seal.

Virginia gasped. It was just the reaction Bits had hoped.

"A full length mink?"

"A *Russian golden sable*," Bits stressed, making a point that this was the grandest of furs. "For Christ sakes, put it on!"

Virginia's long, manicured fingers caressed the folds of the mink. She drew the coat close to her face, loving it. Then she stood and with Bits' help, put it on, twirled, and smiled. "Oh, my, my, my."

"Well, you always wanted a mink."

"This is a perfect size."

"You and I are the same size, so that was easy."

"Oh, Bits! I've never...this is expensive. And really, where can I wear it? It's Texas, after all."

"Didn't you tell me you were going to travel?"

"Well, I guess I can wear it to Alaska."

They both laughed, and Virginia ran to turn down the thermostat so she could wear the fur all day.

As Virginia sat again, she looked closely at Bits.

"What's going on with your nose?" she asked.

"Oh! You noticed. I thought the make up covered it. I'm going to have to have some surgery, I think."

Bits looked so much like Elizabeth Taylor that people would ask for her autograph. But today, her nose was covered with a large moss-like mold of some kind. It was an unfortunate circumstance. "The dermatologist did a biopsy. I have something called lupus profundus. They think they can cut it out, and probably I'll have a nose job at the same time."

Virginia moved closer to Bits and with both hands cradled her face and examined her nose. "Oh, dear, I see that bubble. Is that the disease?"

"Yes, I believe so. It will be OK."

Virginia looked worried. "Do you think they can cure it?"

"Yes, it's nearly 100% curable. AND I'll get a new, slimmer nose."

Bits was always getting something about her changed. She really didn't need a slimmer nose, Virginia thought, but whatever Bits wanted, she got.

"Well, I'm sure you will be happier with that," Virginia said.

It was a red banner day for Bits. She could not have asked for a better outcome. Virginia felt sorry for her, and they spent the rest of the day discussing all the changes that would happen at the ranch—Bits would help Virginia transform the living room into a more modern, less "ranchy" feel.

"Feng shui" Bits explained. "It's the new way to modernize and give this room a harmonious feeling. We'll get rid of the leather furniture and Indian-woven rugs and bring in Roche Bobois white fabric couches and chairs with a new color scheme for the floor rugs and walls. I'll also help you choose the appliances for the new kitchen, and upgrade all the cabinets."

Virginia was thrilled.

Bits did not bore Virginia with her impending tax evasion suit, or the fact that the fur was a present from one of the lovers she was leaving. Her business was on the brink of bankruptcy, and if she could find a buyer, she would sell, move back to the ranch, subdivide her land, start a winery, and live far away from the crowd.

After a long and spirited conversation about more of the interior decoration, Bits brought in an assortment of fruits and cheeses she purchased on her way to the ranch. She also brought a long cylinder and stood it beside the table.

"Mom, I love the ranch. I'd like to move back to the Austin area."

"Really Bits? You would give up your fragrance business and move here? I thought *Mon Ami* was the hottest selling perfume on the market?"

"I could be persuaded," Bits said slyly. "If it were to help you. Anyway, it may be time for someone else to grow that business, and I could diversify."

Virginia did not have a clue what that meant. "What would it take to get you here?"

"Remember after Dad died you gave us all a map of the ranch?"

Virginia nodded, vaguely remembering.

"I did some homework." Bits grabbed the cylinder, popped off the lid, and showed Virginia her handiwork. She had subdivided the land, giving herself the fat of the calf.

As the two schemed into the early evening, Bits begged off dinner because of plans in Austin. She promised to return the next day, and at Virginia's request, meet with Virginia's attorney to discuss land issues.

"You know, you can help interpret for me," Virginia said, not trusting that she would understand John Trudell. Legal matters made her anxious.

They agreed that Bits would pick up Virginia at ten for the 10:30 am appointment.

As promised, the co-conspirators met with Mr. Trudell and discussed partitioning the land.

"I believe you and VF decided which children would share a life estate with you, is that correct?" He directed his questions to Virginia, but Bits answered.

"Mom and I brought this map." Bits unrolled a large plat partition on his desk. It showed six 100-acre plots, with large block letters over each plot, indicating which sibling was to take possession.

The attorney stood, stretched his arms wide to hold the map while Bits and Virginia sat opposite side by side. "This is a moot issue, isn't it Virginia, because you and VF decided on a *life estate* with equal distribution. What this plat partition would do is essentially divide the property now for possible sale." He cocked an eyebrow. "Are you looking to sell?" Now his curiosity was piqued. He had a small law practice in Dripping Springs, but he made a better living as a real estate broker selling ranchettes in this little heaven on earth. This was prime property. The fifteen percent fee he received on the easy-to-sell land transactions far outpaced his attorney's fees for cases that could stretch over years to resolve.

"Oh, if you're looking to sell, I have a buyer ready, willing and able," Mr. Trudell said.

Virginia frowned. This was getting too complicated.

Bits took her hand into both of hers, and with her giant brown eyes turned and looked directly at Mr. Trudell. "What's the going price of an acre these days?"

"It's anywhere from 25 to 100."

"Thousand. Right?"

"Yep."

"So, Mom, if you sold just 50 acres at $50,000 per acre that would be two and a half million dollars. Look at this," she pointed to the area on the plat with a county road easement. "Here's a prime piece, and selling this would not disturb your herd or you—it's way on the other side of the ranch."

"Bits, why would I want to sell anything?"

"Well, Mom, if you were to decide to just give me my piece of land now, I think I could be convinced to come live out there."

"But you're talkin' about sellin'."

"Well, sure, Mom. It's costly to move, build a house…"

Virginia looked at Mr. Trudell. "John, could I do that—give Bits her land now?"

"Miz Landry, you can do anything you want, because you are the sole life estate owner."

"What about the taxes?"

"Any sales under $5.5 million would not be taxed under estate tax law."

"How would I do this?"

"Well, you could draw up deeds for each of your children…"

Bits interrupted, "Everyone except Iris. She got the O-Bar."

Neither Bits or Virginia cared for the O-Bar farm. They both thought it bred ticks and was a sorry excuse for a farm. "That crummy piece of land will never amount to anything," Virginia told Bits. Bits agreed. She called it the Go-Far. As in "go far, far away from it," she would say. Then they would both laugh. They both felt that the money was in the ranch land.

Mr. Trudell paused and looked down at the plat partition. "Each of your *eligible* children…that gives them ½ their portion now, the other ½ to you and you could suggest they sign the deed now rather than wait until you pass away."

Bits nearly jumped for joy. "See, Mom, there's a solution. Very easy. A deed."

"Doesn't that mean they lose ½ their land?" Virginia was confused, but thrilled with this conspiracy.

"In a manner of speaking…but if your lifestyle is suffering and you need the income now, I'm sure they'll understand," Mr. Trudell said.

"Mom, John will draw up the individual deeds and the letters so that everyone understands that you need to be supported now," Bits said convincingly.

"I don't think everyone will go along," Virginia protested, growing tired.

"Let's let Mr. Trudell work his magic and we'll see what happens." Bits then handed the attorney the names and addresses of the sisters and brothers who should receive a certified letter, along with the plat partition.

"So, John, can you 'bibbidi bobbidi boo' this and we'll give you the listing on the first twenty acres?" Bits spoke very fast when she was creating havoc. She extended her hand.

The attorney took her hand and shook vigorously. It served as their secret understanding that he was not charging legal fees, knowing that as their attorney and real estate agent, he would receive fifteen percent on the sale of the land.

"Deal," he grinned.

"How long do you think that will take?" Bits asked.

"To create and send the letters? Miz Landry, are you willing to sign the letters if I have them ready in a couple of weeks?"

"Well, what do I have to lose?" Virginia smiled sadly. Instinctively she knew that once her chicks figured out they would lose half their land by signing it away things would never be the same. It was the beginning of the end of Silvercreek Ranch.

Bits knew it was time for Virginia's massage, and a sip of wine to help her relax. She drove back to the ranch and deposited her at Vicki's.

Vicki's little home was set up like a spa, with soft music, gurgling indoor waterfalls, plush couches, pastels, an atrium full of light and magically attractive acacia and other subtropical trees and plants. Candles glowed in just the right places.

"I'm glad you called ahead," Vicki chided sarcastically when she met them at the door. Bits had not told her she was in town, or that *she* was bringing Virginia by for her weekly appointment.

"What have you two been up to?" Vicki knew that when Bits and Virginia got together, trouble followed. Bits always wanted something and always got her way.

Vicki motioned to her mother. "The room is ready, Mom. Let me get you a glass of ice water."

"And some wine?" Virginia asked.

"After."

Virginia left them to use the restroom, undress, and relax on the warm, comfy massage table.

"We are finding a way to give you your land now, Vicki. We think we've got a solution," Bits said softly.

*Bits—the master message spinner,* Vicki thought.

"Well, the devil's in the details, isn't it?" Vicki asked.

"Yes, and John Trudell is sending you all the information."

Thus began the disassembly of what the neighbors called "El Rancho Diablo." The name came honestly from Virginia's devilish behavior and the evil goings on.

CHAPTER SIX:

# *Please May I Have a Dr. Pepper?*

## A month later, 1996

The sunny pitch perfect March day began for Richard with a bang on his door.

*The parole board again?*

He was into his first month of a two-year parole from his DUI. He had already served nearly a year in several different Texas correctional facilities. Texas was hard on its repeat offenders even when that offender had an expensive attorney, compliments of mamasita Virginia.

Richard unlocked the deadbolts. The letter carrier cheerily handed him a certified letter and a long cardboard cylinder. "Please sign here."

Richard obliged.

Curiously the documents were from attorney John Trudell in Dripping Springs. Something about signing the enclosed deed to take possession of his land at the ranch. Could that be true? He would have his land—all one hundred acres—now? The cylinder held a plat partition. His name was written across the one hundred acres closest to the main house.

This called for celebration!

What to do first—methadone? Eat? Drink a Dr. Pepper? Call his sponsor? Go see the land? All of the above?

He told himself to slow down. He grabbed a handful of chips and a Dr. Pepper, sat at his Chubbie Checker retro dinette set, and re-read the letter.

*Finally.*

*This was real freedom! I'll have a piece of the ranch where I can live carefree, shoot guns anytime I want, grow some weed without prying eyes, and live without the daily condemnation of bible thumping neighbors. I've got to go see it. Feel it. Embrace the freedom!*

But first, he called his sponsor.

"Taco?"

Taco was Thomas A. Comalé. Richard christened him Taco.

"Yeah? This Rich?"

"I really need a hit."

"No you don't."

"I'm finally going to get my piece of the ranch!"

"That's terrific, Rich. You still have the methadone?"

"Yeah."

"Take a small dose. Get some sunshine. Do some gardening."

They both laughed. Taco knew there was no garden at Richard's tiny apartment. Just a 4" x 12" rectangular Japanese garden with sand, a miniature rake, and smooth rocks.

"OK, see you this evening?"

"Same time as always. 8 pm."

"Adios, amigo."

The shower felt good. Hot water—a luxury that went missing while in prison. Washing his thick black hair was a pleasure. He treasured the products he now had access to, and he took his time reveling in the suds and clean water. *Real shampoo, not that jail commissary crap.* He quickly dried off, trimmed his Fu Manchu moustache, slicked back his hair to show the widow's peak that said I'm my father's son, threw on his white t-shirt, Levis, motorcycle boots, and took a dose of methadone.

*This is what I've dreamed of.* Every moment spent at his job as a janitor while in the Del Valle facility and then the Huntsville prison, he thought about having a place at the ranch. His homies, as he called them—Jimbo, Catfish, Rerun—never believed him. Now he would have his own double-wide and when they were finally released they could come out to the ranch and share a cold one. Hang out.

He would plant a real garden, grow some organic weed. Buy an Australian shepherd. He read that Australian shepherds were very smart dogs and loyal companions. He would teach his dog different languages. He'd take his dog for a dip in the cool waters of the creek and be one with the land.

And maybe he'd even hook up with Sharon or Nora, his pen pals from the women's prisons. They promised each other they would celebrate their release together some day. Sharon, the smart and pretty one, would be out in another month. Nora, who always signed her letters *con todo mi cariño y respeto* would be free in another year.

This gave him a new world to look forward to. He needed to feel it, see it, embrace it **now.**

He cradled his helmet, threw in the keys to his bike, opened his safe, pulled out $100, locked it, and closed and locked his front door. The letter and plat partition lay on the Chubbie Checker table.

*       *       *

I-35 was a mess of traffic in Austin. Richard's 1996 Harley Dyna Wide, with heat shields, rear silencer, backrest, saddle box, and spring strut damping valve was his sleek black baby—recently purchased with the final proceeds of a court case adjudicated after he was run over ten years ago by a truck. VF helped him win that case in 1990. His broken leg brought him $85,000 with all medical bills and attorney's fees paid.

Richard's left leg would never be the same, but today he was feeling no pain and the highway was *his*. As traffic opened up so did his baby. Sixty, seventy, eighty….he turned his head to look back. All clear. Ninety. Ninety-five.

The eighteen-wheeler was a half-mile in front of him and slowing down. *What in the world is he slowing down for?* Richard thought he could make out something in the distance in the road—a deer? At this time of the day?

It happened in a split second. He was braking and flying into the H-E-B truck simultaneously. He read the truck's message "Because People Matter." He held on to the handlebars, slammed into the side of the truck, and rolled to the right and down an embankment of wildflowers, over and over, the bike pounding his right arm, the smell of bluebonnets in his head.

The bike was totaled.

EMS arrived at the scene within ten minutes, and pulled an unconscious white male, 40 years old, serious contusions, large laceration on right arm, possibly broken in two places, second degree road burns on his back and right leg, out from under his mangled bike. An IV was administered, as well as oxygen and as much first aid as they could give under the circumstances. The bones in his arm were protruding through the skin.

At the hospital, the admitting nurse opened his wallet and saw his name: Richard Daniel Landry. *I know this guy. He's the Richard Daniel Landry in my high school German class. He was brilliant. And handsome.*

That was before he began his career in the alternative pharmaceutical industry.

She felt someone in the family should be notified. She also needed evidence of his insurance. She looked for more information in the wallet. It was VF Landry's old business card, listing the home number. She dialed it.

"Miz Landry?"

"Yes. Who's calling?" Virginia answered.

"I'm with Brackenridge Hospital. The trauma unit. Is Richard Daniel Landry your son?"

"Oh, good God! What's happened?"

"Can you give me his date of birth?"

"August 15th. What's happened?"

"Well, he's been in an accident on IH35. He's stable, but right now he is being wheeled into radiology for X-rays. Do you have his insurance information?"

Virginia gave her all the relevant information since she paid for his insurance, and then called Vicki immediately.

"That damned motorbike," she said.

"Mom, he's a grown man. Let's find out more about his condition. I'll drive to Austin and be there for him. I have his Power of Attorney."

"Why in the world would *you* have Power of Attorney?" Virginia asked angrily.

"Well, when we were taking care of Dad, we talked about life and death and things like that and he wanted to get his papers in order, so he asked me to be his Power of Attorney."

"Well, that was very prescient of him." She slammed the phone. *Why does everyone have such secrets?* She hated not being in control. After all, she paid his bills, she gave him everything he wanted.

The news of Richard's accident spread throughout the family.

Vicki arrived at the hospital with the Power of Attorney paperwork and spoke with the doc on duty about Richard's condition. He had fractured his arm in two places. The orthopedic surgeon was about to "put him back together again," the ER physician said. "It will take a couple of hours, several titanium pins, and a good stapler."

Vicki was not amused.

The day was turning to night, and she needed a drink and some dinner. The Spanish Village offered both. It was the Mexican restaurant the family had frequented on special feast days, and a short stroll from the hospital.

When she walked up the cool, smooth familiar steps into the bougainvillea-covered courtyard she felt the fond old memories return. Her favorite waiter, Jesse, still there after all these years, seated her at a private table where she could see the brightly colored frescoes of Latin lovers and hear the mariachi band in the distance.

She remembered Orlando, her first lover. They met here, at the Spanish Village. She had taken a break from her studies at UT, and had a craving for "The Village" as she called her favorite Mexican restaurant.

Orlando was also a student at the University of Texas in those days.

It was a very long time ago.

He saw a gorgeous, statuesque young lady alone at a table and asked to sit with her.

"My name's Orlando…or Lando for short."

"Lando…hmmmm…I like that name," she said. She extended her hand to welcome him to her table. The name did have a dreamy sound.

He was taken by her posture, he said.

"My posture?" Vicki asked, laughing.

"Yes, in my country, the way a lady sits is a sign of her breeding."

"Where is your country?"

"I am from Argentina."

"Really? You came to Austin from Argentina? What's your major?"

"Engineering. My family are all engineers."

Vicki was smitten. He was as tall as she and oh so handsome. His close-cropped blonde hair was parted on the side, and his blue eyes twinkled with amusement. Oh! She delighted in his beautiful Spanish accent. They talked all evening about families, religion—he was Catholic, too—their studies, and their dreams.

That night began a year-long courtship. The most delicious time of her life. The chemistry between them made her crazy. All he had to do was to look at her and she felt an electrical current throughout her body.

He took her to ballet, symphony concerts, European movies, and jazz clubs. He showed her how to smoke "like a foreigner." And he made love like a Latin lover—slow, romantic, and skillful. She, in turn, lovingly gave him Swedish massage and then gently stroked his back with her long nails as a prelude to their foreplay. She would trace circles within the smooth sway of his lower back, and outline the large valentine birthmark on his right cheek with her tongue.

She looked at the kaleidoscope of mosaics around her and thought of the first time she made love with him. It was Barton Springs. He craved the icy blue water and she laughed at his crazy dives off the high diving board. He would stand far above her on the board, then slowly—all show—walk to the end and while balanced on one foot, turn and pause, looking heavenward. His long arms would stretch above his head as if in prayer. Then he would breathe deeply and back dive into the freezing water. He would swim to her at the deepest end and gather her up in his arms as she squealed. They would kiss and fall helplessly to the bottom of the pool, then jump up together to get their breath.

On that first day at the Springs, after hours of diving and swimming, they both carried their blanket and picnic basket to a secluded area of the park, laid down the blanket and each other under an old, gnarled oak.

Vicki looked lovingly into his eyes. "What do you see?" she asked.

"I see the most beautiful woman in the world."

Vicki tickled his arm, then his hand, stroking it gently, sweetly, then gradually tickling his lips.

"You are a dream come true," she said.

He kissed her gently on the shoulder, then on her neck. "Then you are my mujer de ensueño."

Vicki smiled, savoring the Spanish. She opened her heart and her body to him in a way she had never done before. She felt secure with Lando. She felt loved.

For a year, he was all hers.

Sitting at the Village this night, she ruminated over that love affair. Lando moved back to Argentina after his graduation. They wrote passionate love letters to each other for three months.

Suddenly her letters were returned "address unknown." She never knew what became of him. She tried to investigate. She called his thesis advisor who only said "things are happening in Argentina that you shouldn't get involved in."

His two best friends disappeared. It was as if he never existed.

It took her years after the Lando affair to trust anyone's love for her. After nursing school, she met a cardiologist she liked. Emphasis on like. He was funny, and although he was shorter and unattractive, she married him.

VF was not amused.

"He is not Catholic, Vicki."

"Dad, not that many people are Catholic. That's a very old fashioned way of thinking. He is very successful. He will provide."

"There will be a day you will regret this," VF predicted. He knew Vicki was marrying for convenience.

The wedding was perfunctory, and after a short time they had two beautiful daughters. Within ten years, though, he died of a heart attack. He left her with enough money from his retirement account that she could move to Colorado where she always wanted to be.

"Darlin'," her father would say, "if I ever had a choice of a beautiful mountain community, I would live in Denver." Well, Denver it was for Vicki. She wanted to experience where her daddy would have lived. She wanted no other regrets.

Vicki pulled herself out of her reflections and focused on dinner. The menu had not changed in thirty years. *Comida corrida* was everyone's favorite—cheese enchilada, taco, tamale, rice and beans with a delicious covering of asiago cheese. That would not be healthy, but it would be comforting. She ordered that and a margarita gold.

Memories of the family conversations in this very room bubbled up.

"If you order it, you eat it," VF would command the family. "I want to see nothing left on your plates."

"Yes, sir, Colonel Landry," Joe would reply. The kids would giggle.

Steaming fresh corn tortillas would be passed, butter and salt generously applied, and consumed as fast as the kitchen could make them. Then the children would order kids' plates of tacos or enchiladas with refried beans and rice.

*Richard. The human vacuum.* Leftovers were passed to him and quickly consumed. He was the skinniest yet the perpetual eating machine.

She thought about his sad life. He had tasted heroin at the tender age of 15 after being incarcerated in a juvenile detention center. One of the inmates introduced it to him, showing how easy it was snort it. It was the beginning of a love affair with that narcotic, and a life within the cruel culture of Texas prisons.

VF thought that since Richard was caught with a stolen car he should be left in the facility at least for a couple of weeks, just to "knock some sense into him."

He was such a smart kid. He was facile in languages—he learned Spanish, German and French in junior high and spoke fluent Spanish to all of the ranch hands. He loved Shakespeare and made As in advanced literature.

She didn't know when he started running guns into Mexico. Probably soon after graduating from high school. A month after his graduation, VF told him "Son, if you don't go to college or get an honest job then don't come home again."

The family didn't see him for eight years.

No one knew where he was. He just showed up at the ranch on a Sunday when everyone was having dinner together. He was sporting a mustache, his black hair in a ponytail, and he was riding a souped up motorcycle. He looked either like a member of the cast of *Easy Rider* or someone from a Mexican gang.

Vicki took him aside to talk. "I've been growing marijuana on the O-Bar," he told her.

"The farm?" she asked.

"Yeah. Since Dad never goes there anymore, it's a perfect secluded venue to grow and harvest weed. Of course, I have to be careful about the processing and distribution, so I have a side business in retail firearms."

"That's dangerous," Vicki said, thinking how risky that sounded, and at the same time how much she admired his entrepreneurial skills.

"Ah, you just need to know how to communicate," he laughed, knowing that his facility with Spanish and his comfort level with guns kept him alive. "My favorite quote is *virtus junxit mors non separabit.*"

"What does that mean?"

Richard stared into her eyes, "What goodness has joined, death will not separate."

"Where did you get that?"

"A pal of mine said it's an old Mason saying. I think it's appropriate for our family, don't you?"

"Are you being sarcastic?"

"No, I love my family. I will always be a part of la familia. I just can't be around you all for a long period of time. All that judgmental crap flying around in the air."

Most of the family was afraid of him. They needn't be. He was a gentle soul in a costume. He just wanted to live and let live.

Virginia was beside herself when she saw Richard that day.

"Richard," she said, as she led him into the study. "Don't you know that I named you after my father? I want the very best for you. Your life on the road, or wherever you are going, it's not good for you. You need to be around family. Stay here. Live on the ranch. We need help here. You can manage some of the ranch hands."

"Mom, that would never work out. Dad hates me."

"Dad doesn't hate you. He just wants you to have an honest job."

Richard looked forlorn. "Dad will never approve of me." He hugged her, got on his Harley, and roared away.

That marked the day Virginia and VF's war of wills about Richard's future began. Richard was not above using his mother as his go-to ATM when times were tough, and VF would always be angry about that. VF's credo is that a man supports his mother, not vice versa.

*   *   *

Vicki felt revived by the food and drink and made her way back to the hospital, found out that Richard was just getting out of recovery and waited in the appointed area to hear more. After an hour or so, she was given his room number.

She tiptoed in to see a thoroughly bandaged brother. He was awake, sipping water, his right arm in a plaster cast with various pulleys and contraptions holding it up. The only piece of him not in gauze seemed to be his head.

"Hey, Richard," Vicki quietly murmured.

"Boss. What's the prognosis?"

"You broke your arm. I haven't talked to the doctor since your surgery. Are you in pain?"

"I can stand the pain right now. Kinda sleepy. I think I danced with a tractor trailer."

"Yes, I think you did."

"Was going to check out my new piece of Silvercreek."

"Oh, you must have gotten the paperwork from Trudell. I got mine, too."

"Yeah, the map and the papers—I got them."

"Well, when you get out of here, I'll be glad to drive you over to see your land. Are you going to sign the deed?"

"Damned right. But if I don't get out of here, you've got the paperwork."

Vicki knew he was referring to his will. She was the beneficiary.

"You'll get out of here. You should rest, and I'll be back in the morning with Mom."

Richard's eyes were already closed.

*   *   *

By eight the next morning, Virginia called Richard's hospital room.

"Richard, it's your mother. How're you feelin' son?"

"The pain is pretty bad, Mom. Pretty bad. I think they're going to give me something for it soon." His voice was strained.

"I'm coming to see you this morning with Vicki. Anything you want?"

"Please may I have a Dr. Pepper?"

Dr. Pepper was always Richard's choice soft drink. It was his grandmother Williams' favorite too. When he was an infant she would sneak it into his bottle, cuddle him up and feed him as she rocked him in her favorite rocking chair.

"Sure. Dr. Pepper's on its way. We should see you in an hour or so."

It took nearly two hours through the Austin traffic to get to the hospital, stopping on the way for a six-pack of Dr. Pepper.

Vicki parked in the hospital garage and she and Virginia went straight to Richard's room. Two nurses were there, cleaning up, disassembling the traction device. There was no one in the bed.

"Where's Richard Landry?" Vicki asked, frightened.

"Are you family?" The nurses were different from the previous night.

"Well, yes, I'm his sister, this is his mother, Virginia Landry."

"Come with me."

Vicki and Virginia marched to a private study. A doctor appeared and motioned them to sit on the sofa.

"I'm very sorry to report, Mrs. Landry, that your son died an hour ago from his injuries."

Virginia was stunned. And angry. "That's incomprehensible. I don't believe it. He just called me." Virginia was beside herself, her voice rising. She stood up. "I need to see the body." She was still holding the shopping bag of Dr. Pepper.

Vicki couldn't believe it either. "I was just with him last night after his surgery. He was talking. He seemed in pain, but he was dealing with it."

The doctor repeated, "We are very sorry."

Vicki was not convinced. There had to be more to this story.

\*     \*     \*

The coroner's report showed that the hospital killed Richard Daniel Landry. He had an unfortunate amount of methadone in his body when morphine was administered for pain early on the morning after his surgery. The doctor never ordered a blood test to check for opioids in his body before giving him pain medication in his IV. He flatlined soon after the dosage was injected into the IV.

The last words he heard were "This should help."

\*     \*     \*

Richard's funeral was minimal, yet touching. Virginia was too distraught to make arrangements, so Vicki took over and met with the director at Harrell's Funeral Home in south Austin. She decided on a stainless steel coffin, a spray of white lilies, and found photos of him as a child in his cowboy outfit to enlarge, frame, and set on easels. Visitation was the night before the service, but no rosary.

Virginia's one ultimatum about the arrangements was that Richard would be buried beside VF. "After all, it seems appropriate given Daddy's dislike of Richard." She enjoyed being contrarian. She was unaware of their bonding during VF's final days. Vicki did not argue. She knew they would be comfortable next to each other because she heard some of their last conversations.

Richard's brief obituary appeared in the *Austin American Statesman* with his high school graduation photo. The family was surprised to see how many people from his past showed up, especially all the pretty women. After all, who were a drug and gunrunner's best friends? Richard's girlfriend, Angélica, was noticeably absent. She was afraid of coming from Mexico to Texas. She mourned in her own way, offering a Sunday mass in his memory at her church in Cabo.

The person most upset with his sudden death was Virginia. She appeared traumatized at the funeral home, barely reacting to friends' wishes as she stood in the receiving line. His brothers and sisters were sad, but they had always suspected he would die of an overdose or be killed by a Mexican drug lord.

Father Joseph officiated a modest service.

Hap strummed *Amazing Grace* on his guitar as people filed in.

Vicki gave the sweetest remembrance.

"Richard and I were a two-person team caring for Dad during his last days. It was a process of changing him, the sheets, giving him medication, carrying him—sometimes physically in our arms—from a chair to see the sunset and then to his bed, and coaxing him to swallow soft food and drink. It was a difficult process. Richard never complained.

"One day Dad saw Richard and said, 'Here is my favorite person.' Then when Richard was giving him a shave he said, 'Why are you so good to me? I don't deserve such good treatment.'

"Richard replied, 'Dad, it's an honor for me to take care of you.'

"Dad whispered, 'It's an honor to me that you are taking care of me.'

"Richard had tears in his eyes when he told me this. He had finally come home, he said. His life had begun to take on feeling and *real* meaning.

He had plans to embrace the land, Silvercreek Ranch, and to build a house and raise a family.

"I think Richard would have been thrilled today to see the Harleys escorting him to his final resting place—the ranch where he hoped to start life anew before he had a tragic accident…."

Vicki paused and gathered strength, looked down at the coffin and said,

"May you start your new life in the arms of unconditional love, Richard."

Hap rose, took his guitar, and said, "I loved my little brother, Richard. He was a cowboy whose horse was a Harley. I've written this just for him." Then he gently played the guitar and sang:

> He said the Lord is coming
> So get ready for the day
> Make your place with the Maker
> Chase that ole devil away
>
> Brother Richard, the silent preacher
> Laid the Lord on me
>
> Faded Levis and Sunday boots
> Took the place of three-piece suits
>
> For Brother Richard
> Laid the Lord on me

As people filed from the funeral home Hap strummed *Amazing Grace* again.

Harleys escorted the coffin to the family cemetery at the ranch. Richard's friend Pardo, a former cellmate, asked if he could say a few words.

Pardo stood beside the grave looking uncomfortable in a black suit with no tie. He straightened his back and put his arms behind him, as if being hand-cuffed.

"Years ago, when Richard and I met as bunkmates, we shared an interest in reading. You may not think that homies read, but believe me the magazines and books sent to us made for all kinds of conversations besides sex and drugs."

The small gathering gently laughed.

"His favorite quote was by Ralph Chaplin: *Mourn not your captive comrades who must dwell—too strong to strive—within each steel-bound coffin of a cell, buried alive; but rather mourn the apathetic throng—the cowed and the meek—who see the world's great anguish and its wrong...and dare not speak!*"

There was a long silence.

"Rest in peace, my homie. Rest in peace." Pardo kissed two fingers, placed them close to his heart and then tapped the casket.

After everyone filed out, Hap turned to Mary. "Well, well, well. There's a surprise! Did you know about Pardo?"

Mary lowered her voice. "Vicki knew. Said he had done time for POC while Richard was doing time for T&T about ten years ago."

"Whas that supposed to mean?"

"Possession of cocaine and Richard was convicted of trafficking and trading."

"The dude's not too dumb," Hap noted.

"Dumb enough to get caught."

"Who is Ralph Chaplin?"

"Dunno. I'll have to look him up. Never heard of him."

Vicki had the tombstone engraved

Richard Daniel Landry
1956-1996
Ride on, Dear Brother

\*   \*   \*

Vicki visited Richard's apartment soon after the funeral. Not surprisingly, it had been ransacked. The safe, with its Clinton/Gore '96 bumper sticker had been forced open and was empty. Drawers and closets were open. Clothes and papers were strewn about. The back screen door was cut. But the paperwork for the deed to his property sat on his Chubbie Checker kitchen table untouched except for a ring from a Dr. Pepper can.

Who knows how much money he had in that safe, or where the guns and weed were stowed. There was nothing left now. Nothing but the land.

She gave his landlord a copy of his death certificate, boxed up the personal belongings she thought his on-and-off Mexican girlfriend Angélica might want, took the deed and closed the door.

CHAPTER SEVEN:

# *Divide and Conquer*

## 1996

As family members received the paperwork from John Trudell and realized upon carefully reading it that they were being coerced into signing a document that would take one-half of their promised land from them, a firestorm of protest began from Vicki, Hap, and Mary.

Virginia quickly doused the flames by making individual concessions. "What the hell, Mom?" Hap asked Virginia when he came to the ranch one afternoon to help her out. "Why would you only give us half our inheritance?"

"Oh, Hap, that's just lawyer-ese. Since Richard will not have his acreage and had no family except us, I'll be sure you get what's coming to you. Anyway, when you give me an outright ownership for half of that parcel, I can sell now to maintain my lifestyle and you can sell yours if you want. It's about immediacy. Do you get it?" There was an edge to her voice.

Childhood psychic trauma is nearly impossible to cure. When that edge in her voice began cutting into his being, Hap backed off.

After that encounter, Virginia needed to cover her bases. She quickly talked with Vicki, Bits, and Joe about Richard's land, promising portions to each, but delivering only to Bits.

Bits explained in her obsequious request to Virginia, "Think about deeding me 25 acres of that property, Mom. It gives me a stake to sell so that I can leave Toronto and built a home to be close to you."

"Would you really move, honey?"

"Of course I would. I've told you that before. It would be my dream to be one with the land again and build my hacienda out there to be close to you. And I'll create my vineyard. I'd be close enough that we can see each other every day if we want, and far enough away that we don't have to if we don't want to."

On the other hand, Mary decided to never sign the deed. Her land was her land; she had no need to take half as much or to sell half as much land as she should have. She could wait until her mother died for her full one hundred acres.   When any of the siblings signed their deed, one-half of their former land immediately went to Virginia to do whatever she wanted. Mary was convinced that Bits was covertly grabbing acreage when anyone sold.

She had no appetite to give Bits the satisfaction of taking anything from her. It was clear to Mary that Bits had alternative plans for this property. So Mary stood strong to wait for her mother's demise to receive her entitled land.

Hap, although he had protested, was the first to sign and sell. He thought long and hard about it. "My retirement plans do not include being a rancher or a farmer," he told Vicki. "I've never had a hard on for that land the way Dad did. I'd rather invest in something that brings joy and amusement to my life. Think I'll buy a little juke joint where me and my friends can play some music, have some fun."

John Trudell was more than happy to take the listing and handle the closing for 15% of two and a half million dollars.

Virginia took the other half of Hap's land for herself. She gave 40 of the 50 acres to Bits as a "welcome home" gift. The remaining ten acres was sold so that Virginia had some spending money for her personal travel, gifts to friends, private piano lessons, and the new interior decorating.

Vicki bargained with Virginia to keep her spa and take the land around her, ceding one-half of her property to Virginia, and swapping her land for one-half of Joe's. This way, she would have the responsibility of the family cemetery, which she felt was an honor.

Father Joe never enjoyed the land and found all the animals disagreeable. "They stink," he told Mary. "And besides, I'm allergic to animals." From the time he was old enough to help out at the ranch, he always found a way to beg off from the hard work everyone else endured. After being thrown from one of the horses at the age of six, he decided there were other means of transportation.

He told his father that he was not cut out to be a cowboy, knowing this would disappoint. After this declaration, he stuttered more profoundly. He told anyone in the family who was patient enough to listen that the cows, sheep and horses gave him hives, and that he did not want to hunt deer. He explained he was a pacifist and never wanted to pick up a gun.

It was not surprising when he agreed to the deed, sold his portion, and deposited the windfall in a charitable remainder trust with Catholic Charities. He felt this positioned him for a nice retirement fund and a special place in heaven. The charity had explained to Father Joe that he could create a gift trust with Catholic Charities and receive an income for life, at a 5.5% fixed rate. After his death the remainder would go to name his favorite program— The Joseph F. Landry Veteran's Welcome Home program for the homeless.

He explained the transaction to Vicki. "I moved my land into a charitable trust designated to Catholic Charities. Then they sold my fifty acres for two million dollars. That way, I received a tax deduction for the gift. The trust pays me at least $110,000 every year, while it grows year-by-year, for the rest of my life."

Vicki was stupefied. "You mean, you gave them the land in exchange for a trust that pays you an income for the rest of your life? And you got a tax deduction?"

Joe was amused that she actually understood the transaction. "Yes, and then when I die, the remainder of the trust, which will probably be more than two million dollars since I plan to live for at least twenty more years, will benefit my homeless veteran's program at Catholic Charities."

"The beauty of smart investment," Joe said when he explained it to Mary. "Catholic Charities makes around 10% on a 5-year average. I get 5.5%. So they seed the trust with the remainder, minus their fees. It turns out about 3-4% gain on the principal goes back into the trust. So the trust grows and grows. And the charity gets a nice gift when I'm gone."

Although Mary understood the legalities of trusts and estates, she did not know the ins and outs of charitable trusts. "Sounds amazing, Joe! How smart of you." She really was impressed with his investment.

"So, does the Catholic church allow you to have an income?"

"If it's a trust, the Church has no say."

"What are you going to do with it?"

"I've always wanted to pursue more education. So, I'll do that and perhaps get a little vacation cottage on a lake somewhere."

"Can you have property?"

"Oh, I've found a way to do that, too."

"How so?"

"I'll give it to the Church through what's called a retained life estate. I continue to stay in the property, pay taxes on it, and maintain it, but it flows directly to the Church when I die."

"So you've essentially deeded it to the Church, contingent upon your demise?"

"Well said," Joe agreed.

"You know, Joe, something occurred to me about Dad wanting us all to marry Catholics. I think you've fulfilled that for all of us. With your marrying the Catholic Church, I don't think we need to have Catholic spouses."

"It's not the same thing, Mary."

"Oh, I think it counts, nevertheless! Many times over."

Soon after her sisters and brothers made their fateful decisions with their deeds, Bits gave the go-ahead to her architect and builder and started construction on her sprawling 10,000 square foot hacienda on her part of Silvercreek Ranch. She was ready to dig in and convince Virginia that at least another 100 acres should be hers, for her winery and to develop a division of ranchettes.

She was on a mission for the next several months. While her bankrupt fragrance business was dissolved, she moved on to another adventure. She visited old, ravaged haciendas in her favorite town, San Miguel de Allende, Mexico and shipped doors, windows, fountains, carved fireplaces and beautiful mosaics for her new home to the ranch.

Bits loved San Miguel de Allende, a beautiful city in eastern Mexico. After her third divorce, she took her settlement and bought a lovely little bungalow in that city. "I've found my winter home," she told her mother.

"Why in the world would you live in a Mexican town?" Virginia asked her, disapprovingly. Virginia thought Mexicans were "half breeds" as she called them. She refused to step foot in Mexico.

"Well, have you ever been to San Miguel de Allende?" Bits asked.

"Never have. Never will. That's your Daddy's stomping grounds."

Bits would never have considered living part-time in Mexico if it hadn't been for VF's devotion to Mexico. He respected Mexicans. He traveled to various Mexican cities when he worked environmental cases for Texas. He would talk about how hard working, romantic, hard fighting they were. He had a sense of their history.

"If you ever get to San Miguel de Allende you must look up the memorials to fighters in the Chichimeca War against the Spanish empire. They defeated the Spanish, much like they defeated the Texans. You've got to respect their devotion to country. And to their land," he told Bits after she had moved to Toronto. She had called the ranch to talk with Virginia that day, but her mother was out with her friends, and VF answered.

The conversation had begun with Bits comparing Toronto's freezing weather with Texas' steaming springtime.

"Do you think that would make a good winter's nest for me? I could manage my business at a distance in the winter."

"See for yourself," he said. "See for yourself."

So she did—she saw what he saw. A beautiful, comfortable, affordable town where she could escape the biting winters in Toronto and enjoy the ambience of a different culture. And have several maids for the cost of one Toronto maid.

Bits was a whirlwind of energy as she supervised the creation of her five bedroom, six bath home with its fountains, mosaics, designer kitchen and wine cellar.

By 1998 her hacienda was complete and she moved to the ranch. Her income came from selling parcels of Richard's land that her mother had deeded to her.

Her plan for creating ranchettes and thus destroying the topography of Silvercreek Ranch was taking shape.

She now shifted her resources to building her winery.

"Mom," she gushed one day as she visited Virginia at the fortress, "I've found my partner."

"What partner? A partner as in a husband?"

"Who knows?" Bits replied.

"I thought you were done with men in your life."

"Oh, who is ever done with men in our lives? I saw you playing coy with Mr. Martin at the town meeting yesterday."

"Mr. Martin is just getting over the death of his wife, Bits. I would never...."

"Oh, yes you would. Anyway, I think I've found a partner for my winery. He's cute, he's smart, and he's single."

"But can he keep up with you? You have more schemes than a Wile E. Coyote."

"I'm sure you mean that in a good way," Bits said with a lilt in her voice. "He's a few years younger than I am, big blue eyes and sandy hair, but I love his accent."

"You love 'em until you leave 'em, Bits. Another notch in your chastity belt. Speaking of chastity, or lack thereof, have you been following this Monica Lewinsky thing?"

"You mean with President Clinton?" Bits asked. "Who the hell cares? We all knew that Kennedy was a skirt chaser, and even LBJ had his secret lovers. So, Clinton is carrying on with his intern and the Republicans are gonna make him pay. As if they aren't a bunch of perverts."

"Men are disgusting. He was probably finger fucking her," Virginia said. "But back to your lover boy. Do you know the size of his cigar?"

Bits was always surprised how vulgar her mother was with her. Unlike her other siblings, she could share all kinds of secrets with Virginia. Up to a point. For example, she would never tell her what fun she had with her new lover just the day before in her hacienda's master bedroom. If her mother only knew the kind of belt she used on him! Definitely not a chastity belt.

"Oh, Mom, don't be ridiculous," Bits protested.

"What kind of accent does he have? Please don't tell me he's Mexican."

"British. He has a British accent. It's adorable."

"What do the Brits know about making wine?" Virginia asked.

"He's been in the wine business for over twenty years. He has connections in Canada who can get us the must from the grapes and then we'll make the wine, bottle it and sell it from here. We'll call it Silvercreek Vineyards."

"Oh, that's original."

"I think it sounds Texan. He likes it. I like it."

"Well, good luck with that, Bits. Just so you don't make that icky stuff your Daddy made. That mustang grape wine."

"This will be the best of Texas."

"Or the best of Toronto if the grapes are from Toronto."

"Don't tell."

Bits felt that her life was finally coming together—she had her dream hacienda, her fortune of ranchettes, and her cute boyfriend who would soon become her husband and partner in the wine business. What could be better?

# CHAPTER EIGHT:

# Good Night Nurse

## 2004

Hap sat at his patio table on Valentine's Day, 2004, surrounded by the Austin vibe, pencil in hand, music tablet in front of him. The brilliantly colored hibiscus framed the arbor above him as he wrote the lyrics that had been whirling in his head:

### Why Do You Believe in Me

Why do you believe in me

And give your very heart and soul to me

When a perfect love

This may never be

And still....

You make it real

You believe in me...

REPEAT

And it makes me try to do

Things that mean so much to you

Knowing you're much stronger

Than I will ever be

Gives me courage

To go on

REPEAT

There are times

You show so much faith in me

It brings out desires

Hidden deep inside

Makes me feel it's my place to be

Close, very close to you

You believe in me.

He felt this deeply—it was his ode to Karen, his "blonde bombshell" as VF called her, of a wife. She was a successful psychologist in town, Ivy-League trained, specializing in couples counseling, and he was forever wondering why she had married him and put up with him and his bad jokes. He loved that lady more than life. He could tell her anything. She understood him, he felt, as no other woman in his life had. As he told his pickin' buddy, Jody, "as in the words of an old Ray Price song 'she's got to be a saint, cause Lord knows I ain't.'"

Hap sighed heavily, pulled out his guitar and started to sing *Why do you believe....* His throat was so raw, he could not clearly articulate the words. He tried again. The soreness was worse. He grabbed a glass of ice water to sip. The trickle sent razors down his throat.

For the past month, he thought his sore throat was due to allergens from the abnormally early spring in Austin. At first, he put on his big boy pants and manned up, week after week. But now, after a month, and after the pain, the cough, and the bleeding that would not go away, it was time to see a doctor.

He called a buddy who was head of admissions at the VA hospital, and got an early appointment for the following week.

The Central Texas VA Hospital in Temple was not so far that he couldn't drive himself so he was alone. *I know what the doctor's gonna say—no more smoking, no more drinking.* He knew it because that's what the doctor said last time he had a physical.

"Hap Landry?" the nurse yelled.

"That's my name, don't wear it out."

*She's a duplicate Nurse Ratchet.* She tilted her head down and looked out at him over her glasses. "Come with me," she scowled.

They marched down the long, tiled, astringent-smelling hallway. Hap followed Nurse Ratchet into the small examination room.

"You here for a sore throat?" she asked.

Hap nodded.

"Let's have you take off your shirt and have a seat on the exam table."

Another 30 minute wait.

"Lt. Landry, I'm Dr. Grossman," the young intern said as he extended his hand and ushered in the transcriber. "This is Paul, our information specialist." All information about the patient was now transcribed during the exam so that more accurate records could be kept—an improvement to VA medical care.

Hap looked at both of them and shook hands. The doctor put on his exam gloves, and took out the otoscope.

"Let's take a look."

Hap complied to all the commands— let's take a look at your ears, first this ear, then the other, open your mouth wide, stick out your tongue, move your head this way, that way, look up, look down, how does it feel when I touch this area below your ears, do you have hearing problems, have you seen blood with your cough, have you been tested for HPV, etc. etc.

Dr. Grossman barked the results he was finding as Paul transcribed: "pharyngitis, palpable mass on neck, hyperalgesia, bleeding in the throat,

persistent cough, laryngitis."

"That sounds like a medical dictionary," Hap rasped.

"Lt. Landry, we're going to put you on a little antibiotic—cephalosporin—to see if that helps give you any relief. I'll order it in liquid form—your swallowing must be painful. I'm also ordering a biopsy of this little lump I found on your neck, we're going to do some blood work, and here's a referral I'm giving you for a throat doctor. It says here," the doctor held his medical history file of past exams, "that you have a history of smoking and alcoholism. You'll have to find a way to modify both of those behaviors."

"Modify? Doc, look, if I can't smoke and I can't drink, I can't live." Hap's voice was a rough whisper.

"Your choice, Lt. Landry." Dr. Grossman closed the file, handed Hap the prescription, the form for blood work, and the referral and left the room shaking his head, with the transcriber fast behind him.

*Good Night Nurse*, Hap said to himself, knowing the irony of the saying. He adopted the adage after he saw the movie of the same name starring Fatty Arbuckle and Buster Keaton. Arbuckle is an alcoholic who is institutionalized after his wife has had enough of his drunken behavior. Keaton is the neurosurgeon who is supposed to lobotomize his patient to cure him. Hap watched that movie many times, laughing uproariously.

He sat on the exam table, puzzled about a biopsy, but knowing it sounded serious.

*Damn it all,* he told himself, *just when I had a little money to sit and write my songs and have some fun with my cars, my plane and my life.*

After making the appointment for the biopsy, having blood drawn, filling his prescription and driving back to Austin, Hap sat with a bottle of Jack, thought about his boyhood, and wrote this:

## In My Dreams

When I was a kid in my

Early teens

I cut off the loops of my

Blue jeans

But then kids—they do

Some crazy things

I didn't have a care in the world

Three blocks over

Lived my best girl

Yesterday….In my dreams

We used to play that old

Juke box all day long for

A dollar,

Run through the back yard

And hear my momma holler

Hey! Keep away from the

Laundry on the line

Go on swimmin' –be home

By supper time

As Hap wrote he remembered the fun of being a boy in the fifties. He felt the bike pedals under his bare feet and the wind against his naked chest as he barreled down Terrace Drive on the way to Big Stacy swimming pool.

He was on his way to flirt with pretty girls and try some daring dives. He was the only diver who could do a back flip with a twist.

He thought about the responsibilities he was given. "Everyone needs to pull his own weight," his father taught him. "The girls clean the house, and you, son, need a paper route."

> Yesterday….in my dreams
>
> School is out, I got a paper route
>
> Gonna get the job done
>
> Then have some fun
>
> Friday night we're gonna go
>
> To the twenty-cent show
>
> After they shut down
>
> The movie machine
>
> We're gonna shut down
>
> That 'ole Dairy Queen
>
> Yesterday…in my dreams

Hap finished the last stanza, tried to gulp down the antibiotic, and took a nap. The instant he awoke, he called Iris, even though it was late in New York.

"Iris. It's Hap, dawlin'. I just had this dream. It was with Dad. I've never had a dream like it."

Iris was so pleased to hear from Hap, she had been thinking about him and his upcoming big birthday—the big 6-0. "Tell me more," she smiled, put on her robe and walked into her study to not disturb her husband.

"Well, he looked wonderful—a full head of hair, strong body, and he was showing you and me how the Pedernales River met our land at this 'secret' place. It was beautiful. Perfectly peaceful. It was spread out like Barton

Springs below us—we were high on a hill overlooking it. I told him 'I've never seen this part of the ranch before—it's breathtaking.' He just smiled. Then he put several envelopes on a table. They were all labeled with names of the kids and '$1K'—things like that—like little gifts.

"I ran to get Vicki. She was in a shower and she wouldn't come out. I kept saying 'hurry, hurry, hurry—you've got to see him—he looks great.' She just cried and hid behind the shower curtain. 'It's not really him,' she said. But it was him."

Iris' eyes filled with tears. "Hap, that's such a wonderful dream. I have an interpretation....You sold your land, right?"

"Sure did. Years ago."

"I think the envelopes are full of cash—like a dream come true--and that by giving us land he's helping our dreams unfold—whether we take the cash or the land. I think that you're seeing him strong and virile again because you know he's in a better place."

"I just finished writin' a song about my childhood, and you know, it wasn't all bad," Hap said.

"Of course not," Iris agreed wryly, trying to envision happiness in the Landry family.

"I thought about the vacations we took. Galveston, for example. We'd pack up the station wagon and head down to Galveston and every one of us would race out of that car and into the surf where we would stay for hours and hours."

"Yes, we were all so ignorant about sunburn. We slathered baby oil all over our bodies. You were so dark brown, Hap, that people called you a Mexican."

"Well, being in the ocean was worth it. And the trip to the Grand Canyon. That was hilarious when Bits and I had that bubble-blowing contest and we got double bubble all over our hair!"

"Mom went wild."

"And the Big Bend camping trips. Dad saved our lives when a sudden storm flooded our campsite."

Iris had a sudden image. "Ewww…remember on that same vacation when he killed all of those scorpions—they were everywhere!" She was cringing.

"I had a dream about Dad last night, too," she said.

"Let me hear it."

"OK. Dad and I were picking beans from a bean tree. They were larger-than-life beans—seemed to be very dark, but when we got closer to the tree they looked healthier. Anyway, I saw a snake and was alarmed and I realized I shouldn't be afraid. It slithered down…all of a sudden it was on the ground. Dad said to my oldest son, 'look Will, this is how we take care of the snakes—grab a rock.' And he hit the snake with a rock and killed it. Then Will hit it with a rock. I turned away so I wouldn't see Will picking up the dead snake.

"My feeling was one of real happiness that Dad was so strong and still such a fighter."

"Hmmmm…. maybe Dad is telling you that there are snakes out there in the world that you'll have to defeat and he's here with you to help you along the way. Either that or something about penises."

Iris laughed as if she was shocked.

"But what about the beans?" She said soberly.

"You think the beans are representative of Jillian's life in heaven—that it's bigger than life…a life everlasting?"

"Ah..Beans! I remember you called Jillian 'Beans.' That's good. I like that!" Iris' tears were dry now. "How are you doing?"

"Aw…just writin' the music, drinkin' the Kool-Aid," Hap said.

"Hap, remember when we were kids and you would buy peanuts and put 'em in your Coke?"

"Yeah."

"Well, I thought that was the coolest thing in the world…And you were the king of seed spitting—remember? All the watermelon seed spitting contests?"

"That was Terrace Drive. That was before you had titties."

"Oh, now I know I'm talking to the real Hap! …." Iris paused, thinking of all the things this little tribe of kids did…" you were always the best at skipping rocks."

"I knew how to find the flat ones."

"How's your plane?"

"Right now, it's grounded for a while. I'm concentrating on my golf game."

"Maybe when I come see you on your birthday we could fly over that dreamscape—over the Pedernales? See if it meets up with Barton Creek?"

"You'll be here in July? Well, good night nurse! It'll be a hot time in the cool city or a cool time in the hot city in July. Just call first. Nighty nite, and remember—it is better to look good than to feel good—and yew look mawvelous."

The remark had its intended effect. Iris giggled.

"Love you, Hap. Take care."

"Yerself."

Iris hung up and even though he had left her with a smile, all was not right with Hap. His voice, always rusty, was peppered with a constant cough and a horrid sound as if he couldn't catch his breath. And he didn't sound drunk. That was a first.

\*   \*   \*

Hap's diagnosis was worse than anyone feared—stage IV throat cancer. The treatment protocol was very similar to VF's—surgery followed by radiation, followed by chemo. He seemed to be resigned to his fate.

The surgery in April that followed his biopsy did not go as well as expected. There was a lot of bleeding, and his larynx was "compromised." The radiation made him very tired and left his neck and face burned.

It became more and more difficult for him to swallow until he had to have a tube inserted into his stomach for nourishment. His good friend and golfing buddy Roger chauffeured him to and from his chemo infusions.

But he kept smoking, joking and cogitating on his golf game.

"Have yew heard this?" He asked Roger as they were driving to his chemo. "Walking to the altar, the groom tells his lady, 'Honey, I've got something to confess: I'm a golf nut, and every chance I get, I'll be playing golf!' She says, 'Since we're being honest, I have to tell you that I'm a hooker.' The groom smiles and says, 'That's okay, honey. You just need to learn to keep your head down and your left arm straight.'"

Hap laughed, slapped his thigh and told another, watching Roger's expression of delight—the 'ole Hap had rallied.

"Roger, I have to tell you, I think my game is showing some arm. Years ago, when I was on a cruise to Australia, I went to the golf nets just about every day. Once, another fella was hitting balls one net over. I asked if he would look at my swing—check it for my familiar 'loop.' Guess what? No loop! He said it was straight up and straight back. Maybe my practice paid off. I discovered I haven't been using my right hand like I should. I've been coming over instead of under. I hope it's true. I can't wait to get on the course and try it out again......

"Roger, let me ask you," Hap said plaintively. "Do you think golfers ever die?" This was an old chestnut of Hap's that Roger had heard maybe a thousand times.

"Hmmmm...I dunno Hap, do they?"

"Oh, hell, no. They just lose their balls."

They both laughed so hard that Roger nearly ran off the road.

* * *

By July, Hap's health was not improving. The pain was excruciating for him, so oxycontin was the pharmaceutical of choice. This made him constipated, a terrible side effect of the drug.

He became more and more emaciated.

He was too exhausted to celebrate his birthday, which left friends and family frustrated. Everyone wanted to do something for him, but they were helpless to provide happiness.

Iris asked his wife, Karen, if it would be OK to could come see Hap when she was in town. "Frankly, Iris, he has his good days and his bad days. I need to prepare you for what you might see. And he may not be able to see you at all."

"I'll take my chances," Iris replied. She had her tickets and she was coming to Texas.

"Well, Hap wants to talk with you."

Iris was amazed that Hap could talk at all. Karen put him on the phone.

"Darlin' if yer comin' over to see me I want.... no tears. And if yew want to stay over I'll have Karen put clean sheets on the bed in the guest room."

"Well, Hap, you know I'm a crybaby and I will promise to try my best not to be. I'm just there to see you, so I'm flying back after our visit. I have something to tell you."

"Yew know, yer my favorite lil' sis. And yew look mawvelous."

Karen took the phone, told Iris that Hap needed to lie down. She said she recently met with the hospice caretakers from Christopher House. She realized that she was unable to care for Hap at home, and it was only a matter of time.

*   *   *

Iris knew that a person with late stage cancer is just a shell of him/herself, but she was not prepared to see what had become of Hap. As Karen opened the front door to their lovely ranch-style home, Iris saw a small old man sitting in an oversized leather chair in their sunken living room. *Could this be Hap?*

Hap was 50 pounds lighter than his healthy, trim 165. His gorgeous blue eyes bulged from his face, his skin tight and burned. His clothes swallowed him. His hair, once so thick and blonde, was white and stringy. He winced with pain. He gave Iris a thin smile, staring sadly at her. She hugged his bony shoulders, and sat on the floor beside his chair.

"I brought you hydrangeas from my community garden in New York, and I have something else to give you for your birthday."

Hap looked deeply at her.

"This is a birthday letter to you, my favorite big brother."

Hap smiled. He was her only big brother.

"Here goes…." Iris glanced lovingly at him as she read, punching certain words for emphasis.

"How can you ever be sad if your name is Happy? Forget that you were named after General Harold (Hap) Arnold, the General of the Army and the General of the Air Forces during World War II, who was trained to be a pilot by the Wright Brothers. That's part of your patriotic DNA, and probably drove you to be a pilot."

Hap smiled wanly and she continued.

"Your fascination with the yin/yang and wordplay began early, maybe in the days of the 'Annie, Annie Over' ball toss over the house with your pal Rusty Weir ....

"Your brilliant pun of naming Vicki the 'family hysterian' still resonates, since she was both the family historian and pretty hysterical at times.

"Listening to you sing with that deep, rich voice (*is that Elvis? Waylan? Johnny Cash? I'd try to guess*) and hearing some of your favorite lyrics from the fantastic album that Karen put together ten years ago made me realize what a remarkable writer you are......e.g., 'the good people tell all the bad stories' 'John McBride—a dream come true, for chosen few' 'Morning coffee with a kiss' 'And I believe in you.'"

Hap smiled and touched Iris' hand. Iris looked into his dreamy light blue eyes and continued.

"From the time I watched you carefully put together model aircraft carriers, airplanes and automobiles of all intricacies and technical skill and then with the utmost patience paint them with your color-coded Testor model paint, aligned on your shelf like a horizontal color-wheel, I realized I was watching a genius of artistic calm.

"One day I peeked into your room and saw architectural drawings on your desk. What were these? I was too young to understand. I just gaped in awe at all the work the proper pencil could do in the hands of an artisan. It was love at first sight with Koh-I-Noor and Pentel.

"And of course you are never happy without your hilarious side. I can count on you to have a joke on hand when we talk, no matter what the color of that joke. And, with your remarkable ear for voices, you always end our conversation with this remark in an uncanny Fernando Lamas (or Billy Crystal, choose) baritone,

> 'Darlin', I got to tell you something
> And I don't say this to everybody
> Yew look mawvelous
> Absolutely mawvelous
>
> It's not how yew feel
> It's how yew look
>
> And yew, darlin'
> Yew look mawvelous
> Absolutely mawvelous
>
> And this is from my heart
> Which is deep inside my body
> It is better to look good
> Than to feel good'....."

Hap tried to laugh. Iris went on:

"And your sensitive side. A person can't totally remodel an '88 Dodge truck complete with original leather interior and trim or bring an ancient mottled and warped Victrola back to life with a sateen finish and not be sensitive and loving.

"And there's your entrepreneurial side—remember those Sunday mornings after Mass when Mom drove to the fried pie factory to get bags of broken pies at twenty-five cents a bag? Who thought of jumping on his bike with the Fried Pies and reselling them to the neighbors for a 500% profit? It was just last week, after forty-five years, that I learned why we hardly ever had any coconut pies when we got home after buying them! What you didn't sell, you ate!

Hap had tears in his eyes. Iris did not know that those tears were being shed for a different kind of memory about the pies.

"So, Happy… I am so grateful to know and be the sister of you--a man who is the embodiment of all these wonderful characteristics—artist, patriot, lover, singer, comedian, and entrepreneur. I love you! Happy Birthday!"

They hugged. Iris felt Hap's tears on her face. Hap stood up and excused himself. She looked around the living room at the books in the built-in bookcases. There, neatly lined up were all the books VF had written—from the early hardback copy of the biography *Davy Crockett*, which Hap had illustrated, to the most recent paperback series VF wrote before he died. She was struck how they stood at attention, so neat and clean. Everything in the room had a precision to it, a soldierly presence.

*  *  *

Hap died peacefully on August 12, 2004 at Christopher House in Austin, with Karen caressing his hand while his favorite Patsy Cline album played in the background. Karen decided to have him cremated and part of his ashes flown out to Silvercreek Ranch in his plane, scattered to the winds.

Virginia was having lunch with Bits at their favorite little bistro in south Austin when Bits' flip phone rang that fateful summer day.

"Yes, Vicki, it's Bits…What?" Bits said loudly, as she looked at Virginia.

"When?...OK. Bye." She closed the phone.

"What was that about?" Virginia asked.

"Oh, Mom! I'm afraid Hap is gone."

"What do you mean gone?" Virginia gasped.

"I mean he died an hour ago. Karen has already decided to cremate him."

Virginia excused herself and got up from the table. Bits waited, sipping her wine and thinking about how she and Hap had promised each other to send a signal from the afterlife.

Twenty minutes passed. Bits asked the waitress to check the restroom. Suddenly there was an outburst and someone called for a doctor. Virginia had collapsed in the ladies' room.

It was a heart attack. No one knew if there was a casual relationship between her faith and the Church's distaste for cremation, or if it was just time for her heart to give out. Virginia was rushed to the Hillcountry hospital, where she was put on life support and given expert attention.

"What a drama queen! Anything not to attend Hap's memorial service," Vicki said.

\*   \*   \*

In September, Karen created a unique and beautiful service with musicians playing Hap's original country western music, a color guard, and a local cowboy preacher, complete with cowboy boots. She had a large marble headstone carved for the family cemetery:

*Lt. Hap Arnold Landry, 1944-2004*
*Served his Country, his Family, and his Lord*
*Long Live Love, Art, and Humor*

After the service, all were invited to The Dive In, the bar Hap purchased with some of the proceeds of the sale of his land. A lavish Tex Mex dinner, margaritas, and coconut cream pie, Hap's favorite desert, was served. There were tequila shots for anyone so inclined and an engraved souvenir shot glass as a parting gift.

Karen was dressed in an emerald green sheath. She greeted Mary with a big hug. "Hap loved you Mary. He said you were the smartest and sweetest of all of 'em. Where's your better half?"

"Oh, Todd's over at the dessert table. You'd think a dentist would stay away from sweets."

"Mary, let me ask you something." Karen was a wee bit drunk, and Mary was trying to act as if she didn't notice.

"Sure, Karen."

"You and Todd have been married—what—twenty years?"

"Seventeen. Seventeen years," Mary replied.

"You still have romance in your love life?"

"You mean, do we still make love?" Mary asked.

Karen nodded.

"Well, yes. Is this some kind of psychological study you're doing? Couples counseling?"

"No, just wondered. Hap and I were married for twenty years and the last few years were pretty loveless."

"Oh, Karen, not for lack of love, I'm sure. Hap loved you to the ends of the earth."

Mary could not help wonder if that conversation had some greater meaning. She knew Hap seemed preoccupied with jokes that had sexual connotations, and that he always loved mimicking Fernando Llamas with his "yew look mawvelous" speech to all the women in his life. Perhaps Hap just didn't need sex after a certain time in life. Or perhaps the lack of libido was due to his cancer. It was clear to Mary that Karen had a lot of love to give, and perhaps she was seeking permission.

"Look, Karen. I know I may be out of bounds in saying this, because you're the psychologist. But when you're ready for a relationship again, please don't think I'm going to judge you. You should feel free to find love. Hap would want that for you."

CHAPTER NINE:

# *My Sweet Virginia*

## March, 2005

The March 15, 2005 *Austin American Statesman* morning paper hit the front door of the fortress with a bang, waking Virginia up. She rolled out of bed and slowly shuffled to the front door to pick it up. It was her connection with her former life. The life of politics and gab.

Headlines included an article titled "Ellis Seeks Legal Help For Counties" and stated that Texas "should boost funding to help counties pay for legal representation for poor defendants." Virginia read this with resignation, thinking of Richard and the money she had spent trying to defend him.

She couldn't help thinking of all three sons, especially Hap. She hoped God would forgive her for not attending Hap's memorial service. She had her own problems to attend to.

After her heart attack, she was unable to drive, became weaker, incapable of walking up stairs. She had to depend more and more on Vicki's help. She worried about herself. She couldn't complete a crossword puzzle and she felt angrier about everything.

You would think that her favorite daughter, Bits, would have cared for her. Bits did not have that capacity.

Vicki realized her mother needed 24-hour care, so she moved into the fortress at the beginning of 2005. She re-arranged the bedrooms to accommodate Virginia's inability to master the stairs, and wound down her massage practice to part-time.

The day-to-day care of Virginia with her undiagnosed bi-polar behavior began to take a toll on Vicki. Her mother criticized everything she did whether it was her hairstyle, her inability to clean the toilet properly, the way she prepared a sandwich, or her voice.

"Daddy used to say that my sister Dorothy had a shrill voice. Well, guess what? You inherited it!"

There were other days when Virginia would want to give Vicki things. "Now when I'm gone, Vicki, this Grandma Moses painting is yours. Put your name on it."

The morning of March 15, Vicki finished her shower while Virginia sat in the kitchen drinking her coffee and reading her newspaper. Vicki was looking in the bathroom mirror and plucking her eyebrows, towel around her wet body. Virginia walked up behind her.

"Vanity is insanity," she yelled, surprising Vicki.

"Jesus Christ, Mom! You scared the sheep out of me. What's wrong with you?"

"Why are you plucking your eyebrows? Have a hot date? No one wants to see you."

"Why are you so angry Mom?"

"Why are you so ugly?" Virginia replied.

"What kind of answer is that?"

"The truth—and YOU can't take it."

Vicki was puzzled. *What brought this on?* She feared she would be prodded to escalate this "fight about nothing." She pushed Virginia out of the doorway and closed the door, pledging to see a psychologist to help her get through this horrible nightmare.

She called Iris, just wanting to talk through the impossible situation.

"Gosh, Vicki, I wish I could help you. I really mean that, I'm not being facetious."

"I think talking about it helps," Vicki said.

"Yes, you need to see an objective party for that. I know too much. It helps to just see the abuse for what it is. That's what I've done and that's why I try to stay as far away from Mom as possible. I can't imagine why you haven't killed her."

"To be honest, I have fantasized. I see myself using arsenic in her coffee. She loooooves her coffee." Vicki paused. "Have you been to a shrink?"

"I've been to psychologists. Yes. And I went to a workshop once on the psychology of dysfunctional families."

"Did you learn anything?"

"I did. I learned that some people find it 'comforting' to stay in a dysfunctional situation rather than leave," Iris said.

"Comforting?"

"Sure. It's difficult to divorce yourself from anything—a bad marriage, an abusive mother, etc. Changing your life is hard. It takes courage. It takes a lot of discomfort to move on, to put yourself in new situations."

"Do you have dreams about our abuse?" Vicki asked.

"Not anymore. Used to. Let me tell you about this funny dream I had just last night. I dreamed I saw this crustacean that everyone said was Mom and thought—wow! How strange for Mom to die in this form since she always loved eating shellfish. Someone was holding her and as I looked at 'the thing,' wondering if we were going to cremate it and spread the ashes, it came to life.

It was a lobster! Wasn't that appropriate? Mom came back to life as something to eat. I think Dad was also in the dream, smiling."

"So, are you saying Mom is dead to you?"

"That's an interesting interpretation."

"Listen," Iris said. "Hire a night nurse. Get the hell out of that frickin' fortress at night. Go back to your home down the street. That should provide some semblance of sanity, at least for ten hours or so."

"That's good advice." Vicki was appreciative.

\*   \*   \*

Vicki hired a night nurse and then got an appointment with a shrink specializing in PTSD.

On a lovely spring afternoon, Vicki found herself sitting on Dr. Helen Earl's ergonomic Scandinavian chair. "Tell me, dear, about yourself and what you hope to accomplish here," Dr. Earl began.

"I'd like to stop hating my mom."

"What is it you hate about her?"

"Where do I begin? She and my dad were married for 52 years, yet most of that time was miserable because she was so cruel to him. She had eight children, yet they all, well, except one, they all hate or hated her. Three are gone. She is diabolical one day and cheerful and happy and trying to give you things the next. Then the next day she'll turn around and try to take those things from you and call you a liar and a thief. She's crude at times, and then other times she's all prim and proper. She's absolutely insane."

"Has she been diagnosed?"

"Not officially."

"Would you like to slap her?"

"I don't know about slapping her. Sometimes I'd like to kill her. More than anything, though, I just want her to be a normal, loving mother."

"She's how old?"

"84."

"I'm afraid it's too late."

Vicki and Dr. Earl looked at each other. Vicki was agitated. She didn't like Dr. Earl's sympathetic eyes. She didn't need sympathy. She wanted resolution. She forgot what hard work psychotherapy was. Many years had passed since her last encounter with psychotherapy. None of the many psychologists and social workers had relieved her anxiety over this mother/daughter relationship.

*These questions make me tired.*

The psychologist got up from her straight-backed chair, grabbed a pillow from the couch and handed it to Vicki.

Vicki stared at the pillow. "For my back?"

"No, it's your punching bag."

"I'm not into that."

"Try it.....Just punch it. Punch out that anger. That frustration. That disappointment."

Vicki held it with one hand and punched it with the other, trying to comply with Dr. Earl's suggestion. It felt silly.

"I'm afraid this doesn't work for me."

"Try again."

Vicki tried, over and over again until the session ended.

At the next week's session, Vicki gave Dr. Earl a long, detailed description of her life growing up in the Landry household and how she came to be the "Boss" and why she was the one caring for her mother.

"I just cannot continue being there with her," she finally told Dr. Earl.

"Have you ever told your mother how you feel?"

"You mean because of all the things she did? I don't think she would listen."

"Well, sometimes it can be therapeutic for you to write your feelings in a letter to your mother."

Dr. Earl gave Vicki her homework: write a letter to Virginia telling her exactly how you feel about your childhood all the way to now and don't hold back. And next time they would discuss the letter.

*   *   *

The evening dusk outside Vicki's lovely home brought a chorus of background music from the critters' zoo as she sat with pen in hand, absent the usual carafe of wine, and began to write:

*Dear Mom,*

*Life should be happy but it seems you and I have been in a slump with each other for some time now.*

*The problem goes all the way back to childhood. I did not realize how conveniently the alcohol masked my agony until I recently lived upstairs in your house sober. The whole scenario of childhood played back to me on a daily basis.*

*I have spent thousands of dollars in therapy trying to resolve my inner mother-daughter conflict and feel I have made very little progress. I have prayed for a solution to our conflict. I have prayed for your welfare and wished good things for you. But my anger about helplessness to defend others and myself keeps creeping back into my mind.*

Memories flooded Vicki's mind, from the earliest times she could remember to the present. She saw and felt vivid reenactments of her mother's wrath: Virginia dunking toddler Hap's head in scalding water, beating little five-year old Hap with a dishtowel, grabbing his gonads when he was six, screaming at him to "find the biggest stick" to beat him with before he was old enough to fight back, and breaking all of his model planes and ships as a young teen. This was hard work, writing these horrible memories. She pushed herself to continue:

> *I carry tremendous guilt about being a silent witness to all the ridiculous and completely unnecessary discipline and harassment you laid upon my brothers and sisters, especially Hap and Jillian. I felt so helpless, so frustrated at not being able to remove them from your meanness. I also felt that frustration about your behavior towards Dad.*

As Vicki wrote the word "Dad," she had an instant recollection of the comforting scent of Juicy Fruit gum, VF's favorite. She thought about many years past, when she and Hap were toddlers, before the other children were born, and she had her daddy all to herself. She could see her handsome hero walking up the steps to the house as she waited at the top, tilting his movie star face up to see her. She smiled as she remembered his wide grin with his perfect teeth closed, a piece of gum peaking out on the side. She felt his strong, capable arms as she heard him calling her his "little vixen," lifting her high over his head and twirling her around.

Vicki's mood grew cloudy when she thought about the things she saw her mother do to her father—flashbacks of Virginia throwing hot coffee on VF because she suspected an affair, screaming at him in front of the children because she wanted a more expensive car, hitting him in the face when he accepted a coveted professorship because "now you'll find your floosy." Vicki continued to write:

> *You seem to harbor the attitude that if you scream louder, pound your fists harder, slap faces, then you can get your way and no one will stand up to you. And it seems to have worked out that way. So you just keep doing it. You keep getting your way.*

*The angels are still crying at the way you wrecked your children's lives. Jillian's death still screams for justice.*

*You go around bragging that you had eight children—your big claim to fame, being a baby-making machine. What you fail to tell everyone is that out of those eight children, five became alcoholics or addicts. Do you ever stop to think that you may have contributed to their disease?*

Vicki stopped writing, wondering if it was fair to blame her mother for the alcoholism in the family. She had read recently that DNA can be affected by trauma in early childhood and she pondered whether alcoholism is an inherited gene, and if the trauma inflicted by Virginia was what turned that gene on. Certainly her grandfather Williams, her mother's father, was an alcoholic. And she wondered if it was one and the same gene for drug addiction. *Why not?* She asked herself. *Alcohol is a drug; it alters behavior.* She thought about the many conversations she and Virginia had had about Richard's addiction:

*You mentioned several times while I was with you that you wonder what made Richard turn to drugs. Well, it doesn't take a rocket scientist to figure that one out. Don't you remember that when you found something that looked like marijuana in one of Richard's dresser drawers you called the police? This was your son and you call the police when you find an unidentifiable substance in his bedroom. You didn't even bother to sit down with him and quietly discuss it. That alone would be enough to start him off on the wrong path for the rest of his life.*

*Aside from the police, I'm sure all the yelling and carrying on with Dad didn't help. Children take those arguments to heart. With you it was a constant stream. One never knew when the volcano would blow.*

Vicki stopped writing. Tears were streaming down her face as she thought about Richard, and how tender and thoughtful he had been to his father when he cared for him before his death. She wished she could change the past.

She looked up at the clock and then noticed the darkness outside the French doors of her study. Hours had passed. Time had ceased to exist while she wrote. She needed a break.

Stepping outside into her sunken patio with a glass of sparkling water, she felt better about herself. *Yes*, she told herself, *this is a letter I've needed to write for a long time. I will send it.* She sat on the chaise, lifted her head to the skies and felt grateful for the wide expanse of navy blue with the swath of the Milky Way. *Please God, help me get through this*, she prayed.

That night, she had a beautiful, comforting dream. She was kneeling at the foot of a statue of the Virgin Mary, in the most gorgeous chapel of Tiffany stained glass and Carrera marble. She could feel the cool marble under her knees. As she prayed, the Virgin Mary, surrounded by warm light, came to life, lifting her up. She began to weep. "Dry your tears, my child," the Virgin Mary said. "I am with you always. You are safe." Suddenly, Vicki felt a tenderness and warmth throughout her body, something akin to bliss. She awoke with one goal: finish this letter.

First thing in the morning after her walk, she continued:

*And Hap. On my God! Why were you so cruel to him? I'm surprised he ever talked to you as an adult. The way you made him dress up like a girl so everyone could make fun of him at the lunch table in the summer. "Since he was acting like a girl, he might as well look like one," you said. That was your rationale. The pain of throwing up after being made to drink a quart of milk that was rancid. The pain of having all his model planes, ships and cars so painstakingly made smashed by YOU. The pain of having his head put under scalding water after getting his finger burned on a firecracker. The pain of having his head dunked in a commode. The list goes on and on and on.*

*And why did Hap look different than everyone else? Is there a deep, dark secret?*

Vicki stopped writing. This would be the hot button.

She remembered the lunch meeting with Faye soon after VF's death, way back in 1995.

Faye was the sister of VF's best friend, Fred. At VF's funeral, she invited Vicki to meet and talk about Hap.

Within a couple of months of the invitation, Vicki drove the 200 miles to Dallas to meet with Faye. She wanted to be far, far away from the ranch.

La Madeleine was a favorite of Faye's. They served nourishing lunches, close to her home on Mockingbird Lane. Faye was dressed beautifully in a baby blue cashmere sweater and matching skirt, with low blue suede heels. Vicki wore her favorite white long-sleeve blouse, white lace sweater and black slacks, with black flats. She couldn't help think upon seeing Faye, *why in the world do I always dress like a nun?*

They ordered—Faye the quiche and Vicki a wholesome salad.

Faye began the difficult conversation. "Vicki, I'm so sorry I brought up this terrible story. I shouldn't have, especially at such a delicate time."

"I'm so curious about this far more serious secret you mentioned at Dad's funeral."

"I shouldn't have."

"You've said that. Faye, I've driven two hundred miles to see you. I would really like to know what you know."

"I don't know how to say this."

"Just begin at the beginning," Vicki gently offered.

"I think this information will help you see why Virginia was so cruel to Hap."

"Faye, we've all wondered about Hap. He never looked like the rest of us, and he was different. He loved singing, and performing. That's not much like us, either. He thought being some kind of singer was his destiny, either that or being an artist. He was always getting into trouble as a kid, or maybe it was just Mom beating on him that caused the trouble."

Faye delicately put her hand on Vicki's arm and leaned in, "Dear, my husband and I were so upset about Hap being abused that we offered to adopt him. After all, we had no children, and we had the means to send him to the best schools."

"Who refused to let you adopt him?"

"Mainly Virginia. She was livid when we suggested that this would relieve the burden of 'mothering' so many children. He was only seven at the time and your mother and father had five children by then."

"Five minus Jillian. Four children," Vicki interrupted.

"Yes. God bless little Jillian. I think VF warmed up to the idea of adoption because he hoped Hap would have a better future."

"So," Vicki looked at Faye's dark eyes, "who is his father?" Vicki knew that Faye knew.

Faye shifted uncomfortably in her chair. She asked for more tea.

Minutes passed.

"Faye?" Vicki asked.

Faye looked at Vicki, and cleared her throat.

"We're not sure—no one tested the DNA, but we think his father was a friend of your mom's from before she met VF, and then she continued to see him."

"So this was when Dad was in law school?"

"Yes, probably even before that—when he was a senior at UT."

Vicki tried to think if she had ever heard her mother talk about another man.

"Was he from Austin?"

"No. He was from a wealthy family from Ohio."

Faye paused. She could see that Vicki was trying to absorb the news.

"Wow. Ohio. You know that Mom's dad and stepmother Ada lived in Ohio, don't you?" Vicki asked.

"Yes, we believe he and your mom met in Ohio when Virginia visited your grandfather Williams and Ada there as a teenager. Virginia also had a stepsister the same age, married to a multi-millionaire, and they would have grand parties. I think they met at one of the parties and were attracted to each other.

"I met Virginia—my mom's stepsister—when we went to Ohio to visit granddad once. She had a beautiful mansion and her husband was crazy about cars. He had two barns of these gleaming cards in popsicle colors—he had Ferraris and Maseratis and Lamborghinis and other cars whose names I couldn't pronounce."

Vicki thought back to that time, and wondered if this guy was around when she and her sisters and brothers visited Ohio.

"So, how old was he?" Vicki asked.

"Oh, he was the same age as your mother, we think."

"Did you ever meet him?"

"No."

"Did Dad ever meet him?"

"No."

"So how could he possibly get Mom pregnant?"

"Well, it's a little bit complicated," Faye answered.

Vicki was annoyed that her mother, who always accused her father of affairs, had carried on such a damaging affair during the war.

"What was his name?" Vicki asked.

"Dan. We only know his first name. Dan graduated from the University of Washington soon after VF and Virginia married, then joined the Navy during the height of the war."

"But, why wouldn't Dad have known about him?"

"Your dad—VF—was on a secret classified mission in Czechoslovakia during the time Hap was conceived."

"I've heard bits and pieces about this mission. Do you know more? Is it declassified now that the War has been over for fifty years?"

"I've just surmised what it was about, from hints from my brother Fred. I think this was a test mission for the US to learn all they could about an SS General Reinhard Heydrich who had become the Nazi's Reich Protector of Bohemia and Moravia. The Czechs called him the Butcher. The Allies wanted him dead, and VF and his fellow soldiers who all spoke Czech were parachuted into a village close to Heydrich's headquarters. They were supposed to gather intelligence on his movements—his activities. But something went wrong. They were only there for a week or so when someone leaked to the Nazi commander that some American soldiers were there. The Nazis captured five of them, tortured them, and finally killed them. VF and another trooper barely made it out of Czechoslovakia. It was considered a failed mission. According to Fred, though, it helped set up a future mission of the Brits that killed Heydrich. Although, I think all those soldiers were killed."

"Wow. Dad never mentioned this."

"As I said this was classified. These were the horrors of the War, Vicki."

They ate quietly for a few minutes, and their drinks were refreshed.

Faye continued, "Virginia lived in Florida alone with you at that time. Soon after VF left on his secret mission, Virginia and Dan renewed their relationship. Within a few months, Dan was shipped off from a Florida base to the Pacific front. Virginia never saw him again."

"How do you know all of this?"

Faye looked down. "VF found a stash of letters from Dan to Virginia when he returned to the States after nearly a year abroad. He was furious. Beside himself. She was nine months pregnant by then. He called Fred and confided in him. VF decided to do the right thing, to keep the baby, and keep the marriage intact."

"Did Mom ever acknowledge that Hap was Dan's baby?"

"Not to VF. She just wouldn't talk about it," Faye said.

Vicki's ruminations felt rejuvenating. She continued writing:

*She said she and her husband at one point offered to adopt Hap since they were childless and it was obvious he was being mistreated, but YOU refused. I suppose that would be admitting the lie. Obviously, your false pride ruled out over Hap's well being. His life would definitely have been more stable if he had loving parents.*

Vicki knew that when she wrote about Hap's parentage she was delving into buried history, and she wanted to confront it before Virginia passed away. *Shouldn't the rest of the family know who Hap's real dad was?*

She stopped writing and thought about what she was doing. Did she really want to send this to everyone in the family? Hap included? *Why would I want to hurt Hap even more?*

She deleted the sentence *And why did Hap look different than everyone else?* She deleted the next paragraph about Faye wanting to adopt Hap.

As she ruminated about the abuse meted out to Hap, she couldn't help but think about Jillian, and the torture she suffered at such a young age. "Little puppy dog needs to learn," Virginia would smirk when Jillian wet the bed as a toddler, as she smashed her little face into the wet bed sheets over and over again.

Vicki remembered waking up in the wee hours of the morning with little Iris weeping beside her. Vicki would soothe Iris by gently tickling her back until she went back to sleep and then she would tiptoe to Jillian and do the same for her. The girls' dorm was set up so that Vicki's single bed was at the far corner of the room, just far enough to hear the rumblings of her mother's wrath and to pretend she didn't. For the rest of her life, she would pay dearly in psychic income for not defending her sister and brother.

Vicki wrote about Virginia's transgressions to Jillian and others including Iris and Mary, her erratic behavior during the final moments of VF's life and the time during which the funeral home employees arrived to prepare the body.

> *Then when Dad died, you and I were in the room. You sat there completely without emotion. Like you had planned it all along and were just waiting for the outcome. You said, "I just wanted him in the ground and out of the way and then YOU come along and change everything." You were referring to me explaining to the funeral director that we need a later date for the funeral since people needed time to get here from out of town.*

> *You were actually joking with the two men from the funeral home when they were putting Dad's body into the body bag.*

> *We showed you Dad's papers that requested what he wanted engraved on his tombstone. You refused. What shocked me the most is what little respect you had for Dad. I realized you were jealous of him and really hated him.*

> *After you had been so cruel to me during Dad's illness, trying to ban me from the ranch because I needed to be with my daughter in Colorado for a brief time, you were then overly generous—like deeding me a pasture and rental property.*

> *Vicki took a yoga break for half an hour and prepared a cup of herbal tea afterward. She looked over what she had written. Here comes the hard part she told herself. She pushed herself to finish what seemed like a thesis, but what would become a catharsis.*

> *I still feel like a child around you because you are so intimidating.*

*How do you defend your erratic behavior?*

*The sex thing bothers me. You had my first born examined at the tender age of five by a doctor who used the metal instrument used to examine the uterus because she complained of her vulva being irritated. You thought my husband was messing around with her? This exam was done while she was left in your care! I found out from my daughter. The irritation had been caused by a bubble bath. How could you do that?*

*Then I found out that you had accused my youngest sister of having sexual relations with Dad. How insane. I think you were jealous of his attention toward his daughter since you weren't getting the most attention.*

*And then there was the potty training obsession. You were convinced that all children should be potty trained by the time they could walk to their potty. This was when I left my daughters in your care. You decided it was time for Tootsie to be potty trained. I don't know what you did; there were no bruises. But she stuttered for six months after that baby-sitting adventure.*

*What was the business with enemas? How you had us children line up on a weekly basis and you would pump hot water up our asses? How did you get pleasure from that?*

Vicki knew this was a fool's errand, but she felt she had to ask Virginia to change. So she pleaded:

What makes the bad less offensive is when:

1. the doer acknowledges her actions

2. says she was wrong

3. asks forgiveness

*If you do not do this in your present lifetime, you will leave that evil lingering and still felt by your offspring, and you will have to deal with it in your next life.*

*I am still doing this—asking forgiveness for wrongs. It's part of the AA program.*

*I have been brave and said things no one else has probably dared to tell you. What you do with the information is your call.*

*Perhaps you could start writing letters to your children and grandchildren and tell them that you are truly sorry for any and all wrongs and that you love them. How about Thanksgiving at the ranch? You could include an invite with your note.*

*This could be the beginning of a NEW FAMILY—a healthy family who wants to live in harmony with one another.*

*For this to happen you will have to drop the false pride and say,*

*'Vicki, yes there were times I was wrong about the way I behaved toward you and your Dad and the grandkids. I am truly sorry for anything I have done in the past to hurt you, your sisters, brothers, grandchildren and your father.'*

*You aren't the only one who has been BAD. I remember when I first sobered up and joined AA. The first thing required by AA is to seek out the people you have harmed by your alcoholic behavior and apologize. Naturally my girls were first on the list. That's when I discovered that they had both gone to counseling because of my behavior. And all the time I had been under the impression that I had been a good mother. It's amazing how a person can be disillusioned.*

*Now that I've admitted my faults and said I was sorry and truly and deeply apologized I think they are beginning to remember the good things about their childhood. They tell me that they feel a lot stronger mother-daughter relationship.*

\*   \*   \*

Vicki sent the letter, minus the part about Hap's parentage, to all of her siblings, and hand delivered it to her mother. Virginia never mentioned it and certainly never asked for forgiveness. However, it was the best therapy Vicki ever had. Sending the letter to her brother and sisters and then discussing it with Dr. Earl helped her to hand over the care and concern of Virginia to her sister Mary. Forever.

"I'm glad you've come to some closure, Vicki, about caring for your mother." Dr. Earl said at the next session. "Did you bring anything with you today that would absolve your mother, like I asked?"

The homework was for Vicki to find anything personal her mother had written that would help Vicki see that her mother was a person with feelings.

"Surprisingly, I found something she had written. It's a little mysterious."

"You want to read it?" Dr. Earl asked.

"Sure. I think my mom had attended a memoir writing class or something like that. I found this in a drawer in her favorite desk when she was out with friends." Vicki held up a hand-written page.

"Let's hear it."

Vicki nodded and began,

## A Train Ride

*Every summer, I had to visit my Dad, who lived in Dayton, Ohio. I would usually take the train.*

*I was married and had a husband and several children at home when I made one trip. On my way home, after my visit, I was sitting in the observation car of the train when a handsome man sat down beside me.*

*We started talking and he held my hand. I think we covered every topic but sex and all that night he kept holding my hand. He never even tried to kiss me. When daylight came, the train was pulling into the St. Louis station. This is where we both had to change trains. He went his way. I went mine.*

*I never saw or heard from him again, but all I can remember is that he had more feelings in his hands than my husband had in his whole body! What a wonderful experience! This experience was a gift, a memory that will always be with me. It helped my self-esteem and made me feel alive.*

"So, what did you think when you read that the first time?" Dr. Earl asked.

"Gosh, well, first I was surprised that Mom would even write about such an experience. It was sweet. Touching. But then I was a little pissed off that she was demeaning Dad and saying that this guy had more feelings in his hands than Dad had in his whole body. That's so mean. That's just not Dad."

"Do you think perhaps your parents' relationship with each other was more complicated than you ever knew?"

Vicki's eyes widened, "Well, of course they were more complicated. She was such a maniac….is such a maniac…"

"Wait, Vicki, let's try not to be judgmental. It could be that your mother has mental health issues and that you could examine what went on in your childhood with that lens."

As they talked about Virginia, Vicki's hatred for her eased, and she realized that just being able to give voice to her story made her stronger.

Soon after reading what the family eventually called "The Crazy Mother" letter, Virginia unexpectedly phoned Iris and told her "I do not dream nor do I cry. You know, you all expect me to be this blubbering moron, all helpless and sad. What is there to be sad about? Life is life. Death is death. Your Daddy used to tell me as I read the obituaries every morning, 'person's gotta die of something.' He was right. We all die. No need to cry. Just a fact of life."

Iris couldn't help writing "I Do Not Weep" after that conversation.

## I Do Not Weep

*I do not weep*
*She told her daughter*
*I do not sleep*
*I do not dream*

*I do not weep*

*I take pride in my pride*
*Of eight*

*Yes, I've sold the land*
*Why not*
*Damned land*
*Filthy land*
*Mostly tho I've given it away*
*I'm a philanthropist*
*For the family*
*Bits—*
*my favorite…*
*I never hit her*
*That I remember*
*So she got the best*
*And the most*
*As she should.*
*She gave me so much*
*Love*

*Unlike her father*
*Wed to his religion*
*And his silly land*

*He betrayed me*
*He died first*

*I've been a good mother*
*Well fed*
*Well clothed*
*Ungrateful bastards*

*They better say I had a*
*Sense of humor*
*I love to laugh*
*I do not weep*

\*　　\*　　\*

Vicki had a long discussion with Mary about taking over Virginia's care. Mary was a well-known, prosecuting attorney in Austin with two sons, a husband wed to his dental practice, and a bruising travel schedule. She had more than her share of responsibilities but regrettably she knew she needed to step in.

"Mary, I'm worn out," Vicki said when she called. "I've cleaned up after Mom, suffered her cruel statements about me and others, fed her, taken her to the bank and her painting lessons, and done everything I can to keep from killing that damned woman."

"What about Bits?" Mary asked.

"Bits? Are you kidding? She and Mom are the same. Selfish. Self-centered. There is no way Bits could care for anyone except herself. And her land-grabbing just continues. Until you step in and do something, Mary, she'll take away all of your bequeathed property."

"Why do you think she'll take my property?"

"Well, she already has taken ten acres in an easement to the creek. Check it out. I talked with the surveyor the other day. She's stealing your property bit by bit, pardon the pun."

"You mean, she widened the road to the creek and took part of my property in that easement?" Mary was paying attention.

"Yes, told the surveyor it was so that her trucks can get into the vineyard."

"You mean the faux vineyard?" Mary knew that there was no wine being created on Bits' so-called vineyard. The wine was shipped in from Toronto, bottled and labeled on the ranch.

"In addition, whenever Mom and Bits get together, Bits gets larger and larger grants from Mom's bank account. I saw a statement the other day that showed $50,000 was taken from Mom's account. I checked with the bank, it was wired to Bits' account!"

That did it. Mary agreed she needed to take over the care of their mom.

Vicki told Mary where she could find the keys to the house, all the legal and financial paperwork for Virginia, and the names and phone numbers of the neighbors.

"I cannot be the boss of a crazy person any longer."

"I understand," Mary said.

Mary immediately made decisions about her mother's future care. She decided to move Virginia out of the ranch house and began working out the arrangements with nurses and healthcare aids to get Virginia the care she needed twenty-four hours a day at a luxurious retirement community close to the ranch.

"You would have thought she would have been kicking and screaming," Mary told Iris one weekend. "But it only took near death to get her out of the fortress."

"Yeah, I didn't think Mom would go gently into the night," Iris said.

Mary agreed. "It was a drama. I found out that Bits was trying to starve her to death."

"What? Bits? I thought they were BFFs."

"Yes, between the time Vicki stopped caring for her and I began getting her continuous care out there and then arranging for a new home, Bits was supposed to just make sure she had food to eat. Her friends would drop in to see her, and Patsy told me after three days that Mom had not had anything to eat or drink because Bits called the senior citizens club and told them to stop delivery."

"You have GOT to be kidding." Iris was incredulous.

"Nope," Mary continued, "by the time I came to pick her up, Bits had taken some of the most valuable furniture and paintings, and I found Mom in a puddle of piss acting very out-of-it, kind of delirious."

"So, that's how you got her to the continuous care center?"

"The luxurious retirement community," Mary corrected. "Yep. I don't think it was a brilliant strategy of Bits' to get her to move. I really think she was trying to kill Mom."

"I don't know why in the world I'm surprised. Or shocked."

\* \* \*

The transition from living at the ranch in a large home to a condo with a lot of people milling around was difficult at first, but Virginia warmed up to it and began to thrive after a couple of months.

As she told Mary one day, "I hated this hotel at first. But I like 'the help' and my friends. Father Gerard is a good man, and my lady friends who play gin with me are good fun." Mary wondered why she didn't mention a handsome older man who looked a lot like VF who ate lunch with her some days. Once she saw them holding hands.

Mary took over the bank accounts so that Virginia would be unable to continue to give hundreds of thousands of dollars away to Bits and bogus schemes; she obtained Power of Attorney.

She also learned that soon after VF's death, Bits covertly created a new will that Virginia signed, giving one-half of Mary's property to Bits upon their mother's death. Making the change back to the original would bring a thimble of justice to her life. She asked a good friend of hers, a wills and estate attorney, to draw up the appropriate paperwork.

"Mom," Mary asked one beautiful day in October after Virginia was comfortable in the plush new life of the hotel, as she called the retirement village, "why would you give the property that is supposed to be mine to Bits?"

"What are you talking about?" Virginia looked truly surprised by the question. It was morning, she had had her coffee, the view outside showed a bright and lovely day. Her mood was upbeat.

Mary held up the will. "This most recent will of yours gives Bits one-half of the land formerly left to me."

"There's been a mistake," Virginia said, smiling.

Mary pulled a corrected will from the file folder. "Mom, are you willing to sign the correct will stating that I will receive the property that belongs to me?"

"Sure."

"I'll be right back."

Mary walked to the office and asked the executive assistant if she was a notary. "Yes," the efficient, large woman replied.

"Could you come to Mrs. Landry's room with me and notarize these papers?"

"Of course."

The two women chatted as they walked briskly to Virginia's overstuffed room, picking up two witnesses along the way.

"Mom, I'm going to read you this will, and if you agree, you initial it and sign it, and these people will witness and notarize it."

"Well, OK, but really I have nothing to give away."

As Mary read each part of the will, Virginia nodded her agreement, initialed the appropriate areas, and signed the last sheet. It was witnessed and notarized. Mary would lawfully have her intended share of the ranch.

CHAPTER TEN:

# *Kiss Me Once*

## 2006

"Iris, do you really think that Hap's cremation led to Mom's heart attack?" Mary asked Iris in a late night call to New York in January, 2006.

"No, of course not. You heard the cardiologist didn't you?" Iris asked. "Remember, when we visited her in the hospital, the cardiologist took me aside and said Mom only had ten percent heart function. He gave her three to five months, remember? It wasn't about Hap or Catholic pedagogy. It was about the abuse of her body—all that sugar! Remember what PJ, her friend, said? That Mom never met a pie she didn't like? Then, her lack of exercise, heavy smoking when she was young...."

"I think Mom just never acknowledged she needed to see a physician for her heart. I'm surprised they found it at all," Mary quipped.

"Yeah, like the Tin Man," Iris snickered. "You read Vicki's letter?"

"I did. It was revealing."

"You missed a lot of that excitement because you're so much younger than most of us."

"Are you angry with Mom?"

"Damned right I'm angry with her. I shall dance on her grave," Iris said with determination. "Why wouldn't she ever apologize to Hap before he died? Did she even visit him when he was so frail?"

"I don't think so. Hap forgave her. That's what's important."

"You mean when he said, 'awww, she didn't know how to be a parent?' You think that was his forgiveness?"

"Probably."

Both sisters were silent.

"I should tell you about a dream I had soon after I read Vicki's letter," Iris offered.

"Tell me."

"OK. Dad had called me and asked me to come back to Texas from New York, so I arrived at a house I bought in Austin and as I walked in I saw that all the curtains were put up and that Mom and Dad were waiting for me. Dad was heavy, and had a short, grey beard—very distinguished looking, with moustache. The curtains were atrocious—and on every window. I was grossed out. I said, 'who did this? I ordered beautiful floor to ceiling white curtains.' Mom said, 'don't you like it dear? I thought you needed a change.' It was obvious she spent a great deal of time working on the curtains. They were huge blobs of bright blue and red and purple. They were short café style—cut in the middle.

"I was so upset. Dad could see that and he walked over to me, using his cane, and hugged me. I felt his whiskers and his warm arm and I said, 'Oh, Dad, I love you so much.' And he looked at me and said, 'Don't be too angry with your mother.'

"I woke up so sad. I just wish I had had a more loving mother."

"Well, did Mom ever hurt you?"

"I cannot say she physically hurt me, Mare. Certainly I was hurt by all the abuse I witnessed. She was unable to be affectionate. Maybe she had already given all of her affection away by the time I needed her love. She told me she was unable to nurse me—that I was born so fast and nearly a month early—she was unprepared. Then she was so exhausted she said that she contracted breast fever. So, I got evaporated milk mixed with corn syrup."

"Gross."

"That's what they did in 1949--infant formula didn't get into mainstream use until the mid-50's."

"I guess it's like Hap said, she did her best," Mary said.

"I think she had too many children too fast and too early. She was in her twenties for god's sakes! And surely it didn't help that…well, losing Jillian had to be traumatizing. It was to me."

"You've never talked about Jillian. No one ever talks about Jillian. I've only seen pictures of a beautiful little doll-like child. Do you want to tell me what happened to Jillian?" Mary asked.

Iris breathed in deliberately.

"OK, Mare. It's time to tell you about Jillian."

\*　　\*　　\*

Born on Valentine's Day, she was the icon for love and affection and the family's most beautiful daughter. Named Jillian as a symbol of youth—a goddess—and Antoinette for what her mother said was their French heritage, this little Landry had a complicated birth.

Virginia was given "special" drugs to allay her 24-hour birthing pains before she delivered Jillian, which paralyzed her. Jillian did not cry at first when she was wrenched with forceps from her mother's womb.

VF paced the "family room" for hours while he was kept in the dark about the delivery. He fervently promised he would pay more attention to this child than he did to her three siblings if God would just give him a healthy baby.

She was healthy, but her mother was left paralyzed for a month.

God bestowed other gifts on Jillian in addition to her ringlets of golden hair and her bright green eyes. A precocious toddler, she learned to read at age four. By the time she was five years old she was a seamstress, impressively dressing her dolls. She taught herself about fabrics, textures, stitches, threads, patterns, buttons, laces, and notions of all kinds.

At six, she created patterns from newspaper if she couldn't find the right Simplicity one for a shirt, skirt, dress, or pants. Her corner of the girls' dorm housed all of her neatly filed and categorized threads (in order of color), buttons, notions, ribbons, and most cherished fabrics in a heavy treasure chest that her VF gave her as a present on her sixth birthday.

By the time she was in Catholic elementary school Hap had taught her how to draw, design and color her fashions. She adorned her homework with sketches of different outfits for the saints, attaching a holy card showing the "before" and a fresh fashion design on the last page of her homework as "after." She thought that would amuse the nuns, whose black and white attire earned them the moniker crows.

She was a thoughtful big sister. She taught Iris, her adoring little sister, to read at age 4 and to write cursive by age 5.

She was vivacious, fun loving, tender and kind. "You have a heart of gold," her father told her, "just like my favorite aunt Julie."

Once she found a feral kitten when visiting Grandpa and Grandma Krejci at the O-Bar, and, worried that it didn't have a mother, she created a little cradle out of a shoebox and nursed it with a doll's bottle until it grew up and ran away.

When Hap showed her a dead mockingbird one day at their home in Austin, she created a funeral Mass complete with Necco wafers. "All God's creatures need respect," she said to little 4-year old Iris, who dutifully dug the grave.

Hap nicknamed her Beans because she was always like a jumping bean. She had one project after another, always on the go.

She also relished embellishing reality. When she was six years old she convincingly told other children and adults that she was adopted.

"My real parents," she said in her sweet precocious voice, hands folded, "perished in a hellish blaze of a car crash when I was an infant, and the Landrys took me in."

How else could the only blonde, green-eyed child fit into a family where everyone else except Hap was dark eyed, dark haired?

Fate caught up with her joyful innocence.

By the time Jillian was seven, Bits had had enough of her "bratty sister," as she referred to Jillian. Bits was nine and never got over what she felt was the loss of her daddy's affection. Bits was supposed to be the apple of his eye. It wasn't enough for Bits to be her mother's favorite. She wanted favoritism from both her parents. Despite seeing and hearing the beatings Jillian endured from Virginia for her bed-wetting, Bits needed to extract her pound of flesh and show Jillian who the real boss was.

The day of the fall began with an autumn shower that let up by noon. It was a Saturday and the kids had their chores. Jillian was supposed to iron ten handkerchiefs that day and then she was going to sew a new dress for her favorite doll. She finished her chores, stacked the ironed hankies on her father's dresser, and ran to the treble sewing machine to work on the doll's outfit. She sang as she worked, just like Cinderella.

"What's this?" she heard her mother scream. "Who burned this handkerchief?"

Her mother was having a tantrum. It scared her. She suffered enough from her mother's cruelty when she wet the bed. She and Iris always had to change the sheets, both of them crying as their mother brutally forced Jillian's head into the wet stains yelling, "puppy has to pay…puppy has to pay."

Virginia appeared in front of her, standing rigidly with one hand on a hip and the other holding a white handkerchief with a large brown and black burn in front of Jillian's face.

"You did this, didn't you?"

"No, ma'am… I didn't," Jillian said in her small voice.

"You'll pay, you little liar. Look at me."

Jillian stared at her mother's twitching eye with her large, sweet blue eyes, and shuttered.

"I can tell you're lying."

This was Virginia's trademark claim to fame. She had read that you could tell if a person is being truthful by the size of their pupils. If the pupils were dilated, they were lying. So she would demand that her child stare directly at her and she would determine if the child's pupils were enlarged, and therefore if she was a liar.

At that moment, Jillian was seized with her mother's strong hand and whacked repeatedly across the mouth, then her back and her legs. Then she felt herself thrown down on the hard floor.

"Little brat."

Jillian lay there, weeping. She waited for her mother to leave and then got up and grabbed her doll.

Bits walked over and shoved her. "Little brat," she repeated, throwing a freshly ironed handkerchief at her. The same one Bits had substituted for a burned version.

Jillian ran outside, weeping harder, tears rolling down her branded cheeks. Iris watched from the large living room picture window.

A twenty-foot wall separated the Landry property from the next-door neighbor's property. After all, they lived on Terrace Drive. It was built with large fieldstone and had a stone lip at the bottom. Jillian and Iris had skipped along that wall many times, never fearing that they might fall.

It looked as if Jillian was about to sit down on the wall but her leg buckled and in an instant she tumbled, the doll in her arms. She disappeared over the wall.

"Jillian fell," little Iris screamed. She raced outside, and screamed louder.

VF was outside working in the back yard. He heard Iris scream. He sprinted to the front and saw Iris standing on the wall, pointing down.

Jillian was at the bottom in a pool of blood. He literally jumped off the wall and scooped her up in his arms. He tried to stop the bleeding with his handkerchief, bundled her in blankets and placed her in the back seat of the family's Ford sedan.

"She had severe, fatal head trauma," Dr. Hunter announced after VF had raced her to his office.

There was nothing he could do to save her.

"I'm afraid she's with the angels now. You'll have to take her body to the hospital for the death certificate. I'm so sorry." Dr. Hunter had tears in his eyes. He was the family doctor. He had known her since she was born. The two men stood looking at each other forlornly.

At her funeral VF was beside himself. "I'll always envision my lovely little girl with her dollie who fell twenty feet onto the rocks…cold fear gripping me because she whispered, 'Daddy, I can't see; it's getting dark.' I remember choking back tears and saying, 'Darling, it will be all right.' And then holding her in my arms in the doctor's office praying she would live."

The next year the family moved.

\* \* \*

It was November 9, 2006. It would have been VF's 90th birthday. Mary was waiting outside the Texas Legislature where she was to report on impending legislation affecting Texas Parks and Wildlife when she got the call.

"Ms. Landry?" this is Ethel, your mother's aide. Mary did not go by her married name. "We've called the ambulance."

"Ethel? What's going on?"

"She fell, Ms. Landry. She's very weak. They'll take her to Hillcountry Hospital."

"I'll be there within an hour."

Mary left her junior attorney in charge and raced to the hospital in her new Lexus hybrid, accompanied by NPR news that Nancy Pelosi was meeting with President Bush and was probably going to become Speaker of the House. *You go, girl.* Such news kept her hopes up for the Democratic party. After all, she was considering running for judge in Travis County.

By the time she arrived at the hospital, Virginia had already been through radiology.

"Your mother has a broken hip," the orthopedist told Mary, very matter-of-fact. They were both standing in the hallway of the ICU. Mary looked down at his Tony Lama ostrich boots. "We can go in and repair the fracture with a pin. Should take about an hour—hour and a half tops."

"Will she be able to walk again?"

"Rehab should take a few weeks, but she should be on her feet almost immediately, and working towards rehab."

Mary agreed to the surgery and then called all of the siblings to let them know of Virginia's fall, her treatment and the prognosis. "I spoke with Mom before her surgery and she said I shouldn't be writing her obituary anytime soon," Mary told everyone. "She's going to live to be 100."

Vicki was not amused. "Not if I can help it," she said. "Mary, do you realize that this would have been Dad's 90th birthday?"

"Of course I did."

"Don't you think Mom is just stealing the spotlight?"

"I don't know. Mom loves attention, I have to hand it to her," Mary said.

After the surgery, things took a turn. Virginia screeched in pain when the nurses tried to get her on her feet, so she stayed in the hospital bed day after day.

Two weeks before Christmas, she acquired a urinary track infection. Then sepsis set in.

"Sepsis is an overall infection and it can be deadly in a hospital environment," the nurses explained to Mary. Virginia had fever, kidney dysfunction, increased heart rate, and confusion.

Mary called Iris, alarmed. "You should come back home for a while."

"What's 'a while'?" Iris asked.

"I don't know. The doctors say she may last several weeks, or a few days. I don't know. She talks. Still wants her root beer.

"Bits arrives and sits by her side staring—so dramatic. Joe was here last night praying with her," Mary said

"What a zoo. And Vicki?"

"Vicki has had it with Mom. I don't think she wants to go near her, except maybe to shut off her oxygen."

"I'll be there day after tomorrow."

Yet again, Iris was on a JetBlue flight from JFK to Austin-Bergstrom. This time, though, she made it a one-way ticket to keep the timeline open. She booked a suite at the downtown Hyatt for a week.

When Iris arrived at the hospital the early evening of December 18, she was met by the social worker, Barbara, who handed her a booklet entitled *Gone From My Sight*. She looked at the subtitle, "The Dying Experience."

Iris was alarmed. "Is my mother dying?" she asked Barbara.

Barbara's voice was kind and deliberate. "I've been with more than a hundred patients in various end-of-life stages, and I've watched your mother over the past couple of days. She is not eating. She is sleeping most of the time. She is disoriented. You'll be able to see for yourself. I think this book might help."

The warning on Virginia Landry's hospital door advised everyone to suit up for a serious infection for their own protection. Booties were available as well as hospital gowns. Iris ignored the warnings since Virginia no longer had an infection, and stood beside her sleeping mother, holding one of her terribly bruised hands and reading *Gone From My Sight*. It read:

One to Two Weeks Prior to Death

- Disorientation—A person can't seem to keep their eyes open…[they] often become confused, talking about places and events unknown to others. They may see and converse with loved ones who have died before them…

- Physical Changes—lower blood pressure, fluctuation in body temperature, increased perspiration…

- Breathing Changes—puffing, blowing of the lips, coughing, and congestion. One minute, any or all of these may be present, the next minute; breathing may clear and be even.

- Surge of Energy—One to Two Days prior to death—a person might sit up, talk clearly and alertly when before there had been disorientation. A favorite meal may be requested.

- Congestion—may be very loud

Virginia awoke and smiled sadly at Iris.

"Mom," Iris said softly, "it's your daughter Iris."

"Oh, Iris. Where've you been?"

"Well, I just came back from New York."

"Nuuuuuuuewwww York?," Virginia said, drawing out the first syllable as if the host of a late night show. The question was familiar. Although Iris had lived in New York for more than twelve years, Virginia always acted as if this was news.

"My parents met in Nuuuuuuuewww York."

Iris pulled up a chair, sat, felt Virginia's forehead, and held her hand, asking if she would like a glass of water.

"Did you know your grandmother was a Jew?"

Iris was surprised, but intrigued.

"I didn't," she answered.

Virginia's eyes twinkled with the glee of someone who has kept a lifetime secret, and turned her head to squarely meet Iris' eyes. "Yes. Finkbeinner was their name. My mother's side. They were from Baden Baden. Moved to New York. Maybe that's why you married a Jew. It's in your blood." Virginia smiled mischievously.

Iris contemplated whether that information was fact or fiction. Her mother was very weak. She spoke purposefully.

"I remember when I met your father. I was just fourteen. I didn't like him much. I thought my sister Dorothy should date him. Then my daddy moved me to Ohio with Ada, his new wife. The high school there was terrible. No orchestra, no journalism. Not like Austin's high schools."

Iris stood and cradled her mother's back to sit her up enough for a drink of water. Virginia sipped the water and fell asleep. Iris lowered the bed to a comfortable position and sat beside her for a few hours, listening to her difficult breathing, marveling at the revelations that her mother actually played in the orchestra and was interested in journalism. She re-read the dying pamphlet, trying to prepare herself for whatever was coming next.

Early the next morning, Iris took a run around Austin's Town Lake, re-named Lady Bird Lake, a reservoir of the Colorado River. Generations past, it was the dividing line between north and south Austin, between white collar and blue collar. She marveled at the beautifully constructed running trail and the Bridge Walk with its copper song belts—western belt sculptures engraved with words from songs by famous Austin musicians, which stretched along the two-mile course of the bridge. It was a mild 60° with a gentle breeze. She hoped each day of her stay would be this beautiful.

She thought about the times after her first horrifying marriage, when she and Miles, newly married, would come to the Congress Avenue bridge and watch the bats fly. They'd talk about the people, him commenting on crowd behavior, her talking about who was wearing or not wearing what or whose hair was green and whose was cherry pink.

She giggled when she remembered the boat tour they went on soon after VF's funeral. They wanted to do something touristy in her native city so they signed up for the bat boat tour. The tour guide was genuine Texan. Nearly a dozen tri-Delt sorority sisters were on the boat, cradling their drinks from the bat guana. "Hey, gals, hold on to yer drinks," he said as the boat came to a slow crawl under the bridge. "These bats don't have bathrooms."

The bat guana dropped loudly into the ladies' drinks and onto their cute outfits as they screamed for him to drive the boat faster. "Awwww.... gals, doan cha know...it's good luck to get a dousin.'" Iris loved that Miles handed the guide a $20 at the end of the ride and said, "keep it weird, dude."

Then they wandered over to Sixth Street and listened and danced to music long into the night. Miles loved the music. Iris loved watching him enjoy himself. He was not only an insightful sociologist; he was a musician who played keyboard in a pick up band. He loved to dance. She was not a fan of country western music, but if Miles wanted to dance, she was game. The two-step was a blast. They would help close down the place, dancing the night away. She never worried about drunk driving, either. He didn't drink. He said he was allergic to alcohol.

Thinking back before their marriage, it was probably his being a musician that attracted her to him.

The attraction began soon after her divorce. One Saturday night friends convinced her to come listen to a new jazz band on the drag, close to UT. She hired a babysitter for her boys and took them up on their offer.

Miles Cohen was there, playing keyboard. One of her friends knew him and introduced them.

Thus began the longest romance in the Landry family. As Iris explained to Vicki, "the first night we made love, we didn't just make love. We devoured each other. We couldn't stop making love. He was such a great lover—so sweet and caring, and so knowledgeable! I never knew sex could be so much fun!"

They were married within two years, and along with Iris' two sons from her first marriage, grew their family to three beautiful boys.

On the run, thoughts turned to the present situation and the hatred of her mother's behavior. Childhood flashbacks entered her mind—especially the day Virginia tore through Hap's bedroom and demolished every one of his perfectly crafted model planes, cars and ships, leaving Hap sobbing in a corner with his arms folded around his jean-clad skinny legs. *I remember the loops were cut off those jeans.* She could see every detail of her mother's tantrum. The cold, white walls of the room. The strings dangling from the ceiling where the magnificent model planes had flown. The plastic shards of the models in clumps on the floor. One decal stood out: the Flying Tigers P-40. His favorite plane.

Iris' meditation coach was teaching her how to take those negative thoughts, turn them into clouds, and let them float away. She did so with this memory, and for the rest of her run, delighted in being able to name singers of some of the lyrics she passed.

Day after day, Iris showed up at her mother's bedside, listening to the doctor and nurses talk about her care, confiding in Mary about what to do if Virginia died that day, and helping to manage the family visitors.

Even in such a dire situation Virginia still had some anger to throw around.

"Take me out of here!" she seethed at Iris one afternoon. Her eyes could have burned holes in a blanket.

Iris listened to her inner self and let the anger drift away. "Mom, we cannot take you out of here. You need constant care."

"If you don't take me out of here immediately," she hissed, "I will take you out of my will. Did you hear me? I will take you out of my will."

Iris had a hard time holding back. What she wanted to say to her mother was "Well, bitch, I'm not in your fucking will."

Instead she said without the slightest hint of mockery, "Mom, we're working on it. We'll try to get you out of here very soon."

Virginia wasn't eating, refused even water, and she was complaining how much her body hurt. Her eyes would suddenly open wide and she would call out to no one "It hurts so much."

Day after day, Iris grew less angry with her mother and more aware that she was on a journey to the other side.

On day five, Virginia asked for a chocolate malt. Father Joe was summoned to pick one up at her favorite burger joint, Sandy's. When he delivered it, Iris, Mary, and Vicki's daughter Jessica were there. Virginia was very lively.

"I wondered if that Chinese doctor was young enough for me," she said.

"Dr. Ng?" Joe asked. "He's Vietnamese."

"He's a handsome one. I like his uniform." She smiled.

"Mom, that's his white coat. He's a doctor."

"Yes, I know," she continued, "and do I have a new definition for white coat syndrome."

The room erupted in laughter. Virginia was being bawdy again, even as she lay in critical condition.

She couldn't drink the malt. She fell asleep.

Long after everyone left, the nurse's aide asked Iris if she would help bathe Virginia. She brought sponges, warm soapy water, and a soothing after-shower powder. She lowered the shades, turned on the soft lights. They lifted Virginia gently to a sitting position in the bed, removed her hospital gown, and covered her with warm towels. "You take that side, and I'll bathe this," the young aide said. Virginia sighed.

Iris uncovered her mother's right breast and saw how small and shriveled it was.

*So this is the breast that couldn't feed me,* Iris thought sadly.

She saw the smooth, unblemished skin on Virginia's back, noticed her long, slim neck, and her terribly bruised hands and arms from the intravenous needles. As Virginia breaths grew longer, she dipped the large sponge into soapy water and gently bathed her neck, under her arms, her back, her bottom, between her legs, those long and pretty legs, her feet, and noticed her recent pedicure.

When she softly towel dried her mother's body she longed to hold her. To be still with her. To love her.

The only instance of being held by her mother that Iris remembered was when she was about four years old. The family was traveling in the old Ford "Woodie" station wagon, heading back to Austin from a visit at the O-Bar farm, VF driving. With five children at that time, there was no room for Iris in the car except on her mother's lap. She cuddled into a ball in her mother's arms, and felt her warmth for the two-hour trip. As she lay her head on her mother's breast, she smelled baby powder mixed with a hint of Chanel No. 5. Dreamy.

Iris helped the nurse put a beautiful baby blue satin nightgown on Virginia that Mary bought to help her feel pretty.

The nurse took all the towels, sponges, and wash pan and tiptoed out.

As she stepped back and looked at her mother dozing quietly, a deep sense of love and forgiveness washed over Iris.

It could only be described as bliss. It was similar to an experience she once had as a Eucharistic minister. When she was handed the chalice, she felt an all-consuming warmth throughout her body, and a desire to fall on her knees. *Was this rapture?*

The next morning, Virginia, in a deep haze, told Iris and Mary about a bassinette.

"It was there," she whispered in a raspy voice, pointing to the sky with her manicured finger, "a white basket-weave bassinette with light blue beads and a blue satin lining. It was there. They said the baby was gone. They can't find the baby. I need to help them find the baby. I saw my mother."

"Your mother?" Mary asked.

"Dan, Dan, Dan…." Virginia answered mysteriously, then she fell asleep.

Mary and Iris stared quizzically at each other.

"Who is Dan?" Mary asked.

"Beats me," Iris said, "you think she said 'Dad'?"

"No, you heard her. She said Dan."

Mary plugged in a CD player for Virginia to listen to her treasured 1940's hits, and put in her all time favorite CD of Bing Crosby. They hugged and Mary left for work.

Iris settled in for another long day of brushing her mother's silver-streaked mane, listening to her breathing, and discussing her care with the doctor and nurses. They agreed to remove the IV from her hand, which had occluded. When the nurse gave her the five injections to reverse the damage, Virginia screamed feebly.

Her kidney function had returned to normal, and except for her fever, her lack of appetite and her congestive heart failure, she was doing well, the doctor said when he appeared later in the day.

Iris pulled a chair closer to Virginia, and sat at its edge, watching her mother sleeping and breathing heavily. She had brought along her favorite prayer book, and quietly read the scripture for Thursday:

> May the God who gives us peace make you completely His,
> and keep your whole being, spirit, soul, and body free from all
> fault, at the coming of our Lord Jesus Christ.

Every few minutes Virginia's breathing stopped—as if she had apnea. Then it would continue. Her eyes were closed, her mouth wide open. Iris gently wiped her brow. She kissed her cheek. *Not a single wrinkle, and no plastic surgery for this girl! There's a testament to skin care compliments of Lancôme and her favorite facialist.* Iris sat uncomfortably, not knowing what else to do. The music played softly in the background.

Iris thought about the dramatic scenes in movies where the offender and the offended have their come to Jesus moment. She wished Virginia could talk to her. There was so much she wanted to ask, and words she wanted to hear. She wanted more than anything for her mother just to say "I love you, Iris."

Virginia's breathing stopped. Abruptly. A hard stop.

Simultaneously, the music stopped.

All was still.

*This is it?*

Iris held her breath. Listened. Watched.

She saw her mother's body lie quietly as a whirlwind of gauzy iridescence materialized above her, then hovered briefly and disappeared. Iris immediately felt she had witnessed a cellular transformation. She felt a lightness of being—as if being witness to this passing lifted her, too. She was not afraid. Not angry. She was in awe.

She stood up, put her ear to her mother's chest, and then looked at the CD. It had stopped on the song, "It's Been a Long, Long Time," Virginia's all-time favorite. She felt like she could hear her mom sing, "Kiss me once, kiss me twice, and kiss me once again…" *How appropriate to die hearing her angel Bing Crosby.*

Iris kissed her mother and calmly rang the nurses' station. No one came, so she covered her mother and walked up to the desk.

"I believe my mother has died."

The head nurse hurriedly followed Iris back to Virginia's room, checked her vital signs, and nodded.

Iris phoned Mary, pulling her out of a meeting. Mary, who had Power of Attorney, called the funeral home. Everything else happened in quick succession. The doctor signed the death certificate, Mary arrived, the funeral home employees picked up the body, and family members were all alerted that Virginia died December 23, 2006.

Iris did not cry.

# CHAPTER ELEVEN:

# Oh Death! Where Art Thy Sting?

## Christmas, 2006

Mary and Iris worked with the funeral home and with the pastor at the Dripping Springs Catholic Church close to the ranch to re-create the service that Virginia had arranged years before. The church allowed Father Joe to officiate. Virginia's instructions included an open casket, no rosary, a church service but no communion, "nice" music, flowers, and burial next to VF in the family cemetery. Virginia had thought of almost everything, but the sisters felt it needed a little more panache.

"Should we entitle the program, 'Oh Death, Where Art Thy Sting?'" Iris asked Mary while meeting with the funeral director. *Mom's last words to me before I moved to New York. So cruel.* She was ruminating more than proposing the title of her mother's funeral program. She knew her mother didn't get the words right. She just couldn't help herself.

The director grabbed his King James Version bible and turned to the verse. "It's here," he said, "1 Corinthians 15:55-57 'O death, where is thy sting? O grave, where is thy victory?'"

Mary kiboshed that idea. "No, Iris. No." Iris just couldn't help it. She smiled, and then she suggested holy cards with St. Anthony's image on them "because St. Anthony is the patron saint of loss."

It was true that during their childhood Virginia made the magic of beseeching the saints to intercede for a special cause into a weekly ritual. She made all the children pray to St. Anthony when anything in the house was lost. Most of the time, the prayers were answered since all the family needed was a quiet minute or two to contemplate where the item was last seen.

There were more global requests. She told them to pray to St. Jude when she felt there was an impossible cause, like the Vietnam War. Vicki took up the practice with gusto and created a shrine to the Blessed Virgin Mary in the girls dorm. A one foot statue of the Blessed Virgin held a jeweled miniature rosary in her hands, with smaller statues of St. Teresa of Avila, patron saint of headache suffers, and St. Joseph, patron saint of carpenters, at each side. Jillian was only six when she made the alcove part of their built-in bookshelves, and lined it with blue velvet.

The funeral was set for December 26, the day after Christmas. Both Iris and Mary hurriedly ran errands, chose stunning lingerie, a cerulean blue dress, wrote the obituary and designed the program. Virginia may have been a horrible mother most of the time, but they were going to have her dressed in style because they were not vindictive. That and she was going on a date with their dad.

Vicki asked to arrange the reception. Their families wondered if there would be a Christmas that year. Mary had two children in middle and high school, and Iris had grown, married sons and grandchildren. They told their families that Christmas would have to wait. Iris asked her kids and husband to come to Austin for the funeral, where they would celebrate Christmas.

Mary and Iris decided that Iris would give the eulogy. "Years ago, I *so* wanted to tell everyone what a horrible human being Mom was. I looked forward to that day. Now, I feel very different. It's as if a great burden is gone—I think I understand some of what she went through with so many kids and having them one after another, with all the demands of raising hellions, and having such a complicated family herself. I just will never understand her cruelty, the over the top abuse she meted out. The rage. I'll never get it. But perhaps the times in which they lived from the beginning set the stage for chaos in Mom and Dad's lives."

"Yeah… marrying Dad during the War" Mary offered.

"I can imaging that was frightening and exciting at the same time."

\* \* \*

On December 26, the church accommodated a small crowd to celebrate Virginia L. Landry's life. Most of Virginia's Wild Women friends were there. The last funeral Virginia had attended was her good friend Dottie, who had passed away several years before in an auto accident. Dottie was driving her brand new Mercedes when hit by a 19-year old whose car veered across the median at 90 mph. The teenager escaped with bruises.

One of Virginia's favorite songs, *Amazing Grace*, opened the service. The organist was Virginia's piano teacher. Mary read scripture and Father Joe led the singing of *An Old Rugged Cross*, something Virginia requested in her funeral arrangements. Finally, Iris approached the lectern, and looked out over the friends, family and neighbors who had gathered.

"Thank you for being here with us today and celebrating Mom's life. I'm Iris Landry Cohen, number five of the Landry Tribe, and I had the privilege of being with Mom when she drew her last breath. I'm sure some of you are wondering if she passed with any last words or revelations. Frankly, I think she had said them months ago.

"That was when I got a call from her as I was walking home from work. No one was more surprised than I was to hear *her* voice because she NEVER called *me*. 'Well, hello Iris? It's your mom. You doing OK? What are you doing?'"

"Well Mom I'm walking home from work."

"Where do you work?"

"I work in New York."

"After the niceties of asking about my family, she went on to tell me what a magnificent sunset she was watching, and how colorful the wide, Texas sky was."

"'I'm looking out the back porch window now. Your dad would have loved to see this. I think I see a deer out there.' She told me she really loved Dad and missed him terribly. I was speechless—you just had to know my mom—she was a tough cookie and she would never ever let anyone know she had such emotions.

"Mom's greatest pride was her eight children. 'My chickadees' she used to call us. And we would call her 'Mamasita.' Our wake up call was 'Good morning breakfast lovers, good morning to you!' in an off-tune lilting voice, throwing open the bedroom door and sashaying into the room as if she was in a Broadway show.

"Her father was an engineer and she made the trains run on time in our family. She was master planner of our activities and our shuttle service—to music, dance, tennis, tumbling, etiquette lessons, cooking classes, Scouts, Y-Teens, and hair appointments.

"Because she had attended nursing school, she was very attentive to us when we were ill, making sure we had all the necessary comforts to bring us back to health, including her favorite, of course—ice cream. She made sure we had regular dental appointments, and would call Dr. Hunter to our home when a child had a raging fever.

"She spoke sign language. She learned it in order to communicate with the owners of the dry cleaners we frequented.

"She was mysterious. What was it with the violin she kept most of her life? She had played it as a child, but why had she given up playing it? She loved painting, but never took us to an art museum. She took up painting china, then watercolors, and oils—usually with like-minded gentlewomen, finally joining the Palette Club.

"Her favorite color was blue. Her favorite cookbook was that red plaid Betty Crocker cookbook, of course. Favorite food? Lobster, with Cheddar Bay Biscuits as a close 2nd. Favorite restaurant? Red Lobster. Just last week she told us her favorite movie was *Cool Hand Luke*. Her favorite ice cream flavor was vanilla and her favorite soda was root beer.

"I never saw her ride a horse, although she lived many years on a ranch. She was afraid of horses.

"Her genealogy as a descendant of Roger G. Williams, the founder of Rhode Island, gave her some claim to fame, but she never told us more about the Williams' clan. The only thing she clung to from that family was the enigmatic Williams family bible from 1891.

"Her life, it seems, was to create and celebrate the lives of her children.

"Although there were a LOT of birthdays to remember, Mom always made sure that birthdays were celebrated. That didn't mean there were expensive presents, but it did mean cake and ice cream with candles and Happy Birthday sung out of key.

"Catholicism was an adopted religion for her, and although she preferred Baptist hymns, she made the best of the pageantry and ceremony of the Catholic Church. She made sure we had our prayer books, mantillas and our rosaries and that we attended Catholic school. And, I'm sure none of us can ever forget that she would have us pray to St. Anthony immediately when any of us lost something—miraculously, those prayers would be rewarded.

"She enjoyed tunes from the 1940's and could sing every word of many of them.

"She was a nuanced person--Mom LOVED to laugh—sometimes so much so she had tears in her eyes, and us on the floor. She loved to joke—sometimes bawdy. When she was in the hospital recently, the handsome doctor asked her if there was anything he could do for her. 'Hmmm…. she paused, 'maybe if you were a little younger.'

"Her flip side was that she believed in never sparing the rod. It would spoil the child.

"So she was a strong lady. And she had to be obeyed.

"By today's standards it's a miracle she lived to be 85. Exercise for her was going shopping. Sugar was a main staple of her diet. Despite the lack of diet and exercise, she rarely needed glasses, she could hear a person from 20 feet away, and she never had a broken bone until age 84 when she fell and broke her hip. She also had the best handwriting of all of us.

"She was an optimist. 'You can do anything,' she would tell us kids. 'You can be anything you want to be.' She was perfectly happy to be a wife and a mother. However, when she planned her obituary about 20 years ago, she noted that she was Past President of the American Legion Auxiliary Post #76, a real estate broker, and a housewife.

"The mother of eight, grandmother of 16 and great grandmother of 23.

*"And she loved us all."*

The church was silent but for an elderly lady seated with her friend. "Is this the same Virginia you and I knew?"

The funeral proceeded to the Landry family cemetery with prayers and lowering the casket into the ground beside VF's grave.

Vicki walked over to Iris. "So that was enlightening."

"The eulogy?" Iris asked.

"Uh huh. Sweetened. Lots of sugar."

"Oh, come on, Vicki. You can't tell people the bad stuff at a funeral. When I said that she was a tough lady and didn't spare the rod, did you see Joe's face? He was so afraid I'd say more."

"Where did you find all that BS to talk about?"

"It was true. It's just that it was 10% of her mean, cruel life. The positive 10%. The 10% that her Palette Club saw. Anyway, Mary told me she had a last confession with Father O'Keefe. So, who am I to judge?" Iris asked.

"Purgatory. That's where she is."

"Oh, really? Purgatory? For how long, God?"

"Only God knows."

Iris laughed at the remark. She had forgiven her mother. Clearly Vicki had not.

There was more work to be done.

# CHAPTER TWELVE:

# *Hold Back the Dawn*

## 2007

Mary knew exactly what was needed—a top to bottom cleaning of the fortress as everyone called it. The great house on the ranch outside of Austin, which now belonged to her, along with 100 acres. She called the estate movers, the organizers, and the Viet Nam Veteran's Services and began putting furniture, clothes, personal artifacts, and artwork in various piles in four separate rooms: GIVE AWAY TO CHARITY, SELL, HOLD FOR FAMILY, and THROW AWAY. After four days with three professional organizers working with her, she made her way to the basement.

The Army Air Corps trunk caught her eye. She didn't remember ever seeing it. It seemed to glow. The name Lt. Vincent Frank Krejci was engraved on a silver plaque on the lid. She unbuckled the straps and pushed it open. Among photographs and jewelry-like mementos were letters tied with satin ribbons and lovingly categorized from 1938 to 1969. From her dad to her mom, from Grandfather Williams to Mom, from Mom's sisters to Mom, and from special friends to Mom. Underneath all was VF's leather bomber jacket.

She chose a silver embossed "Lowry Field" letter and read:

*Lowry Field*
*Saturday*
*Denver, Colorado*
*Oct 19, 1941 2:30 pm*


*My Darling Baby Doll:*


*Enclosed you have $5. Sorry I couldn't get it sooner. As I once told you, you don't need fear or feel awkward about asking me for money—but be sure you 1. Use it wisely and 2. You don't pull such stunts as the last one—paying on that note for your expensive watch. We just can't stick our necks out too far.*

*Going on duty at the hospital will place you in a position to meet all sorts of people—some no doubt young men in the hospital who will hound you for dates after they recover. Well, I don't worry about that. By now, if you don't know your job and "career" you never will.*

*Here is something I want you to get straight. Listen closely.*

*It seems to me that you have been talking to people or someone who knows a little about Lowry Field. Get this—Lowry Field is U.S. Army Air Forces Restricted Area. No one in civilian life knows a thing about Lowry. Army men know little. Those who go thru Lowry don't talk. They can't! Lowry (now this may be censored before you get it!) Lowry Field is the only Air Corps School of its kind in America. Perhaps the world. Since June 1941 when the Air Corps became a distinct unit apart from the regular army, it became the U.S. Army Air Forces in 3 parts—men are taken out of flying and placed into special training like here for very highly specialized training. Right now I am not flying. I am undergoing very rigid specialized training for the purpose of supervising our fighting air forces when I become an officer. Right down my line!*

*Flying is only 1 of 3 parts of the U.S. Army Air Forces. I am telling you dope that civilians do not ordinarily know.*

*As for my specific work—please don't ask me—I can't talk—we study and work like blazes all week. Then study over the weekend. If we leave post like Sunday we don't talk. Some cadets get tight and do and they go out. This is very vital and restricted stuff we are in. Our country is on the verge of war and we can't take chances. Can you understand? If you were my wife and here I might be able to say more. When I see you I can say more about our future. Keep quiet about Lowry and don't ask people about it because they don't know. If they pretend to they are liars.*

*The UT Thanksgiving game—I would like to send you money and say "ask Faye and Grace to take you." Virginia, please don't expect me to go that far—I must think of Christmas and of getting home. Why, we will see the best games to come. I haven't seen one this year and don't expect to.*

*As to home—Let's just forget it. I will try to straighten out things when I get down. I will have to dig into things myself. Really all is OK on the surface.*

*I must send this now so you get it Sunday.*

*Keep up your good marks and Benedictions, etc. My 97% daily average last week came thru prayer.*

*You are my wife-to-be. Never forget that and that your true love is*

*Vincent*

*I'll send pictures later and will try to send you some stationery.*

She was mesmerized! *Look at that beautiful handwriting! The curve of the letters just oozes longing and desire. The words were so lawyerly and yet so lustful.* She spent all afternoon reading story after story of VF's desires, dreams, work in munitions, bombs, chemical warfare, his friends and enemies, the struggle with the "Yanks vs. the boys from the South," in his barracks, his dutiful fulfillment of his Catholic faith, his descriptions of the sunrise and sunset in the Rocky Mountains, his health, his exploit with a flying buddy who fell asleep at the controls, and most of all his ambition to marry Virginia and raise a family and someday have a beautiful ranch.

He described his flying:

*The east is only momentary; we turn west. That is where that unforgettable beauty of nature's wonderland sleeps under a carpet of fresh snow. Way up, up towards Echo Lake nestled in the pit of a pre-historic crater. All around the snow is multicolored. From the tip of Mt. Evans (14,245 ft.) where it is a deep orange red to the shores of Lake Echo where it is a pale rose it is awe inspiring. Nature's catastrophe descends and suddenly, into a blinding snow storm we plow. The flakes are huge fluffy balls, full of tiny crystal balls. Gosh it is cold. That was only momentary, a sweep to the right and we are back heading for that glowing East. I don't remember who said it, it does not matter, one of the cadets, but the words were "Hold Back that Dawn" and I know that every soul within hearing felt way down deep every sentimental inch of it.*

Some letters were touching, ending in "Baby, I miss you tremendously" and telling Virginia how much he treasured the times they spent together. Others expressed his concerns about receiving a paycheck or getting proper clothing from the Air Corps. Often he encouraged her to stick to nursing school, pray, and "be a proper Lady" (with the capital L).

*Baby Doll, I am proud of you. You know I was in a tight situation when we paid for your registration, but now you have done well. An A at UT is something—you are an ex-UT, or rather UT ex. When we go to the Big Roundups, we can both sign among Ex Students—See!*

*Pictures and Ring covered in previous letter. But again I see they go over Big. Willcox got a snap of his Waco girl in bathing suit today. Mine won out in comparison. Both the framed one and one at Barton Springs.*

*Guard House is where the officer of the day stays on duty 24 hrs per day. There cadets sign in and out mail comes there and is put into alphabetic boxes two times a day. Laundry has been coming there and going out. No, it is not a jail. We all go there to get mail, etc.*

*The $45. Well, it will be tough and will keep me from two things:*

1. going to LA as all the fellows do pay day open post. I don't need it;

2. seeing you between shifts in Sept. This I want and need. But we will manage to get the money some way. You just make up your mind that you are going in to do good and don't let on that we are going to marry Christmas or shortly thereafter. I am for married life as never before. Just your head on my shoulder and kiss your back and hair.

*You have made up your mind in proper directions—keep on the point like I have to keep the nose of #7 on a point every day. I get mad, uncertain, and flat at times, then I almost cuss a streak, grit my teeth and take over the controls. Every day—1,000, 2,0000, 3,000—above these mountains; dive, spin, etc.*

*You are the center of my life and my all. I could not admire and love anyone more than you. Yes, darling you are the answer to a life long prayer, dream and ambition for an ideal mate. Our test of love will be the finest thing in the world because we have God for us. We will live head and shoulders above the average. We are keeping it up and we will continue for life and a day. There is a place for all my salary and if any left over it goes into my Dream Ranch.*

*"You surely did make a changed woman out of me." That statement deserves expansion and specific explanation. Taken in general: Virginia, remember this, you too deserve credit for the part you took, the effort you put out and the sound judgment you exercised in deciding between the finer, the better, the real and brave—the Lady—head and shoulders above the mire of common people—and the determination to face life, i.e., becoming a Catholic—that you did. Without your cooperation*

*though lacking at times, I could never have done it! I could have never finished law school!*

*When you go on duty, remember this—you are going through and doing things young ladies before you have done for ages. Yes, young ladies with a whole lot less to them than there is to you. Yes, and pray to Blessed Virgin Mary. Remember, you can do not only as well but better than the next person—be better than the average, your roommate, your class. That is something we will have to demonstrate to our children.*

He worried about his best friend, Fred, who had grown up with him, gone to college with him, and who was then stationed in the Pacific:

*I have no idea where Fred is. Either Atlantic or Pacific. Perhaps on one of the newly captured Islands in the Atlantic that the public press has not been permitted to publish. Pearl Harbor where he was initially stationed really was shelled by the Japs. Those Japs will pay for every fragment let down a hundred fold.*

VF was such a patriot! He expressed his duty to his country so beautifully, and he loved his uniform, called the pinks.

*I put on the pinks and blouse and the Eagle (garrison hat) for the first time in my life. It was a complete uniform as Lieutenant in the US Air Forces—all except the Bars. I drove two fellow cadets downtown, one for his date, stopping by the cathedral I expect us to be married in. I went up front inside to spend a while with my maker. Giving thanks for His innumerable blessings, I asked Him that that uniform never see dishonor, disloyalty, or shame, that it be worn for the greatness of our nation and the greater glory of God. Asking Him for guidance I prayed that he unite us and for our future happiness and good fortune.*

One letter made Mary blush. In it, VF reminded Virginia of the time they had a spat when he "pinched [her] boobie." Imagining her mother and father in such a playful, sexual encounter was both touching and hilarious.

*Remember about a year ago Friday we went walking to the State Cemetery—you brought meat (Friday—a no no) and Bur Oak acorns (for nuts)? That lady wanted us to leave—we made her so mad! We had a word because I pinched your boobie on the porch at 1710. Then I came back after studies (10:30) and we were such nice lovers in the Texas moonlight.*

*You know Darling, Saturday nite and everynite I realize how much I miss you. The feel of your fingertips on my face, holding you in my arms, kissing you. It seems so near I can taste it, yet so far away.*

*I think a thousand times of you each day. I recall every detail of last Fall. It seems to register minutely from day to day. Your waiting for me in the Model A by the Capitol or leaving a note—morning, noon, evening nights together. We never did tire of each other. A spat here and there because I wanted (1) to see you become a real Lady and (2) to make absolutely sure that we belonged. I tried your patience often, I know, but for the better.*

He seemed very intent on converting Virginia to an officer's wife. *The mention of becoming a Lady over and over again,* Mary wondered, *why did he think she wasn't already a lady?* She was from an upper class family and yes, they had fallen on hard times when her father left her mother and moved to Ohio with his secretary. But she had poise and polish. At least it seemed so in the photos Virginia kept.

Some of the letters told of going to movies during that tumultuous time, and his evaluation of those big screen blockbusters.

*Last nite I saw my third show "Remember that Day" with Claudette Colbert and John Wayne. Truly a great work. Half the audience broke down and cried when the two had to part, then never came back. I could not see the second run. But I want to see it again.*

*"Waterloo Bridge" and "Remember the Day" are two great pictures—so real this very day.*

*I don't care for movies anymore unless really a good show is playing. Too, I want to write you. Before reporting, I saw "Meet Mr. John Doe"--pretty good, much like "Mr. Deeds Goes to Town."*

She saw a rust-colored envelope marked "TELEGRAM" with the following message:

HOLIDAY GREETING BY WESTERN UNION: TELEGRAM 1941

DEC 15 DENVER COLO

MISS VIRGINIA WILLIAMS

CARE SETON SCHOOL OF NURSING AUSTIN

FROM SNOW BOUND DENVER TO TELL YOU CHRISTMAS IS INCOMPLETE APART. DARLING, A MERRY CHRISTMAS. PROMISE WE WILL MARRY SOON. VINCENT

Mary's attention turned to the little jewelry mementos. She held the silver wings that had adorned her father's uniform sixty-three years ago. Then she picked up an oval miniature photo of VF in uniform attached to a straight pin—a sweetheart pin. She wondered if her mother wore this while VF was away chasing Nazis. She opened a velvet box and there was a silver charm with a Longhorn icon at the top, two wrestlers in a circle, and the words #1 Texas Intramural. On the back was engraved V.F. Krejci '37. She clutched it tenderly, then immediately added it to her key ring.

And then, the bomber jacket. It had been saved all these years and was the softest leather imaginable. Mary couldn't help but caress it. *Where had it been? What adventures had it known?* It had flown miles above the earth, and seen failure abroad. It had the characteristic Juicy Fruit aroma she remembered from her father. She searched its pockets—sure enough, an ossified pack of Juicy Fruit gum was in one of the pockets. She then found a clean, white (although faded) handkerchief in another, and a silver dollar in another. That must have been his lucky piece. She smiled, feeling her eyes well up with tears, and thinking about her father's loyalty—whether it was to a brand of chewing gum (his most successful stock had been in Wrigley), his country, his friends, his religion, or his family.

Those letters told a story of frantic lovers, of wartime angst, of two people planning for their future. They gave Mary a window into her parents' values and hidden secrets.

Most interesting, though, is that they seemed destined to be found. *Why would her mother have saved them? Was she holding them hostage for an impending divorce suit because they would prove his love for her and she imagined that she would be able to exact revenge in assets? Did she read them when she felt lonely and unlovable after VF's death? Did she think that someone would find them long after her demise and see how these lovers cared so deeply for each other?*

Finally, Mary carefully examined the bottom of the trunk, and ran her fingers across the felt cover. There was a subtle bump. She found a corner, tugged, and the material loosened. Underneath was an unusual letter postmarked Seattle, on gold embossed University of Washington letterhead. She gingerly opened it and read:

> *April 15, 1941*
> *In Memoriam to "Gina,"*
>
> *I received your card the other day.*
>
> *Am sorry that I have not written sooner to offer congratulations on your engagement. I remember your telling me about your fiancé last Spring when we were back in Ohio. I believe you said he was quite a serious chap with a feeling of great social responsibility. More power to him.*
>
> *I have bid fond farewell to the "Gina" I used to know. I could hardly believe that such a charming, pleasure loving, carefree character who*

*lived for today and didn't give a damned for the morrow, was gone. But then I thought—who am I to say that the age of miracles has passed?*

*I just had one disturbing thought. I wonder if she is sure that this character change is a permanent thing. The world will suffer a loss because the man who marries "Gina" will have his hands so full and his personal responsibilities will be so great that he will not have time for any social responsibilities. Oh, well, the world's too far gone to be saved anyhow.*

*I guess I haven't written since we moved into an apartment. Three of us fellows have a honey of an apartment with the latest modernistic furnishings. Please note the change of address.*

*You said something about going back to Ohio. Did you mean to visit or to go to Ohio State? Is your dad still in Columbus?*

*Don't be as negligent about writing as I was. Please don't take offense at anything I have written. I was only kidding. Hope to hear from you soon.*

*Lovingly,*
*Dan*

Mary read and re-read the letter. Was this Dan? The same Dan that Iris said their mom whispered upon her deathbed? There was no last name. Just the postmark Seattle, the embossed letterhead, the well-written letter with impeccable penmanship. April 15, 1941. The day 200 German bombers, known as the Luftwaffe, bombed Belfast, Northern Island. Hmmm…Wonder what Daddy was doing that day? Preparing for the Germans one would think.

Dan. Oh, Danny boy!

Mary was thinking—if this is THE Dan who was Hap's father, perhaps she could find out by tracing Hap's DNA. She had just heard of a company called 23 And Me that could take one's DNA and tell you who was related, with names and everything. *Karen kept a lock of Hap's hair! We should have it tested! And Vicki kept Dad's hair. At the least we can find out whether Hap and Dad matched.*

Mary was on a mission. She carefully folded the letter, putting it aside to copy and send to Iris. She reorganized all of the other letters, tied them with the appropriate ribbons, and placed them back in the trunk with the bomber jacket. This may have solved the mysteries of her mother and father's relationship. She couldn't wait to talk with Vicki and Iris about these discoveries.

And she couldn't wait to visit Karen and get some of Hap's hair.

CHAPTER THIRTEEN:

# *Horatius The Cat*

## March, 2010

In the ensuing years, there were various changes in the Landry clan. Children were born to daughters of the Landrys, sons and daughters married and their children grew up, and everyone except Bits stayed in touch on the remarkable new discovery called Facebook. Jason, Iris' middle son, created a "Silvercreek Cousins" group page, and brought all the cousins together every other year in Austin even though some cousins lived as far away as New Zealand.

But Bits was another story.

Vicki, Mary, and Bits all had property on Silvercreek Ranch. Although Mary did not talk to Bits, she saw that parcels of Bits' land were being sold, and she often heard from Vicki that Bits was developing ranchettes and running her vineyard. The sisters' respective acreage was large enough that they could go months without seeing each other, but Vicki kept in touch regularly with all of her sisters. She had a favorite saying. "Hope springs eternal." She would say, "Someday we will be one big happy family again. That's what Dad would want."

"I'm an optimist, but I don't think that will ever happen," Iris said when Vicki called one beautiful Texas Saturday morning repeating her favorite mantra. Vicki was on her back porch at the ranch where the reception for her new iPhone was strongest, watering her camellias. Iris still lived in New York and worked at the American Museum of Natural History. This call interrupted her meditating in the Shakespeare Garden in Central Park, on her favorite bench. Iris continued, "especially after what Bits did to all of you—how she stole property from Richard's estate particularly. Who steals land from someone who is dead?"

"And from your son," Vicki blurted out.

"What are you talking about? Which son?" Iris had three sons.

"Your oldest son—Will. Didn't you know?"

"No!" Iris sat straighter, rather agitated at this disturbing news.

"Dad and Mom gave Will twenty-five acres after he came back from the Gulf War," Vicki said, proud of herself that she had the scoop.

"Where was the acreage?"

"A prime piece across from the creek."

"On that hill? Overlooking the ranch? Inspiration Point?" Iris asked.

"Yes. Yes. And yes."

"How did she steal it?" Iris voice grew strained while she imagined that beautiful piece of property taken from her son.

"I'm not sure how this works but this is what someone at the deeds office in Drippin' told me. Evidently Will didn't file the deed soon enough, so when Bits took over a lot of property soon after Dad died, she enveloped his acreage within hers, with no easement. Essentially, she stole it."

"How could she do that? That is pure evil."

"She got Mom to sign off on it. They had Trudell do the paperwork, and the result is that Will can never get access to his property unless he pays Bits to create an easement—at today's going rate that's about $100,000."

"Damn damn damn. I wonder why Will never told me. I know he's been very upset about the ranch and angry at Bits, I just didn't know what happened. I thought he was so angry with her because of all her land grabbing habits overall. He and I talk all the time. He often says she'll have a sad ending. This makes me feel terrible. Maybe this is why he seems so happy when I discuss the changes I'm going to make at the farm. He understands he'll have a third of that land after I die."

"Don't you ever talk to her?" Vicki asked.

"Why would I talk to such a thief? I have nothing whatsoever to do with her or her ransacking of the ranchland. Since my property is the farm, thank God, I don't have to think about talking with her. I want nothing to do with her. By the way, whatever happened to her and the IRS? Wasn't she in arrears?"

"Oh, you'll love this," Vicki said. "Did you hear about the guy who flew his plane into the IRS building in Austin after he set fire to his home? I think his name was Andrew Stash—or something like that."

"Stash works…" Iris laughed, skipping a beat while Vicki got it.

"Anyway, that was just last month and Iris had a hearing at that same building *on the same day*. It turns out all the paperwork on her case was destroyed in the kamikaze blaze!"

"No. She just can't be that lucky!" Iris was incredulous. "Do others in the family talk to her? Joe? Your daughters? Isn't she your oldest daughter's godmother?"

"I'm afraid the rest of the family feels the same way you do. I talk to her because she is out and about on her golf cart at the ranch, but she rarely picks up her phone. She says she's writing. Her winery isn't doing so great after that article in *Texas Monthly*."

"Tell me more," Iris asked, happy about Bits' misfortune.

"There was this investigative article in *Texas Monthly* about her winery, pointing out that the wine was not from grapes grown in Texas, but in Canada. It had a negative effect on her sales immediately."

"Can't say I feel sorry for her."

"Then her husband took off with that pretty young artist who has the llama ranch down the road."

"Whoa….Whaaat? A llama rancher? This is news." Iris rolled the words *llama rancher* over and over in her mouth and grew more delighted with Bits' misfortune.

It turned out that Bits' husband had grown tired of their years-long sleeping arrangement—she in master bedroom #1, him in master bedroom #2 and no skin between them. He was a wine salesman and had met the pretty llama rancher who was half his age when he sold her a new wine cellar for her expansive ranch house.

*Serves her right,* Iris thought. *Who would want to live with such a cruel, self-centered jerk?*

"Want to hear what she's writing about?" Vicki asked.

"What?"

"Cats."

"Cats? Does she have cats?" Iris asked, incredulous.

Bits hated most animals, except for horses, and she never rode anymore.

"In fact, several." Vicki added, "feral cats. I think from various other ranches. She feeds them. She's a member of the Cat Writer's Association."

"There's actually a Cat Writer's Association?" Iris was smirking, and began to scratch her arm. Just the thought of cats made her itchy. She was horribly allergic to cats and wasps. Carried her epi pen everywhere she went.

No surprise really that Bits would fall for cats—*cats need little love. Mostly they just need to be fed. But writing about them? So strange. Bits had become a cat lady. A bona fide member of the Cat Writer's Association.*

"She's writing a book about one of the cats. It's called *Horatius the Cat.* Want to read some of it?"

"Hell, no! Why would I want to read anything she's written? She's just a greedy, horrible person."

"Iris, everyone has two sides. The yin and the yang. Even Mom had two sides."

"In Bits' case, Vicki, it's evil side one, and more evil side two. I know, Vicki, that you want to get the family to love one another and be together as a family, but frankly, Bits is not family to me. Now that I know what she did to my son Will by taking his property….I want nothing to do with her—ever…."

"Think about it, Vicki. You've told me how she's schemed and stolen property from nearly everyone—the way she took the largest section of Richard's land after Mom told Mary she could have that. Then she took parcels of everyone else's land that mother didn't sell when she made people sign off on half of their land. Altogether she has taken, what? Three hundred acres?"

"About that."

"Damn, Vicki. You are too forgiving. This family just pushes all of the dysfunction under the rug—hiding all the anger and frustration. I think it builds up and manifests itself as addiction, health problems and mental health problems." Iris' voice was deliberate, nearly pleading.

"I think we're on pain overload. I think we don't face what's going on because we just can't take any more pain. In massage therapy school you learn that the body has various pain centers, but when a person has massive pain, only one pain center is prominent, the others shut down, and the therapist can work on that area to relieve pain in the other areas."

"So, you think that Dad's death, then Richard's death, then Hap's death...all of that pain in a relatively short time together with our childhood baggage—you think we all just shut down our *feelings*? Is that what you're thinking? You think that's why no one took you up on a group therapy session?" Iris asked.

"I think we all still *feel*, but we just can't talk about it—it's too painful. And I think it goes all the way back to Jillian," Vicki said.

"Vicki, I can't believe you mentioned Jillian. Now *there's* a reason to hate Bits if I ever heard one."

"Why? What?" Vicki was sincerely confused.

"Oh, give me a break. You didn't know about Bits setting up Jillian for a beating before Jillian fell off that wall?"

"No. This is news."

"About 60 years too late," Iris said. "I think our sister Bits is a psychopath."

Characteristically, Vicki changed the subject. She and Iris talked about the upcoming reunion that they and Mary were going to have at Iris' farm, which she had renamed Thunder Valley Farm. Iris was excited about the plans. "I've got each day planned out—we're going to study the farm parcel by parcel and listen to Dad's audio tape as we do."

"Well if anyone can put together an organized assessment of 300 acres, it's you, Iris."

Iris' anger over Bits' pathetic life had softened. She was curious about Bits' writing if for nothing else to see how a psychopath writes. She didn't know if it was the scientist in her, trying to unearth fossilized creativity, or if she was genuinely curious to see what exactly a creature like Bits would about.

"Vicki, email me one of the chapters of Bits' book. I would like to read it, even if it's for a laugh."

Iris thought about what Vicki told her about the article in *Texas Monthly*. Now, *that* was a revelation. Iris knew very little about how Bits ran her winery. She had heard that Bits cultivated grapes in Canada and had the *must*—the skins, juice and particulate matter—sent to her wintery in Texas, and then she processed and bottled it. Iris felt a little thrill that justice might prevail. *Truth will out.* One of VF's favorite sayings.

Shifting her focus to the luscious beauty of the Shakespeare Garden around her, Iris breathed in deeply the scent of spring. The explosion of tulips, crocuses, snowdrops, daffodils, and the hint of cherry blossoms wafted before her eyes, like a Monet pastel. *When I die and am cremated, I want some of my ashes to rest here, with the beauty of this garden.*

\*     \*     \*

After a few days, Vicki sent Iris an e-mail with an attachment. It was chapter one of Bits' book, *Horatius the Cat*.

She opened and read:

Down the rocky path he came. Gray head and body, large yellow eyes. He has a black stripe from the tip of his nose to the end of his tail. I just stood still and gaped at this beautiful creature. I judged him to weigh about fifteen pounds. The hair on his body was short—but heavy. I tried to stop him at the gate. Observing me as a barrier, the big cat opened his mouth and screamed.

The days drifted by and I'd forgotten about him. Food scraps were placed outside for the birds. A long, low bench sat under the trees for the food. Late one evening, I could see something moving around near the bench. When I investigated the next day, I discovered the food gone. Well, birds sleep nights—they don't prowl, I thought.

Once again I put food outside. This time I watched and waited.

Something terrible had happened. He was crippled. He seemed all twisted. The hair on his body had been cut. Had someone hit him with a car? Had he been shot?

*It's quite ordinary,* Iris thought as she stopped reading. *No. It's awful.* She wondered what those Cat Writer's conventions must be like. *Women, mostly women, for sure. Some wearing cat glasses and sporting cat jewelry? Some with silk cat scarves tied neatly around their necks or dangling from their purses? Sponsored by cat food and cat product vendors? Maybe even cat cemetery sponsors. Do they award a cat writer of the year trophy?*

While Iris contemplated the Cat Writer's conventions, Bits sat in her golf cart overlooking Inspiration Point, just a small part of her kingdom of ranchland. She was viewing her newest development, The Wild Side of Barton. This division of thirty new homes on fifteen acres with hike 'n bike paths and manmade streams and waterfalls were what made her day. She should have been happy.        Instead, she felt defeated. *What had become of her life?* She wondered. *How did all of her hard work on her winery go to hell so fast just because some baby-faced writer found out the grapes are really from Toronto? Who the hell cares what kind of grapes I use?*

Bits used to confide in Virginia, when Virginia was still alive. She could tell her anything. They would sit on the vast screened in porch at the fortress and drink wine all afternoon and laugh about all those silly men Bits had been married to, and the stupid things they did. One of her favorite phrases about one of her husbands was "I had to put a bag over his head to make love with him." That would crack Virginia up so much that she would nearly fall off the couch laughing, one hand on the crystal wine glass, the other at her throat, chortling.

At that time there had been six. Now the sixth was gone to a llama rancher.

One of the last times they were together like that, as sunset approached, Bits confided she was selling another piece of the property. Another million dollars.

Virginia always said, "Bits, you know best. Go ahead and do what you think is right."

Bits looked at her right arm, covered with deep scratches. It seemed her skin grew thinner every day. Her favorite cat, Gertrude, used her arm as a scratching post. She drew a finger over the long scabs and felt the bumps. The arm appeared as if it had been burned, with dark pink and red blotches surfacing throughout.

Now that Virginia was gone, Bits talked to her cats, and when any of them would join her in her golf cart, she would usher them around her compound. "Come, Gertrude," she would say to the orange marmalade feline, "gimme some shugah." Gertrude would stretch her back and say "yeow" loudly and jump up beside her. Today Gertrude sat nobly beside her, looking out over the vast estate. Bits looked down at Gertrude and grabbed her paw, staring at it. Gertrude screamed and jumped from the golf cart, running like a tiger to the creek below.

Horatius would have never done that, Bits thought. He had killer instincts. Bits saw herself in Horatius. He stood up to anyone and anything. But even Horatius could not give her love.

Today, she felt more alone than at any other time of her life.

# PART III

CHAPTER FOURTEEN:

# *Horse Fever*

## 1920

A young boy who has nothing has everything.

That's what VF's mother used to say before she put him to bed at night.

Actually, she would say, "mladý chlapec, který nemá nic, má všechno."

VF was five years old, going on six. He was the spitting image of his slim, beautiful mother with her widow's peak and wavy black hair and dark eyes. Everyone in his family spoke Czech. It would be another year until he began to learn English. He would dutifully kneel, say his Catholic prayers under the watchful eyes of Jesus Christ on the cross, and jump into his bunk, with its flour sack pillowcase and rough sheets. He would lie there thinking of the things he wanted so badly: a horse to ride to school that year, books to read, paper and pens to write with.

Mainly, he wanted a horse to ride. He was willing to find a wild one and break him. That way, the horse would be his forever. He had no money so the only way he could have a horse was to find a wild one and train it. Ever since he was two years old he had watched his neighbor, old Hortus (pronounced Hor-tush), and his dad break wild horses and he knew that once you broke a horse it would follow you to the end of the world if you fed it and cared for it.

That night he dreamed about himself and his horse.

It's neck felt creamy and smooth as he caressed it with long, long caring strokes. He held the end of the rope he made from discarded feed sacks and mounted the strong, dark purple colt. There was no need of a saddle. The colt smiled, cantered around the corral, and opened the gate with his teeth, pulling it wide with his front leg.

VF felt the wind at his back as he and his colt galloped through the night. The wide expanse of dark skies amplified the meteorite shower above and around them. "This is a beautiful night, don't you think, Colt?" VF asked his steady steed.

"I feel free!" the colt answered. "I feel free with you as my guide."

VF was laughing as he awoke. He had never had such a beautiful dream.

In the morning, his father, who towered over him at 6'3", said, "Son, I know you've wanted your own horse, and when you start school later this year you'll need a horse. I think Hortus has a colt that can be trained."

VF was beside himself thinking of all the places they could go together. He and his colt would ride to the mailbox; pick up the ice for his mother's icebox down by the railroad tracks and race to his favorite hideout on Rustler's Hill. All of the adventures that would happen between now and age 18 when he would go away to college would be enhanced with a galloping horse by his side.

"Will you promise me that you will take care of your horse? This means you'll have to be sure he's shod properly, and has enough grain to eat, and is watered daily down by the creek. You have to brush him down every evening, and hang the ropes and the saddle in the right places. These things are important, son. Do you hear me?"

"Yes, sir," VF answered. He knew what was necessary and if he could train this horse, he would do whatever it took to care for him.

"OK, then, let's see what Hortus has for us."

Together they rode over to Hortus' farm on their wide-backed bay, named Kráska, Czech for "beauty" because she was.

Hortus was in the corral with two other horses—a mare and a high-strung colt. VF was stunned. This colt was smaller than in the dream, but other than that he was a dead ringer.

"Vincy," Hortus said after he and the father had talked for a while, "come here. Take this rope. Let's see what you can do."

Hortus handed VF the lead that was tied around the colt's face and head.

The young boy felt the electricity between him and colt. Immediately he held out his hand and the colt snipped at him. He held it out again and again. The colt snipped again and again. He stroked the side of his neck, touched his front leg. The colt snipped.

Hortus and VF's father laughed as they stood against the wooden rails of the corral, arms crossed, pinching snuff.

"Got to try to canter him, Vincy" Hortus yelled.

"I'm gonna call him Snip. He needs a name first," VF yelled back.

The day was getting hotter and VF's head and neck were already soaked. "So, Snip, let's walk." VF led his colt around the corral, over and over for a half hour. Then he began to get the colt to run by command.

Within three hours, VF was bareback riding Snip in the corral.

"OK," Hortus said, "he's yours."

VF's father looked at him and said, "you will care for him or suffer the consequences." VF knew that this was a magnificent gift, even though no money had exchanged hands.

"Yes, sir, I will care for him."

Even at this tender young age, VF was determined to be the best guardian of his horse.

Over the years they grew up together, Snip and VF were inseparable. When he started first grade that fall, Snip was his best companion. Even when he formed a binding friendship with Fred Wiseman, VF thought of Snip before all else. Snip had the best horseshoes, was washed weekly and brushed nightly. Snip ate the farm's best grains, and wasn't worked too hard. VF saw to that. Snip even learned to drink from the ladle at the well.

On his tenth birthday, VF was given a hand-sewn Indian blanket for Snip that was so strong and beautiful that VF had tears in his eyes when he saw it.

VF trained Snip to gallop like a racehorse—with complete abandon. Snip had a velvet stride and VF often rode him bareback. He even taught him tricks he saw at the local annual circus. Snip could rear up on his hind legs and smile. He could dance at VF's command. VF loved to show him off, and once he learned that Snip was a chick magnet, he taught Snip to "talk."

In high school, VF liked to show the cutest girl in the class that Snip could say hello. Darla was her name.

"Darla, you want to hear Snip say hello?" VF asked her as he dismounted one morning.

Darla giggled, "Sure, Vince, show me what Snip can say."

"Snip, say hello to Darla," VF said.

"NEEEEEEEE....HAHHHH."

Darla peeled over in laughter. "That's the funniest thing I've heard."

"Snip can count to three. Watch this, Darla."

"Snip," VF commanded, "count to three."

Snip looked at Darla and lifted his right foot, held it high in the air, and brought it down once, twice, three times.

VF gave Snip a loving pat on the nose. "Good boy."

Darla was more than amused. She was entranced.

The following year, leaving Snip behind gave VF more stress than having to leave his mother when he went off to the University of Texas at Austin. It seemed a universe away from Snip.

When he first got to the campus in his overalls and work boots he felt pangs of guilt that he would not be talking with Snip and riding Snip each day.

He signed letters to his mother each week with "Prosím, dejte nějakou čerstvou kukuřici," which meant *please give Snip some fresh corn*.

When the semester ended, or a major holiday like Christmas gave him time to get back to the farm, VF first ran to find Snip, saddle him and take him for a long, long ride. Then he would greet his mother and father.

He would talk to Snip, share his dreams and secrets, and end the day brushing his beautiful satin coat`. But those days became fewer and far between semesters and summers of hard work selling bibles and picking cotton to pay for his college.

VF's mother and father did not ride Snip, nor did his grown stepbrother or stepsisters he left behind. Snip grew older and suffered from arthritis, according to the local veterinarian.

VF was beside himself when he saw Snip on a holiday his senior year before starting law school.

"Snip," he confided, "I miss you. I'm so sorry I haven't been here for you. Are you in pain?"

Snip looked at VF with his giant black eyes, blinked and lowered his head as if to say, "it's over."

"No, it's not over. I'm older. I'll be away more. But that's all. Just wait for me. Wait for me. Two years. I'll always be back. I've been admitted to law school. Do you know what that means? Snip! Be happy for me."

Snip reared his head, snorted and nodded twice, as if to say, "I am happy for you."

Two long years passed as VF became a law graduate and Snip became lame from his arthritis. VF was certain that horses suffer from depression. That was his diagnosis. If he could only come back to the farm permanently, or bring Snip with him on his adventures in life.

But he would never be able to do either. The clouds of war were brewing and Snip certainly could not join him in the war, nor could VF permanently come home to the farm ever again.

After his graduation, VF visited his parents and Snip. He was about to join the Army Air Corps and his future was uncertain. What was certain was his love of Snip.

He walked from the farmhouse and spotted Snip in the back pasture.

He whistled that high-pitched, singsong whistle that said, "I'm here, Snip! Come let's play."

Snip galloped over, no sign of arthritis.

"Snip! You're healed! What have you been eating? Can I have some?"

VF didn't need to bridle Snip. They walked over to the barn as old friends, seemingly holding hands. VF's hand on Snip's neck.

"Snip. I have some news. I have to go into the Air Corps. I'll learn to be a pilot, Snip!"

Snip stopped in his tracks.

"What's the matter, boy?"

Snip pulled up his front hoof and brought it down once. Hard. Then twice.

VF understood. "Ahh....you're right. Two. Two years. Yes, it's been two hard years. Hard for both of us. And now I don't know how many years it will be until we see each other again. I have a steady girlfriend. I don't know how long it will be until I see her again, either."

That information did not seem to amuse Snip. He brayed.

"Snip, I'm sorry. I'm so sorry. Everything is uncertain. I don't know what to do, except my duty to my country. If I have to fight, I'll fight to keep our country safe."

Snip calmed down and followed VF into the barn. It smelled of mold and sunshine. They walked over to the faded Indian blanket, where the ropes and saddles hung. It was twilight, and there was a large hole in the roof. The moon was rising.

"See that, Snip? See that full moon?" VF motioned to the roof. "Same moon we saw the first night you learned to gallop. Remember?" VF paused. "Those were good days. We've had a great time together, Snip. Wherever my duty takes me, I'll be thinking of you. Those times we had together—well, they'll give me strength, Snip."

VF cradled Snip's head in his arms and kissed him on the nose. He slept beside Snip in the old barn that night.

A rooster woke VF the next morning, crowing nearly in his ear. VF stood up, dusted off his jeans and long sleeve shirt.

"Snip? You ready for a ride to Cady Creek?"

Snip did not get up.

"Snip?"

VF didn't think twice. He drove his dad's Model A to the vet and brought him back to the farm.

"He's gone," the vet said to VF after examining him, as they both looked at the lifeless horse. "Looks like a fever."

VF had his own diagnosis. He knew Snip died of a broken heart.

VF would never love a horse as much as he did Snip. He would never love any animal again. He would treat the animal as an animal—a cog in the wheel of future fortune. That day VF dragged Snip's body behind the Model

A all the way to the culvert below the railroad trestle. There the carcass would have exposure to the vultures. VF removed his hat and said a prayer.

That was the day that VF promised himself that, come hell or high water, he would have his own land. A ranch. With horses, cows, sheep, deer to hunt, and a back pasture to ride. He heard his mother's words "mladý chlapec, který nemá nic, má všechno" and decided it was not true that a boy who has nothing has everything. A boy who has nothing has nothing. He decided some day he would have it all.

# CHAPTER FIFTEEN:

# *Thunder Valley Farm*

## April, 2010

VF Landry was a prescient person. Growing up on the O-Bar, a 300-acre farm located between Houston and Austin, he knew when and what kind of storms were brewing, when drought would set in, and what the land could bear. He understood the whisper of the wind, the tell tale sign of paw prints and footprints.

All of his life, he heard stories that the farm held some serious gold. There was an old Indian burial mound believed to be from Shoshoni or Comanche Indians on the far corner of the O-Bar's hills. Rustler's Hill, he called it. He felt, from the time he was a child, that gold was buried close by, mainly because his neighbor Nate Hortus said he saw it buried there in 1911.

After he purchased the land from his ailing father, and moved him and his mother into a house in Flatonia, he bought a hand held metal detector called a Bounty Hunter to see what he could find. He spent a week on the land sweeping every area he thought could contain that treasure chest, coming up with old spoons, some tin cans, a few quarters, bullet casings, and quite a bit of garbage.

Then one day he decided the best use of his time would be to walk the land and describe his feelings to his children, who he hoped would take up the exploration, in an audiotape. He gave the tape to each of his kids. Except for Vicki, Iris and Mary, no one listened to it.

After his death in late 1994, Iris acquired the property as the bequest from her parents, with her mother's approval. She was so busy with her job in New York and her family that she wasn't able to do much with the farm except to lease it for grazing rights to a fellow from Houston in order to pay the real estate taxes. She thought about it constantly, though. In her spare time she mapped out various things she would do with the land after her mother's passing. She asked agricultural specialists for their opinions on the best crops to plant and began to talk with neighbors about her plans for the land.

One day when Vicki was caring for Virginia, she found Grandpa Krejci's farm journal from 1905-1930 in one of VF's file cabinets, and gave it to Iris. The crumbling leather-bound book was a carefully constructed, handwritten month-to-month diary of tabulations of the growth of various crops on the farm, along with monthly rainfall, temperatures, and soil quality. It was all in Czech.

When she received it, Iris opened it appreciatively, gently touching the skillful handwriting of her grandfather and noticing what focused attention to detail it showed.

She held on to the journal, knowing it would be helpful in her research to discover how best to use the land.

Over sixteen years since she acquired the property, all she accomplished was to have a lot of mesquite and huisache underbrush cleared from a 100-acre pasture.

Iris decided to interpret the journal when Google translate was born. She learned that her grandfather had planted everything from vegetables to grains. She knew that feed corn, wheat and oats were staples. She was surprised to find he had also grown sugar cane (to make molasses), cotton, and rice—some with greater success than others.

This new insight gave her inspiration to invite Mary and Vicki to spend a work week in early April 2010 exploring the 300 acres and listening to their father's history lesson. Each sister made a commitment to stay in Flatonia (the closest town, since the boyhood house on the farm had been razed years ago) at a B&B and each day spend four to five hours driving around the land, learning about its history and its capabilities.

Iris was hoping for some approval about her ideas for the farm from her sisters. Their land on Silvercreek Ranch was outside Austin; this land was closer to Houston. She wanted them to know what she was planning, and get suggestions for the future of the O-Bar, which she had re-named "Thunder Valley Farm."

Iris had VF's tape converted to an MP-3 file, and sent it to Mary and Vicki so they could bring along their iPhones and all three would be able to sync as they rode the property in Iris' rented Jeep.

"Where should we start?" Vicki asked.

"Let's begin at the main gate," Iris suggested, as she drove up to the property. They turned on the narration.

> *This is where I first saw him. That black infant, held closely in the beige blanket as he passed by in his mother's arms in the little horse and buggy the family kept. I've never seen a young woman with a sadder face. She looked like she had been struck by lightening. She was lily white. The Valley didn't take kindly to mixed races. My mother was always kind to them before they left the valley. She gave them blankets she made, and fresh bread and eggs.*

"What do you think happened to that baby?" Mary asked.

"I heard he grew up in Houston. Then became a football star for Texas Tech. Got his business degree. He went into the refinery business in Texas City I think." Vicki knew a lot.

"Speaking of refineries," Mary interrupted, "did you all hear on NPR this morning about that the Deep Water Horizon oil rig exploded last night? Tons of oil have been released."

"Well, that just shows we should pump more from the land," Vicki said.

"OK, girls. Back to the O-Bar. Do you think because grandma was kind to the mother and black baby was the reason Grandpa Krejci was visited by the Klan?" Iris asked.

"Let's find out—what does the tape say?" Vicki jumped from the Jeep and opened the large gate. They drove to the middle of the property and listened.

*I was about 10 years old when the white sheets came on horseback. I recognized the horses, and at first since it was October, I thought maybe this was a precursor to Halloween. Then Daddy told me, my mom, and my half-siblings to stay put. He came out of the house, asking what was going on. I heard them say ugly things to him about being a Catholic, about not wanting anyone on this land who worships statues or takes orders from Italy. I didn't know what they were talking about, since we were descended from the Czechs, and there were many other Czech families around. They spit on him, rode around him in a circle. I thought they were going to harm him, but he was a big guy—6'3" and strong as an ox. Nothing scared him. They finally rode off. The next day we found a burned cross down by the fishing tank.*

Everyone got out of the Jeep and looked around. "Remember, Vicki, where the barn was, before Dad razed it and all the other buildings?" Iris pointed due south, took a stick and ran past an old stone water well. "It was here." She made a line in the sandy loam, beside a large Texas oak. "Remember? And the silos—the silos that held wheat, barley and that awful corn—they were over here. Oh, those silos—they were claustrophobic!" She ran 20 yards to the south and dug another line in the soil.

"Of course—the barn had stalls for the horses, and hay covered the dirt floor." Vicki remembered it well. "Remember hiding up in the loft when we played hide and seek? I remember when granddaddy had a big celebration dinner one Sunday. I was 13 or 14. Friends of theirs came from all over. There were long tables stretched out with all kinds of food—a real feast. A really cute guy, one of the Haas brothers, and I were playing in the loft. I remember he kissed me. I think I was hoping to fool around more, but Dad called for me."

"And remember the wretched outhouse? It was over here." Iris walked another 10 yards to the northeast.

"Who could forget it? The Sears catalogue! Sometimes I became so engrossed in that catalogue. I hated to use it."

Mary was horrified. "What did you use it for?" She looked at the exasperated expressions on Iris and Vicki's faces. "Really? You wiped yourself with pages from a Sears catalogue?"

Iris nodded. "You missed out of a lot of adventures, being the baby. Let's hear what Dad had to say about the house. It would have been about here." Iris was north of the outhouse and marked a big X in the dirt. They turned on the narrative.

*Grandpa Krejci and his friends built every one of the buildings on this farm. That's what people did in their day—they helped each other. I'm sorry the buildings didn't live long enough to stand up to the abuses of nearly 100 years of seasons. They were built of pine and oak, tongue and groove for most of the interior work. There was a two-story house with three bedrooms, a kitchen, a living area, and front and back porches. The front porch wrapped around the side of the house. The back porch opened up to Mom's carefully tended garden.*

*She grew all of her herbs, poppies for poppy seed, carrots, onions, toma-toes, peppers, squash, pickling cucumbers, red and white potatoes, Brussels sprouts, cabbage, lettuce, and green beans.*

Iris turned to Mary. "The 2-story house was a miracle of human inge-nuity. For many years they had no electricity. It was horribly hot in the summers, so they built the house with a lot of windows so that there would be a cross-breeze. They planted shade trees next to the house for cool shelter. Grandma Krejci plotted her garden so the vegetables would have enough sun, and she had her own shaded spot on the back porch where she churned butter, made her cheeses and crafted soap. She kept chickens in a large chicken coop back here."

Iris walked about 50 paces. "When we came to see her on special occa-sions she would let us gather eggs. It was like Easter—some eggs were blue, some yellow, some white. And watching the chickens preen and cackle at each other was hilarious. I remember when Hap would chase them around. Even Grandma giggled sometimes. When Grandma was ready to cook a chicken, she'd come back here, take her largest hen, break her neck, throw her in a boiling pot, then start plucking the feathers. There is nothing that beats a fresh roasted chicken with Grandma's homemade dressing."

Both Iris and Vicki were quiet for a while. The wind stirred, they walked, searching the perimeter. Mary was absorbing all of this news. She was born after the buildings were razed, and she was trying to imagine what this must have looked like.

"Inside the house was an icebox, not a refrigerator," Vicki told Mary. "It needed a block of ice to keep things cool. Grandma kept her butter and eggs in the icebox. She had a potbelly cook stove. She baked her bread, roasted her chickens, made her kolaches, and cooked her vegetables all on a potbelly stove. Holy cards were pasted on the walls in the bedrooms, like wallpaper. The pillowcases were made from flour sacks. Her sewing machine was a Singer pedal foot. She washed clothes in a galvanized steel wash tub and hung them on a line in the back of the house, away from the chickens."

"She worked her butt off," Iris interjected. "Four kids and no running water or electricity! Can you imagine trying to iron your husband's shirts with a heavy cast iron block on a hot stove on a hot Texas day?"

"What's ironing?" Mary laughed. They all laughed.

"Sometime, Mary," Iris began, "we need to tell you how it was in the Landry family before you were born. Every one of the girls had to iron clothes—it was a communal job. We had a weekly schedule. We would sprinkle water on the shirts, skirts, pants (usually our uniforms for Catholic school)…"

"Dad's handkerchiefs," Vicki interjected.

"… and roll them up a certain way and then refrigerate them. Then we'd iron them. The only clothes taken to the dry cleaners were Dad's dress shirts and anything with a 'dry cleaning only' tag."

"Looks like we need to get back to the B&B," Vicki said, as dark clouds approached. Time had flown by. They were expected at an intimate gathering with the local historian and drinks and dinner back in town. They waved their goodbyes to the imaginary Grandma and Grandpa Krejci and sped back to Flatonia.

On the way back, Vicki pointed out a little farm on Highway 95. "That's where the Scott's School was."

"Dad's school—where Mr. and Mrs. Wiseman taught?" Mary asked.

"Yes, and lived. They had a home next to the school. I have the funniest story—on second thought, not funny, a rather odd story about Fred's 4-H Club heifer, Beauty."

"Bring it on," Mary laughed.

"Well, Fred Wiseman, Dad's best friend, evidently loved this Jersey heifer he raised for 4-F Club. He named her Betty, and his routine was to put Betty on a rope, take her out of her pen during the County Fair, and just romp around. One year, Fred needed to find a restroom, so a fella asked if he could walk Betty around, and Fred agreed......"

"Then?" Iris asked.

"Hmmmm…evidently Betty was inadvertently choked to death in a sexual encounter with a mentally impaired young man."

"Ewwwww….." both Iris and Mary said in unison.

The next day they continued the narration from the same spot with VF's tale of the Cracker Jack box.

*My half-brother Paul was a real jerk. He was 7 years older than me, so of course he was bigger and stronger. Whenever he goaded me into fighting him, our daddy whipped both of us. Getting a box of Cracker Jack back in those days, the 1920s, was a very special occasion. It was better than Christmas because you got a sweet treat to eat and a present. Well, I saved mine in my pillowcase in our room upstairs. Paul found it, ate it all, stole the prize, and filled the box with dirt. Of course I was furious when I saw what he did and fought him until we were both bloody. Your Grandpa beat us both, and wouldn't let us eat for a day.*

"Wow!" Mary said. "That's so sad. So what's the story with Paul being a half brother?"

Vicki explained that Grandpa Krejci's first wife died of TB and left him with three children—two daughters and a son. "Bessie Vala came to the farm in answer to his ad requesting a nanny for the kids. She and her twin brother were teenagers when they came to the US from Prague. She stayed here on the O-Bar taking care of Grandpa and his kids and eventually they married and she had Dad. Later she became a US citizen."

"What happened to her brother?" Mary asked.

"He returned to Prague after working in the US for many years as an accountant and a translator. He was multi-lingual—Czech, Russian, German and English. I never met him. People said he was very smart. Dad did not like him, though. Said he was a cheat. Said he abandoned his sister to get social security payments abroad." Vicki sure was the family historian.

Iris was standing by a large cypress with a rock wall built around its lower trunk. "Remember this tree, Vicki? The butchering shed was close by." They listened to VF's description:

> *If you stand by the old cypress with the stone wall and look northwest imagine seeing the butchering shed. That was a low-rise structure made of a white freestone rock base with wood siding and concrete floors. It held your Grandpa's large round foot pedal stone sharpener, all the knives and tools for butchering and making sausage, the heavy long butchering table, hooks in the ceiling for holding the carcasses. This is where beef, pork, turkey, and venison were processed. Some of the meat was dried in the small smokehouse that was close to this structure, and other meat was stored in the salt cellar, below the house, close to the cool well waters. We sold the hides.*

Iris remembered a lot of flies in that slaughterhouse. It was a scary place for her and she stayed away from it. The smokehouse, though, had a delicious, flavorful aroma and memories of beef and venison jerky with their unusual spices swirled in her mind.

Back in the Jeep, they drove to the railroad tracks on the far east side of the land. This is where they used to pick dewberries. People outside of Texas called them blackberries.

"Last time I picked dewberries with Dad I got such a bad case of poison ivy! My hands swelled to twice their size. I had to soak them in ice water three times a day. Nothing helped. No holistic medicine, no prednisone. Nothing." Mary looked at her hands.

"When was that?" Vicki asked.

"About two years before he died. He and I were visiting Grandma in the nursing home and he had the hair brain idea to pick dewberries."

Everyone remembered Grandma Krejci's tragic death.

"But there's an unusual ending to the poison ivy story. Before the horrendous experience with poison ivy—which lasted for two months—I had premature arthritis in my fingers. It hurt even to shake hands. After the poison ivy, no more arthritis. See?"

Mary held up her smooth, unblemished hands.

"JAMA." Vicki observed.

"JAMA?" Mary asked.

"Yeah, it's one for the medical journals."

The huge plump masses of sweet berries grabbed their attention. "These always stained your fingers and clothes when you picked them. No one knew why they grew wild close to the railroad tracks. Perhaps it was the rocky soil that gave the berries room to roam," Vicki said.

Both Vicki and Iris remembered coming to this area of the tracks with its wooden trestle bridge over Cady Creek and picking pails and pails of ripe dewberries with their dad. They parked the Jeep and hiked up to the trestle bridge and sat, dangling their feet over the bridge.

"Vicki, do you remember we called this Candy Creek?" Iris asked. Vicki smiled and they listened.

*Here at the trestle bridge of the railroad tracks is where the Vala boys and I would put a penny on the track and watch the train roar by, then pick up a flattened coin and celebrate. That passed as entertainment in those days.*

*We also picked dewberries and mustang grapes. The grapes were used to make sweet wine, much like Manischewitz.*

*The greatest entertainment the tracks brought were ice and the circus. Ice was delivered here at the railroad tracks every week. We would meet the railcar, and Grandpa Krejci would get those giant tongs and hoist several blocks of ice onto our wagon. Then we'd drive the horses and wagon back to the house, give your Grandma a block of ice for the icebox, and put the rest in the cold cellar. Sometimes we'd cut up a block and ice down watermelons for dinner.*

*The Vala boys (no relation to your grandmother) and I would follow the railroad tracks to the annual circus, set up just outside of town. We would sneak under the tent and watch the tricks and the riding magic of those horsemen. Later we would try some of those ourselves on my gelding, Snip. Oh! We loved the circus. For a boy who never had movies, television, or a zoo this was spectacular—the color, the liveliness, the smells, the pretty ladies, the action, the strange animals.*

The sisters looked at each other with amusement.

"Can you imagine what a circus must have been like in the 20's in Texas?" Vicki asked. "What a big deal for those little farm boys."

"Just think the Hardy Boys meet Federico Fellini," Iris offered.

Mary laughed. "Can't you see Dad as a little boy, practicing standing on his horse Snip as he trotted around this farm? Maybe they also practiced juggling, and walking on a wire!"

They laid out the blanket with a delicious picnic--cold drinks, assortment of deli meats, cheese, fresh bread, lettuce and tomatoes. From their vantage point high on the eastern edge of the farm, they could see far across the land nearly to the Indian mounds. "See Thunder Valley? That's it!" Iris said. "Right below us. That's what Dad talks about later in his narrative about the thunder rolling in over the hills and lightening striking and the hellish sound of hail, then buckets of rain. Or the thunder and no rain in those years of drought."

"Hard way to make a living," Mary said. "You've got to be a gambler to be a farmer. Dad was no gambler, and I think that's why ranching appealed to him."

"But ranching demands that you have feed. And in order to have feed you either have to pay a fortune for pellets or you have to have rain and good pasture," Iris countered.

"So, what are you thinking?" Vicki asked Iris. "Would you use this land for pasture? Would you run cattle?"

"I'm too old for that. I'm thinking something more up-to-date. Solar farming. Wind farming. Perhaps grow aloe. Still food for thought."

After their late lunch, they drove back to town to chat with the director of the Arnim Museum, which holds artifacts of the town's history, and to see the Railroad Tower, a three-story tower used to signal the trains. They read the rail fan pamphlet:

> Flatonia was one of the earliest busy railroad junctions in the state of Texas, hence Tower 3. Tower 3 has been moved from its original location and preserved. There is also a caboose on display next to the tower.

The next morning they stopped at the town's cemetery and found the Krejci family gravesite. Grandpa Vince and Grandma Bessie Krejci had head stones, the stepsister and stepbrother Esther and Paul Krejci had stone markers buried in the ground. They cleaned the site and laid fresh flowers on the graves.

"In the name of the Father, Son, and Holy Spirit," Vicki began, clearing her throat, and bowing her head. "By Your grace and goodness, oh Lord, let us appreciate and celebrate those who have gone before us. Enlighten us with your grace, and show us the way to help Iris reinvent the land our grandparents lived for. Give her wisdom and blessings in her pursuit. Amen."

"Amen," Iris and Mary repeated.

They continued to search the cemetery.

Martha Krejci, VF's half sister and his protector, who became Martha Redding, had lived her adult life in Chicago. Her grave was not in this cemetery. It was in that smoky city as VF had described it.

Mary noticed all the other Krejci markers. "Who are these people? Are they related to us?"

"Probably," Vicki said. "We didn't know them because Dad just wasn't close to his relatives. He hated Paul so much, and Paul married and had six kids. We never met them. Paul was a troubled man. He eventually killed himself. His oldest son became the town sheriff."

"Well, looks like I have some family history to learn," Iris said.

Flatonia seemed buried in its past. It was still a one-traffic-light town with a small hardware store, one bank, a large Catholic church, antique shops, a coffee shop, and a couple of B&B's for the drivers who needed a break traveling from Houston to Austin.

The sisters drove out to Thunder Valley Farm, opened the main gate, and stopped in a large, pale yellow pasture filled with buttercups and phlox. "I call this the Easter pasture," Iris said, "because this is where Grandma would hide the eggs." They all got out of the Jeep. "Listen to what Dad said about this," Vicki insisted.

In 1970 Easter came early. The bluebonnets were just opening and the dewberries were budding. The married daughters asked for an Easter Egg hunt—Vicki and Iris brought their little ones. Grandma was waiting with a noon dinner of delicious ham, sausage and all the trimmings. Grandpa was severely arthritic—he could hardly walk, so he stayed at the house. Dishes were put away and everyone else headed to the living carpet of the front pasture. A crisp breeze whipped the budding pear trees and waved the Indian blankets. I remembered my old home--the green grass, deep soil, hard work, good times and bad.

"I vaguely remember that Easter." Iris said, "I was still in PTSD mode."

"Splain yourself, Lucy," Mary said. This was her way to make fun of sad times—just take a page from the *I Love Lucy* series.

"During the first few years of my early marriage to my rapist husband I was numb, and caring for the babies and going to school and working full time all at the same time was a continual bout of sleep deprivation. So, really, my clearest memories of Easters here at the O-Bar were when I was a child with Jillian, when she was still alive, Bits, Hap and Vicki. We would all be dressed in our finery, usually wearing either white or black patent shoes. There would be an unusual amount of food, always with fresh bread. After dinner, Grandma would hand us these hand-made 'baskets' made from coffee tins with colorful crepe paper glued to them. We would race out to the pasture and start finding eggs and little hard fudge-like candy wrapped in tin foil that Grandma made special for Easter. I saw Dad and Grandma talking Czech, and laughing, always laughing. It was so sweet. One Easter Jillian found a sweet little feral kitten behind the barn and she brought it home with her, hidden in her blouse."

"After the hunt I would head to the teepee fort I made every Easter in the calf pasture, down by the tank," Vicki added. "We would be full of ticks. Mom was always so irritated. She made us bathe before we got in the car. We'd have to undress outdoors and jump in a huge galvanized tub, soap off with Grandma's lye soap—the water was so cold! Dad and Grandma would hold up blankets around the tub for privacy."

Iris was giggling. "Do you remember the time Hap found the key and started up Grandpa's Model A? He must have been 10 or 11 years old."

"Right…yeah…I do," Vicki said with a smile. "I thought for sure he'd get a whippin'. But Dad surprised us all and threw us in the rumble seat and took us for a ride around the farm. Jillian wasn't with us that year."

"He must have had some of that mustang grape wine he always talked about," Mary said, amused.

"Let's take a look at the tank," Vicki suggested.

They drove over to the western side of the farm to look at the large earthen tank, bulldozed years ago to hold catfish and provide water for the livestock.

When you come to the large tank, stop and look at the eastern side. You'll see pecan trees that are some of the best in Texas. We harvested pecans, peaches, and acorns from the oaks at that tank. We had it stocked with catfish by the Texas Game Commission. I remember teaching Vicki and Hap how to fish from there. This is where the KKK burned that cross. It's also where lightening struck a cow and killed it.

The tank still held water; the pecan trees stood stately, limbs full of nuts. The oak trees were grand, their gnarled roots holding firm the berms of the tank. There were no peach trees left—they had either died during a drought or had been struck by lightening, which was very likely.

"Water's dark. Did you ever swim in that tank or canoe in it?" Mary asked.

"Too muddy to swim in and probably too polluted. No one had a canoe," Vicki answered. "I remember Dad teaching Hap and me to fish. We had bamboo fishing poles with corks. We'd put a tiny piece of Vienna sausage on the hook and throw it out. I'd usually sit on that huge boulder by the oak tree," she pointed across the tank, "and Hap would be where we are and he would never be able to sit still. Even so, he caught the biggest catfish."

"So, this was before Dad bought Silvercreek Ranch?" Iris asked. "I'm trying to get a sense of the time."

"Yes, you were about five or six, and Mary you were a mere gleam in your dad's eye!"

"Right. When I was eleven or twelve, that's when Dad bought Silvercreek. Then we hardly came to the farm," Iris said.

"Well, by that time, Dad spent most of his weekends at the ranch—and so did all of us…well, except Mom and the babies. Then Grandad became too old to run the farm, so Dad bought him out and moved him and Grandma to Flatonia."

Iris became contemplative and turned to look at Vicki. "I remember you caring for Granddad on his deathbed. I remember the day he died. I had just driven down from Austin with Dad and walked into the bedroom in their little house in Flatonia. Dad placed quarters on his eyes."

The three sisters sat beside the tank, under the shade of a large pecan tree, quietly thinking about those times.

"Just think, Vicki, you've nursed both Dad and his dad during their deaths. That must have had an effect on you."

Vicki was matter-of-fact. "It's just part of our mortality, I think. If I think about it too much I'll get depressed just knowing I won't get out of this game alive. Granddad lived a very long life. Dad not so long. Surely I was much more upset about Dad's death, with Mom being so crazy and accusing me of killing him."

Iris jumped up. "OK, babes, enough of the sadness. I have a treat for you. No more farm stuff today. I'm taking you to Shiner to hear some music and drink a cold one."

Shiner was a tiny town about 20 miles from Flatonia known for its Shiner beer brewery. A new hole-in-the-wall dance hall called Cyril's had opened up next to the town's Catholic church. It served Shiner on tap in various flavors, smoked sausage, and up-and-coming musicians for a minor cover charge. That evening's show was a cowboy who played jazz piano and sang intermittently. No dancing on Thursday nights, just music.

Vicki, Iris and Mary took a quiet booth far from the cowboy, and ordered—Shiner blonde for Iris, Shiner bock for Mary and a ginger ale with lime for Vicki. They decided to share a large plate of smoked sausage with jalapeño and cheese, Czech bratwurst, bread, pickles, and potato salad.

"So, what's up buttercup?" Mary asked, after sipping her Shiner and feeling no pain.

"I didn't bring you here just for the music and sausage," Iris admitted. "First and foremost we need to toast to Mare's judgeship. Your highness."

The server delivered the drinks and they raised their glasses.

"No, Iris, it's 'your justice,' and I'm not there yet. I'm running for judge."

"Well, if I lived in Texas I would vote for you," Iris said.

"She's got my vote," Vicki chimed in. "I heard the polling is trending your way."

"It's an uphill battle. It's still a Republican state," Mary said.

"Here's to democracy! Here's to Mary Landry, Texas State justice!" Iris declared.

They clinked glasses and said, "Here, here!"

"Now, let's get down to business. Mare, remember sending me a copy of that letter Mom had stowed away at the ranch? The one from Dan?" Iris asked.

"Yes. Quite the shocker. And I have news. Let's talk about it."

Vicki interrupted, "A letter from Dan? Are you talking about the same Dan that Faye told me about?"

Mary looked surprised. "What did Faye tell you?"

"It's a long story. I had to travel to Dallas to have lunch with Faye. She was very reticent to tell me but I patiently listened. The bottom line is that

Mom probably loved this guy Dan more than Dad. She knew him from the time she first met Dad, which was when she was 13 or so."

"We don't know for sure if he was Hap's father," Iris said. "I really want to understand Mom and Dad's relationship, why they always seemed to be fighting, why Mom was always accusing Dad of having an affair, and how Hap's birth may have ruined a love story."

"Well, for one thing Hap didn't ruin it," Vicki was agitated. "Mom did. From what Faye said Mom had an affair with someone named Dan while Dad was on a secret mission in the War. Then Dad comes back and finds that Mom's pregnant." Vicki was agitated.

Iris took a folded page from her pocketbook. "Let me read you this letter that Mary found at the fortress and see what you both think, in light of Vicki's meeting with Faye. So, this is from a guy named Dan, no last name, on University of Washington embossed paper, and he's damning with faint praise her engagement to Dad:

*I believe you said he was quite a serious chap with a feeling of great social responsibility. More power to him.*

*I have bid fond farewell to the 'Gina' I used to know.*

"He called her Gina? He said 'chap'?" Vicki asked.

"Yes, he also called her Regina—his rendition of the name Virginia. I think he was making fun of her adopted Catholicism by taking Ave Regina—the canonical hour of prayer before bedtime—and turning it into his pet name for Mom. This was a bright guy."

"Clearly Mom liked bright guys," Mary interrupted. "Wonder if he played guitar? Or loved to draw or make model airplanes?" She was smiling broadly.

Iris nodded in agreement. "This is getting a bit deep, but remember how Mom used to say that when she told guys her name was Virginia they'd say 'yeah, Virgin for short but not for long?' I think this was Dan and Mom's little inside joke. Remember, Vicki, from your Catholic school days, the words to some of the Ave Regina…..?"

Iris began to sing, "Glorious Virgin, Joy to thee, Loveliest whom in heaven they see."

Vicki joined in, "Fairest thou, where all are fair, Plead with Christ our souls to spare."

"But think about what he's saying. He bids her fond farewell. Why? Were they in a serious relationship and her way of breaking it off was to send him a note telling him she was engaged?" Iris asked, and then continued to read:

I could hardly believe that such a charming, pleasure loving, carefree character who lived for today and didn't give a damned for the morrow, was gone. But then I thought—who am I to say that the age of miracles has passed?"

"Wait a minute," Vicki said, "let me see this." She took the page from Iris and re-read aloud "…*such a charming, pleasure loving, carefree character who lived for today and didn't give a damned for the morrow…*Wow!" she laughed. "Our mother? Charming? Carefree? She must have been fun to be around once upon a time. Maybe that was Dad's attraction to her—she was so different than the women he briefly dated during law school. Like the future governor's wife."

"You mean Nellie Connolly? Dad dated her?" Mary asked.

"Yes. She was sophisticated, wealthy, and probably too smart to be controlled by Dad," said Iris, taking the letter back from Vicki and reading purposefully, slowly, to let the words sink in.

*I just had one disturbing thought. I wonder if she is sure that this character change is a permanent thing. The world will suffer a loss because the man who marries 'Gina' will have his hands so full and his personal responsibilities will be so great that he will not have time for any social responsibilities.*

"Damn. He had her pegged." Vicki put down her fork. "Was this the only letter from Dan? Faye said Mom had a sheaf of letters from Dan."

"The only one," Mary said, "and it was hidden under the lining of the trunk."

The waiter returned and refreshed the drinks. "Ice water for me," Iris smiled and raised her eyebrows, "driving."

"Could I get you dessert?" the handsome waiter offered, "pecan pie, butterscotch bread pudding, poppy seed cake."

In unison the sisters answered "poppy seed cake. Three forks."

"Gotcha," Mr. Handsome smiled.

"Prophetic, don't cha think?" Mary asked.

"The poppy seed cake? Because it was Dad's favorite?" Vicki questioned.

"No, no, no. Back to Dan. Yeah, this guy could predict the future, because it's exactly as he said. Dad had his hands so full after he married Mom that he wasn't able to become the person he wanted to be—a man of social responsibility like a state supreme court judge," Iris answered, talking rapidly.

"So, how did this work if this Dan was the same Dan who was Hap's father? And to answer your question, Vicki, this was the only letter from Dan. No last name. Darn it!" Mary said.

"Faye said that Dan was in the Navy and about to ship out of Florida. I was an infant with Mom in Florida. So she clearly got pregnant while Dad was away, and then Dad comes back Stateside and Mom is nine months pg!"

"Jeez ah peet!" Mary exclaimed. "Can you imagine how that changed Dad? He has this terrible, horrible near death experience in Czechoslovakia where his five buddies die, then he's told he has to change his name, then he comes home to his 'Sweet Virginia' and she is about to have a child he did not father. And it was so early in their marriage."

"He couldn't divorce her! Catholic church wouldn't like that," Vicki noted.

"He had been so devoted to her. She hung the moon for him. I read all the letters she saved from before he enlisted in OTC through the war. She was his all. He was going to make her an Officer's wife. He kept saying she was going to be a 'real Lady'—with a capital L." Mary felt enlightened, but sad for this couple she knew as Mom and Dad.

"Can you imagine what this did to both of them—the trust was broken. Maybe Mom's accusations of Dad having affairs with his secretary, then with his students—maybe that was all about her guilt." Vicki was on to something.

"Why do you think Mom married Dad?" Mary asked.

"Especially if Dan was a great lover," Vicki quipped.

"Exactly," Iris said. "I remember Mom saying once that Dad was a 'slam bam thank-you mam' kind of lover."

"Yeah, Mom was so subtle in her criticism. I think he had to be a fast lover—so many kids could interrupt at any time," Vicki laughed.

"I'll bet if Dad was pressuring Mom to marry him like Mare says the letters show, and the war was about to begin, she probably wanted some stability in her life. Don't you think?" Iris was trying to understand the dynamic.

"What do you mean pressure her?" Vicki asked.

"You'll have to read the letters for yourself. I'll have them copied and put in a little book for you. You'll see—Dad constantly talks about how she'll be an officer's wife, and then he talks about how badly he wants to get married. And then various dates will go by and he'll talk about the stress of being in the Air Corps and how his officers don't tell them anything and that he doesn't know when he'll be home, etc. etc.," Mary said.

The waiter interrupted with a large slice of poppy seed cake and three forks, placed the plate in the middle of the table, bowed and left. The sisters grabbed a fork, took a bite, and sighed....

Another thought occurred to Vicki, "You think that's why they both beat up on Hap? Because his birth and the affair ruined their trust?"

"Undoubtedly," Mary said.

"I dunno. I think Dad just wanted Hap to be more like him—very rigid and devoted to his studies, his religion, his country," Iris noted. "And in the 50's parents slapped their kids around. That's what Dad did to him and Joe and Richard when they misbehaved. But Mom's treatment specifically of Hap was ugly, tortuous, seemingly premeditated. She targeted Hap."

Vicki agreed. "As they got further and further into the marriage they couldn't divorce. The assets were so important to both of them."

"Right," Mary interjected, "Texas is a community property state, meaning that when couples divorce the property has to be divided equally. I can see that Dad NEVER wanted to divide his property."

"His land was his mistress," Iris said. "He wanted to keep both the ranch and the farm together."

"And he needed to keep his dignity," Mary said, "Can you imagine his pals at the American Legion, his friends at church, his associates in the AG's office, his colleagues at UT Law School—any of those people—can you imagine how they would take his divorcing her or vice versa?"

"Well, we're talking and talking about Dad, but what about Mom?" Iris mused. "She must have had all those feelings so bottled up. This is just a slice of explanation for her erratic behavior. You think Dan was the love of her life, or just one of many? And why was she so horrible to Jillian?"

"I think it's because Jillian was the spitting image of Evelyn, her sister who was in the State Hospital. She was helpless to take care of Evelyn, probably was mad as hell about that because Dad wouldn't let Evelyn live with us, so the thought of seeing Evelyn's face every day when she looked at little Jillian probably made her crazier. But we will never know," Vicki frowned, and finished the cake.

Iris was pensive. "OK, so why aren't we crazy as well, after going through such a crummy childhood and seeing all this abuse?"

"Maybe because *all* of our childhood wasn't terribly abusive. There were fun things we did. We had vacations, we had our horses on the ranch, we had our Friday night dances, and we had each other," Vicki said, tickling the top of Iris' hand. "Or, maybe we are all crazy."

Iris smiled, remembering how Vicki would gently tickle her back when she was very young, to put her to sleep. She would say she was practicing the piano on her back.

The bill appeared, Mary paid.

"OK. I've been waiting all night to tell you this," Mary said soberly.

Vicki and Iris paid attention.

"I had Hap's DNA analyzed and Dad's DNA analyzed separately."

"And….." Iris pleaded.

"That's what you did with the lock of Dad's hair I gave you?" Vicki asked.

"Yes, and I got a sample of Hap's hair from Karen. Sent them off to a company called 23 And Me." Mary paused. Iris and Vicki held their breath.

"And they are **not** related."

"Well…well…well…" Iris said. "Mystery solved."

In the background, the cowboy pianist announced, "*Closing Time* is one of my Lyle Lovett favorites."

"Mine, too!" Iris yelled, and began to sing along as he played his jazz rendition, "*The night she is a true companion…I shuffle in…….*"

Everyone got up singing in unison and adding serious bills to the singer's tip jar, "*closing time…unplug them people, and send them home, it's closing time.*"

✷  ✷  ✷

Day 4 of the Thunder Valley Farm adventure brought them early in the dewy morning to the far west side of the farm, the other side of Cady Creek. There the water ran clean and deep through an area that looked unlike any other part of the farm.

VF explained.

*If you drive to the far side of Cady Creek—completely opposite to the trestle bridge—you'll find land that is terraced. After taking an agriculture course in high school, I convinced your Grandpa that we needed to terrace the land if we were to grow melons and a lot of other money-making crops, in addition to the corn, oats, and wheat in other fields. I rented the equipment and put in the hard work to terrace the land. Then I planted. The crops did well.*

*Notice where the creek makes a U. The hill above that is the Indian Mound. Take a walk around, but leave the arrowheads if you find any. Our neighbors said the Shoshone tribes left those mounds, but I found out later that they were Comanches, who were descended from Shoshone. The Comanches were fierce warriors, fluent in many languages, usually elegantly dressed, and loved to steal horses. Your Grandpa told me of the time he had to buy back one of his horses from the Comanches. This is where I think there is buried treasure.*

Vicki, Mary and Iris started looking around the creek. "Maybe the treasure is gold in the creek?" Vicki wondered.

"Well, if it's buried treasure, we'll never find it," Mary said. "Remember that Dad said Mr. Hortus was captured by the Comanches and saw bandits bury what he thought was treasure? Well, I tried to contact Mr. Hortus soon after Dad told me that, and he was already too demented to talk with me. When I would ask him a question, he would point upwards and say, 'Kanuna.' That was his Comanche name that meant bull frog. Perhaps it also meant bullshit!"

They hiked up the tall hill to the burial mound and felt a comforting presence. The day was cool, an anomaly for south Texas in the spring. Large cumulus clouds floated in exaggerated alphabet shapes. At the top of the hill, without speaking, they clasped hands, bowed their heads, and spent several minutes in silent respect for and awe of the Comanche Indians buried below. Iris sat down, crossed her legs, closed her eyes and meditated for half an hour. She did not hear the gurgling below her, or the call of the eagle above. She felt a gentle wind, and welcomed a warm, invisible embrace. Finally, she opened her eyes, lifted her arms wide and screamed, "Yes!"

"What?" Mary and Vicki asked.

"I've got it. I know what I must do with this land. Thank you. Thank you for coming with me on this tour, for helping me find what I've got to do." She hugged her sisters. She had work to do. She could clearly see the transition her land was about to undergo.

CHAPTER SIXTEEN:

# *A Dream Come True*

## Christmas Eve, 2016

It took six years for Iris to complete her dream for Thunder Valley Farm. It was nearly a generation since that GBM had killed VF. The Landry Clan had flourished.

Iris' sons Will, Jason and Thad were 48, 46 and 32 years old. Will, a forensic accountant, had a beautiful 22-year-old daughter, Brittany, who attended Stanford to be close to him in California. He had divorced many years before.

Jason, the computer entrepreneur, and his wife who taught French had twin 18-year-olds, LJ and VF. They lived in Austin. The twins were graduating high school next semester. Both hoped to attend UT Austin.

Thad, Iris' youngest, had finished law school and together with his wife who was also a lawyer lived and practiced law in New York. They had three-year-old Misha, a spitting image of grandfather Landry.

Vicki's daughters Jennifer, who was 49, and Jessica, 42, both lived in Austin. Jennifer, an interior designer, was married to a carpenter who specialized in restoring old homes and her 20-year-old daughter, Marilyn, was a costume designer. Jessica was a jewelry designer who swore never to marry, although she had a long-term relationship with her beautiful friend Hope. Celebrities from near and far wore her creations at the Oscars.

Mary was still married to Todd, her dentist husband. Their sons Luke and Larry were 26 and 22. Both were married. Luke had graduated Texas A & M and was a veterinarian outside Houston. He and his wife, a nurse, had three-year-old Mason. Larry, a real estate broker, was recently married to his Australian sweetheart, a farrier, with a little "oops" infant, Monica. They lived in New Zealand.

Joseph lived in DC, where he was getting his doctoral degree and still serving a parish in the city.

The oil lease was key to Iris' accomplishments. Texas gold. No one could have dreamed that this land had oil, but oil was there. Deep down. Buried treasure. It began with a phone call Iris received at her office in New York.

"Miz Landry?" the voice asked, in an almost cartoonish Texas accent.

"Yes?" Iris answered and asked, wondering what in the world could this be about?

"Miz Landry, I'm Chuck Thompson. I own a little oil company here in Houston called Thousand Oaks. Are you the owner of the property in Gonzales County—three hundred acres, used to be owned by VF Landry ne Krejci?"

"Hmmm.. Yes. How in the world did you find me?"

"Wasn't hard. LinkedIn tells all about you....Well, Miz Landry, I'd like to talk with you if you don't mind about some drillin' we're doin' here in that area."

After the eighth call, Iris agreed to meet with Mr. Thompson in Houston.

"I'm goin' down to check on my farm in Flatonia in a couple a weeks, so I'll come see ya." Iris amused herself when she picked up on her native language. She told her New York friends that she was bilingual. "I speak Texan as well as English," she would say.

\* \* \*

The Thousand Oaks Drilling Company was nestled in large oaks and carpet grass on a dead end street in a little community outside Houston called Katy, Texas. Iris was not surprised to see a commercial business with its gaudy sign on a residential street. *That's Houston.* For years she told friends she felt Houston was the armpit of Texas, and this was proof.

Mr. Thompson was prepared for the visit.

"Come on in, Miz Landry," he said, standing outside his office just as she introduced herself to the cute young assistant in his starched button-down shirt who told her all about his studies in animal husbandry at Texas A & M.

"Just call me Chuck," he clasped her hand to shake it and pulled her into his leathery office. An enormous plat map lay on his massive worktable, held at the corners with diamond drill bits. He pointed to it, "Lookey here, Miz Landry, see these plats? There's your land here…" He took a colored map pin and skewered her property. "And beside it is the old Hortus property to the north and the Vala property to the south…"

"Why are you showing me this?"

"You need to see where the action's at. These other properties are drillin' as we speak. It's horizontal drillin.' You know what that means?"

"I think I know what it means, Chuck. I think it means that they're probably getting oil from my land."

"Yessirree. That's what it means. And we want to be fair to you. You own the mineral rights to your place, don' cha?"

"Yes, I do."

"Well, I got to tell you. The drillin' won't stop, but you sure as hell won't see a penny of that oil money if you don't let us lease your property. It'd be a shame, Miz Landry, if you let that money go to waste."

Chuck motioned to her to take a seat. She noticed his MBA diploma on the wall. "So, you graduated magna cum laude from UT Austin with an MBA?"

"Yes, m'aam, hook 'em!"

Iris smiled, "I'm a UT alumn, too."

"Yep, that's what yer LinkedIn profile said. Well, then, you know I'm talkin' straight here. I can show you plats that cover all of Texas. The oil's not gonna die out. We've done our homework on these high sedimentary fields. There's no reason you shouldn't profit from the drillin' in Gonzales County."

"I get your point, Chuck."

"I've drawn up a standard contract. You'll see we are being fair, just ask your neighbors. We have clauses for clean up, for any damage we do to fences, and actually you'll see we usually improve the land where we drill."

Iris was skeptical, but she would talk with the neighbors.

"And I have somethin' for ya, since ya came all the way out 'ere." Chuck handed her a key fob with a polished piece of petrified wood dangling from the lock.

Iris was touched. "How in the world did you know I love petrified wood?"

"Lucky guess. This one's from one of our sites in East Texas. Beautiful stump. We're told it was two hundred million years old. Just a reminder that your land will continue to produce long after you are gone."

"I'll have my attorney take a look at the contract, Chuck, and I will be back in touch."

She found it distasteful to accept oil money, but since she learned that the horizontal drilling would happen whether she agreed to the lease or not, and since the oil company was going to intrude on her land in that way, they should pay for it. Knowing that the royalties would flow to her heirs also helped her agree to the lease.

So, after carefully reading the lease and making amendments to it, which were agreed by both parties, she signed it.

At least the dividends gave her the opportunity to manage the land the way she wanted.

*The treasure. This is what Dad was talking about all along*, she reasoned.

*      *      *

Transformations of the good earth can take generations, or in the case of Iris Landry Cohen, they can move at warp speed. While holding down her job in New York, Iris managed to find land managers and partners to help her realize her vision for Thunder Valley Farm in just six years.

The seventy-five acres on the east side of the farm became Thunder Valley Solar Farm, helping to provide electricity to 2500 homes in the small town of Schulenberg. Another seventy-five acres in the south pasture held Thunder Valley Wind Farm, which provided power to offices and homes throughout a large swath of valley in south Texas.

Since she knew that crop and land use diversification was essential at a time of climate change, she consulted the local ag association for a premium plant to harvest. "Sotol," a fellow named DJ told her. "Sotol can withstand the brutal summer heat, and it conserves its water intake. I'll help you test your soil for he acidity levels to see if it will thrive."

After spending several months testing the soil concentrations in various areas of the farm, and the dye was cast.

She learned that sotol was the up-and-coming alternative to tequila. The sotol plants are a variation of agave. After a few years of experimentation with the plant, she and her sotol partner began to farm sotol on fifty prime sun-drenched acres. By 2016, she had a 51% stake in her distilled spirit brand, Thunder Valley Sotol.

She leased the 20 acres surrounding the big tank and the tank itself to her other business partner, Ned Vala, who grew koshihicari (koshi) sushi rice. There were few distributors other than Iris' partner who knew how to grow this temperamental kind of rice. Ned was a local farmer who came to her with his great idea, and coincidentally was a distant relative by way of her grandmother Bessie Vala Krejci.

Over the past few years her manager at the natural history museum in New York allowed her to spent "winter recess" on a beautiful 80-acre spread on the farm that included the terraced area of Cady Creek. This gave her the time and space to write up her paleontological research for academic journals, and to tend to business at the farm. Miles usually did not join her, at her request. She loved having the solitude of being one with the land. He said the time and distance made their marriage stronger. She agreed.

Her platinum LEED-certified freestone "farmhouse" was built within inches of the discarded 2-story shack her father grew up in. The open-air ranch style home with its bamboo floors featured multiple accessible guest quarters, fireplaces, running water and six compostable toilets.

The day after Thanksgiving, 2016, Iris sent hand written invitations from New York to her children, grandchildren, sisters, brother, in-laws, and their children to come feast and celebrate Christmas at Thunder Valley Farm outside Flatonia.

Everyone except Bits.

Bits was persona non grata at her house.

"No presents," she wrote, just as VF had done, "just bring love, a covered dish or wine, a story about the family and a sense of humor."

*   *   *

Christmas at Thunder Valley Farm was perfect. A norther blew in the day before, making it a chilly 60 degrees. Faery lights illuminated live cedar Christmas trees lining the entry to the farmhouse, and freshly harvested mistletoe hung above the doorway, encouraging hugs and kisses for each person who entered. Miles sat at his expansive keyboard he had brought along, and played Christmas music from his favorite songbook.

"The Jews knew how to write Christmas. And I can say that with pride as one of the tribe," he said gleefully, as Iris handed him a glass of wine and kissed him on the forehead.

The front of the house was wrapped like a Christmas gift with fresh greenery around the pillars accented with wide red ribbon and bows.

Inside the house, ruby red poinsettias in their gold baskets filled the hallway and outlined the steps to the sunken dining area.

Twenty-seven family members showed up—four siblings, one spouse, a partner, widowed sister-in-law, seven grown grandchildren with six spouses and seven great grandchildren. Iris drew up a family tree and printed it on the back of the menu, placed at each seat so everyone could get to know each other better. After all, they were dispersed around the United States and New Zealand. All of the cousins got along well and were always glad to see each other and listen to stories about the ranch and the farm.

Bits, who had no children, still lived at the ranch outside of Austin, in an even larger hacienda than her original home. Long ago, she had alienated every one of her siblings by stealing Silvercreek Ranch property and selling it, creating her mini empire of ranchettes. It was common knowledge that she dare not show her face. Everyone knew she was not invited, or welcomed.

The family tree diagram looked like this:

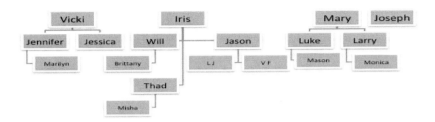

The attention to detail was reminiscent of the historic days of the O-Bar. Tables were set with Comanche-style earthenware. Nameplates were holy card replicas with pictures of saints and the person's name on the back. Tables and chairs had been hewn from downed old oaks on the property. Silver dollars were placed beneath each plate, just like VF had done at the ranch, and his mother before him right there on the farm.

The youngest grandchildren (who were VF and Virginia's great grand-children) jockeyed for seats at their table while the infant Monica dosed in her car seat.

The menu was organic and local: fresh game hens, dressing made with fresh sourdough bread, local eggs, and fresh herbs, garden vegetables of cabbage, broccoli, sweet potatoes, and a large arugula salad with Thunder Valley pecans and tangelos. Only the fresh tamales were not local—Mary brought them from Austin.

"My favorite," Iris gushed, as she hugged Mary, and accepted the large platter of pork and cheese tamales.

Dessert was Grandma Krejci's Czech recipes: poppy seed kolaches, poppy seed cake, VF's favorite, pecan and peach pies. An enormous bowl of hazelnuts sat on the fireplace mantle.

Iris wore VF's old "Bah, humbug" Christmas stocking hat as she brought out a large Top 10 chart with nine questions and set it up on an easel.

"Something to chew on," Vicki chimed in, referring to the Top 10 as everyone gathered in the large dining room with massive skylights.

Some sat quietly while others murmured or giggled.

Father Joe stood and offered the blessing. "In the name of the Father, the Son, and the Holy Spirit. Dear Lord, we thank You for this feast and we ask Your blessing upon these hyperactive children and soon to be stuffed adults that we may all learn the meaning of Your words, 'Love one another as you love yourself.' May we learn to love ourselves and treat each other with dignity and kindness all the days of our lives."

Everyone said "Amen" in unison.

"In the name of the Father, the Son, and the Holy Spirit." Father Joe ended the prayer.

Father Joe no longer stuttered in front of family. Sometime after Virginia's funeral, the stuttering ceased. Later he confided in Mary that he had found his true love. At age fifty-five he was getting another degree, a Ph.D. in anthropology. He wanted to teach at a Jesuit college. "Hopefully Georgetown," he told Mary.

"In DC?" Mary asked.

"Yes, I love it in DC," Joe answered, big smile on his face.

He continued, "I always wondered why I loved comic books when I was a kid. Now I know—comics are really an anthropological study. You read about different cultures and people. They are abbreviated, yes, like graphic novels but they are anthropological nonetheless. So, now, I get to really slice and dice the analogies."

Now, he was so much more confident than before he began his doctoral studies. He sat, unfolded his napkin and began the conversation. "Mare, how's the Pony Camp?"

"Joe, it's an equine assisted therapy center for people with learning disabilities." She laughed. "It's going great guns!"

She paused, enjoying a bite of farm fresh salad. "Did you know I opened the Silvercreek Dispute Resolution Center?"

"I didn't. I need to send some of my former parishioners there!"

"I housed it in the fortress, after the renovations. I built more bedrooms, baths, a larger kitchen. It holds up to 30 people. We've had a lot of traffic in just a few months."

"I'll have to come see it one of these days. By the way, congratulations Justice Landry on your election to the Texas Supreme Court! And how's your better half? Did you get him to vote for you?" Joe asked, referring of course to her husband, Todd.

"Thank you. Thank you. I think he did cross the line and vote for me. He had an emergency dental surgery to take care of. He's good. He's thinking of specializing in elder dental care, so he's taking courses in that. He'll be here tomorrow and you two can chat, if he doesn't arrive sooner. And...how are your studies going?"

"I'm defending my thesis in January," Joe replied. "I'm very excited about being finished. I've found a thrilling subject within anthropological medicine."

"Is this since you worked in Mozambique?"

"Yes, Mozambique and Zimbabwe."

"What's your thesis?" Mary asked.

"It's about HIV and altering anthropological habits of the males of Mozambique."

"Really? I had no idea you were interested in HIV."

"Well, the priesthood brings a lot of trials and tribulations to the forefront, Mary. One learns things one never imagined when one is in the religious order."

"I'll bet," Mary said as she raised an eyebrow, thinking about one of her court cases involving a young beautiful parishioner and her confessor.

Vicki's daughter, Jessica, sat beside Mary and thought it time to change the subject. "Mary, have you seen my mom's wildflower farm?"

"I saw it last week, Jess! It's gorgeous! Forty acres of beautifully cultivated Texas wildflowers. She said she just got the Whole Foods concession for Central Texas. I'm so glad she decided to do something with that part of her land. Just makes sense. It is the most fertile piece of the property—Dad had a huge vegetable garden there."

Jessica motioned to the nosegays at the table. "All these Indian paintbrush bouquets are from her greenhouses. After last summer's intense heat wilted the crops, she built state-of-the-art greenhouses, using the topsoil from that pasture. Now she grows year-round."

Jason, Iris' middle son, turned to Jennifer. "Driving down to the farm today I kept thinking about how Granddad used to show us how to string fencing on the ranch."

"Uh huh… he held the barbed wire with his teeth and would pull it!" Jennifer smiled broadly.

"Yeah, the Paul Bunyan method," Jason said, laughing hard and loud, clapping Jennifer on the shoulder. "He never had a cavity!"

The cousins remembered a lot of their time with their grandfather.

"He was larger than life," Will gestured as he overheard his brother, "I still think about the time out at the ranch when I was about 4 or 5 and he gave me this big metal pail and told me to fill it with stones around the fortress. So I filled it with all these pebbles. Took me about an hour in the hot sun, dragging the damned pail all over the yard."

"I was there," Jason began to laugh, "and he took the pail, emptied it and then gave it to me to fill. Told me there might be gold in the rocks so I should examine each one carefully. Oh! I did think those sparkles might be gold—I didn't know it was fool's gold! So, I picked up where you left off, Will, carefully picking up the stones, examining each one, spending hours on my task. Much later in life I realized this was his way of babysitting."

Everyone laughed, thinking of their own stories about VF.

Vicki asked anyone who would listen, "Did you hear Fred's stories about your granddad?"

"Who's Fred?" a chorus asked.

"Fred was his best friend from first grade throughout his life. He told great stories about himself and other kids, including your great granddad, who went to the 2-room school where Fred's mother and father, Mr. and Mrs. Wiseman, taught. It was called 'Scott's School,' located about three miles from this farm, and it was there that granddad Landry learned to speak English, learned how to argue cases, learned how to care for his health and well being, and learned to believe in himself," Vicki answered.

"What do you mean he learned to argue cases?" LJ asked.

"Mr. Wiseman had been the county justice of the peace before he taught school, and he held court once a month to teach the kids what plaintiffs, defendants, witnesses and a jury of one's peers meant. Want to hear about one that your granddad was a defendant in?"

"Sure!" everyone said at the same time.

"Ok." Vicki looked at the youngest children, "Your great granddad had broken another kid's pencil. His testimony was that the other kid had broken his first. VF pleaded not guilty, and he ended up sawing wood—the punishment, because he was found guilty. To his dying day he contended that he was a victim of a miscarriage of justice. However, his sentence was handed down by a jury of his peers—his classmates."

"What other stories did Fred tell?" Mason asked.

"He told us about the leghorn chickens they kept for eggs. And the turkeys. They raised turkeys at the school. Once a big chicken snake tried to swallow a turkey. He gulped down the turkey's head and killed the turkey, but he couldn't swallow that big bird. Also, there were copperhead snakes that would bite Fred's family's rat terrier dogs every now and then. The bite would swell the head of the dogs horribly, but they didn't die."

Food continued to be passed around the table.

"Do you remember that time granddad killed the rattlesnake in the middle of the back pasture on the ranch?" Jason asked.

Thad, Iris' other son, nodded. "Shit! Gives me chills thinking about it. That was the biggest rattler I've ever seen—must have been eight feet long...."

"Then he cut off the rattlers to show everyone, putting them in the bottle of formaldehyde. I was only about four or five years old then—just a little older than you, Misha," he said to his son across the room. It made an impression," That shuddered.

"And he strung the damned snake sans rattles on the fence at the entrance to the ranch," Jason said.

"Yeah, something like the Romans did with their traitors!"

The grandchildren giggled. They had no clue what their daddies and uncles were talking about, but it sounded exciting.

As food was consumed, there was the usual, "this is delicious," and "pass the dressing and gravy, please." The activity around the table increased by the fuel and drink, dialing up the volume in the room. Vicki, being the boss, wanted everyone to focus on the stories of VF.

"So, does anyone remember the story about Dad and Trigger?" she asked. "It's such a great tale. Kids, ya wanna hear this?"

All the kids looked at her in anticipation. "YAAA."

"OK. This happened nearly fifty years ago on Silvercreek Ranch. It's a true story. Trigger, your great granddad's prize Angus bull, was being bullish—he wasn't going to move into the adjoining pasture to join the cows."

Vicki was talking in her most animated voice—loud and a bit shrill—while she stood and recreated the drama.

"Whoa…whoa…whoa…," Iris interrupted. "I know remember this day! It was Jo Jo, not Trigger."

"I stand corrected. Jo Jo. And to continue…

"'Come on, Jo Jo' VF ordered, 'don't you want to join the girls? …. Let's go,' he stretched one arm straight and motioned with a gloved hand for mighty Jo Jo to move into the pasture with the opened gate.

"Both bull and VF stood their ground.

"He yelled, 'Move, Jo Jo.' And waved his arms.

"Jo Jo stood there, unmoving. Staring at VF.

"VF walked away, and then picked up the largest, heaviest log he could find with one hand.

"'Damn you, Jo Jo. I said 'MOVE!'

"There was a heavy thud as VF hit the bull right between the eyes with that enormous piece of wood.

"Immediately, Jo Jo fell—legs splayed in four directions.

"Dead.

"All of us stood, mouths open, shocked. Even your great granddad was stunned."

The children giggled, some of them pantomiming hitting a bull over the head and twitching.

"I remember," Iris said suddenly, "saying to Dad, 'That was your best bull.'"

'And now he'll be our best steaks,' Dad said."

"Yeah…" Will, Iris' oldest, mused, "I'm sure he hooked that damned bull up to his tractor and dragged its ass to Johnson City for processing."

Will, Thad, Jennifer, Jessica and Jason looked at each other and laughed heartily.

"He was so strong and fearless, with energy like a teenager," Jessica said, smiling brightly. She recalled a series of mental snapshots of her grandfather on Silvercreek Ranch. Years ago on his horse in the back pasture. Pulling up enormous turnips in the vegetable garden. Showing her how to crack pecans with a rock. Giving her a thimble full of his homemade mustang grape wine. And the snakes.

"He even showed us how to kill a coral snake," she said, while the family grew still. "He said it was important to chop its head off. But first, you had to be sure it was a coral snake. Red and yeller kill a feller."

"Red and black, venom lack," Jason chimed in.

"Once when we saw one, he got a hoe, ran over to the snake, and chopped off its head," Jessica continued, as the little kids grimaced.

Jennifer jumped in. "Remember those black racing snakes? Granddad used to run over them when he saw one on the road."

"OK, everyone, this is getting a little icky," Joseph said as he shuddered.

As the plates were cleared Vicki called for everyone to have a seat. "Iris has something to say before dessert."

"Thanks, Vicki." Iris was happier than she had been for the past twenty-two years. "We have some toasts, and I'd like to start with Karen."

Hap's widow stood and raised her glass. "I just want to say that if Hap was here, God love him, he would tell you, each and every one of you, that *yew look mawvelous.* Just remember, it's not how you feel, it's how you look, and *yew look mawvelous.*" Everyone laughed gently.

Karen's eyes welled with tears, her voice more somber. "He would also tell you how much he loves you. I've read letters he wrote when he was in the Navy. He loved his little brothers—Joe and Richard—so much. He'd say 'I can't wait to come home and see how much they've grown. I have some presents for them.' Because I feel his presence here among you all, he and I thank Iris for making this day possible."

Everyone in unison said, "Here. Here." And sipped their appropriate sparkling water or wine.

"And now, Vicki," Iris announced.

Vicki raised her glass and cleared her throat. "I'd like to toast Richard. Richard, my dear brother, may the road rise up to meet you. May the wind always be at your back. May the sun shine warm upon your face, and rains fall soft upon your fields. May God bless you and keep you."

"That was Dad's favorite," Mary noted.

Again, everyone said "Here. Here." And sipped.

"Mary?" Iris motioned as if moving the trains along.

Mary stood, and raised her glass. "I'd like to toast to our mom, Virginia Williams Landry."

Everyone groaned.

"Now now. She loved to laugh and she lived for her children. Truth be told she could be horribly abusive. Let's just let facts be facts. Bless her heart. But everyone deserves her place in that eternal space. May she feel peace and love in her blessed heaven above."

All said "Here. Here."

As people sipped, there was a quiet echo. And then a polite stillness.

Iris stood. "And finally, as we have dessert, I'd like instead of a toast to Dad, and your granddad, and great granddad Colonel VF Landry," Iris looked lovingly at the children, "that we have our usual Top 10 Quiz in his honor."

Everyone raised their glasses. "Here. Here." And sipped.

Iris added, "I have a little book about him for each of the great grand-children, and Luke wrote the introduction."

Luke, Mary's oldest, saw this was his cue. He stood to read. "I didn't think I'd feel so shy about this, especially since I never really knew Granddad Landry. I was just four, a year older than my son, Mason, is now, when he died. But I've learned a lot about him, so I wrote something," he smiled softly, his hands slightly shaking. The room grew calm.

"Here's an excerpt that Iris wanted me to read…OK…here goes:

*What this book tells you is how committed Colonel Landry was to his faith, his family, his country, and the land. If you find even a smidgeon of DNA begging you to grow something, or smiling when you've worked yourself into a sweat, or feeling warmth and love in a church pew, or holding dear the hand of your mother, father, sister or brother, or tearing up when you sing My Country 'Tis of Thee, you may be feeling the glow of your great grandfather Landry smiling within the universe."*

Luke smiled, set aside the page, and saw that his mother's eyes were welling with tears. He walked over to Mary, knelt and hugged her.

Iris and Jason handed out the books to the great grandchildren and/or their parents. One of the great grandchildren, Misha, three years old, giggled as he looked at what seemed to be ancient pictures of his ancestors. "Who's this old man?" he said, pointing to VF in an old photograph.

Thad, his father, said, "The man on that tractor is your great-grandfather."

"OK kids and children! Are you ready?" Iris walked around the table and stood beside the poster. It read:

1. Trump's hair

2. Where are the Democrats?

3. Senator McCain

4. Should sugar drinks be banned?

5. Liars and Cheaters

6. Super Bowl bets already

7. Sean Spicer

8. Healthcare in the USA

9. What are you doing to make this a better world?

"Let's get started. It's gonna be a wild and woolly new year with our newly elected creepy president. Who takes topic #1?" Iris asked.

"Who wants pie? Cake? Kolaches?" Vicki cried out as she and Father Joe began to serve dessert while the children and adults started their lively discussion on each topic.

"Me!" a voice yelled out loud and clear above the prattle.

## "Moi! I...want...pie."

Everyone turned to look at the landing above the large dining room towards the sound of the foreign voice. Towards the open front door, as wind whipped around the intruder.

Bits stood on the top step looking regal in the Russian sable she had once given Virginia.

Holding a bottle of her Silvercreek wine, she raised her arms wide and shouted "Merry Christmas, ya'll!" to the surprised gathering.

"What the hell?" Will asked.

"I'd like to start the discussion, too" Bits yelled, Manolo Blahnik heels planted on the steps.

Iris walked angrily towards her and stood her ground. "You are not invited to participate in this discussion, nor are you invited to have pie."

The vibe in the room was electric. It was time to do something, to stop the madness. Stop the politeness. To unleash the buried anger.

Vicki held her pie server like a knife and walked towards Bits. "Go home, Bits."

Then Mary got up and started walking towards Bits, moving her hands and arms as if brushing her away. "Please leave."

Then everyone stood, walking towards her as Bits' expression turned from conqueror to feared captive.

At once, they all yelled, "Go home, Bitch, go home!"

Bits stood still, not knowing what to do.

"Go home, Bitch, go home!" They chanted, louder, and in unison.

"Go home, Bitch, go home!"

A generation of anger seethed.

"Go home, Bitch, go home!"

Bits' eyes grew large as she absorbed the taunts. Then, just as surprisingly as she appeared, she turned and raced to her Mercedes SUV, started the engine and disappeared into the deep Texas night.

There was a group gasp and then a long exhale before everyone laughed and applauded simultaneously.

Iris asked everyone to sit again.

"*That's* what we call rich white trash," Joseph announced, knowing that he would be confessing his sins later that week.

Suddenly, the sound of sirens filled the air.

"Whaaaa…?" the boys asked. The sound grew closer and louder.

"Not to worry," Iris answered. "I half expected Bits to show up so I let my friend Sheriff Frank alert the Rangers. Evidently there's a warrant for her arrest."

"From the wine scandal?" Vicki asked.

"You'd think, right? No, it turns out she's been abusing cats and her neighbors turned her in. They found ten dead cats in a dumpster, some with their paws slit open…." Parents Thad and Luke ran to their toddlers and put their hands over their ears.

Iris continued, "and some with missing paws…."

Everyone gave a disgusted "ugh…." And imagined the scene down by the cattle guard to Thunder Valley Farm, where Bits was being arrested on Christmas Eve.

"And with that….what *do* we think of Trump's hair?" Iris asked, smiling broadly and continuing with the political discussion, just as VF would have done.

Jason began, "It's a wig."

"No, it's a metaphor," Luke insisted.

"For what?" Joseph asked, as he served pie.

"For what he's hiding. He's hiding his insecurities by covering his head with strings of bleached hair." Luke loved to dissect people's behavior.

"I get your point. Perhaps it's a metaphor for the big lie," Joseph said.

"What big lie?" Jennifer asked.

"Liar, liar, pants on fire," little Mason chimed in. Mason was Luke's three-year-old son.

"I'll take 'Where are the Democrats,'" Thad, Iris's son, who lived in NY, announced.

"OK, Thad, where are the Democrats?" Iris asked with a smile.

"They're here, in Texas, coming out of hiding, and they're moving here from the blue states. I think Texas is going to see a resurgence of Democrats. I think the Republican stronghold on Texas will not last. You'll see…"

"One can only hope," Vicki interrupted, "after what has happened to Lloyd Doggett. He used to be the Congressman from Austin—Jake's old job [very few people at the table remembered Congressman Jake Pickle, VF's good friend from his college days]. They gerrymandered his district and shoved him way the hell over to the far eastern corners of Austin and the surrounding counties over nearly to San Antonio."

"I'll take Senator McCain," Will announced. Will was a Navy vet. "I think he's gonna fight enormous battles with Trump the liar. McCain will live to regret that he took on failin' Palin as his running mate."

"McCain will stand up to him," Jennifer, Vicki's oldest daughter, who also served in the Navy, said. "McCain is a helluva lot stronger than anyone thinks. He should have been a democrat. I want to know what people think of Sean Spicer."

"Who?" Larry, Mary's son, asked.

"He's a Trump truth spinner. Trump's not even in the White House and he's already spinning," Jessica, Vicki's youngest daughter, said. "I don't trust 'em."

"OK, I think we've covered the liars and cheaters. What about sugar drinks—anyone think they should be banned?" Iris asked.

"I've been thinking about sugar," Joe answered. "Sugar is a demon."

"Interesting choice of words," Vicki motioned to Mary.

The youngest children were now getting up from the kids' table and running around.

"Sugar messes with your mind," Joe continued. "I think Bloomberg is right on wanting to ban large amounts of sugared sodas. We all need to eat less sugar. I have this theory about Virginia and sugar." Joe now referred to his mother as Virginia when he talked about her.

"What's that, Joe?" Iris asked.

"I believe that some people are allergic to sugar in that sugar does something to the chemistry of the brain for some people, deregulating their reasoning and hormones, creating a cocktail of confusion and anger."

The room was listening.

"So, you contend that Mom's dysfunction came from her ingesting large amounts of sugar?" Iris continued.

"If you think about the times she had those rages and correlate them with what she was eating, I think it would lead you to wonder," Joe said.

"It's a theory, Joe, but it seems that Mom was **always** making pies, especially those with a lot of corn syrup, and.."

"Fudge with a lot of sugar…" Vicki added.

"And pecan pralines which are all sugar," Will noted. "They were my favorite!"

"And, it did seem she was addicted to the stuff," Joe added.

"So, her sugar addiction was in place of an alcohol addiction, but had the effect of a mean alcoholic?" Iris asked.

"Yes, I think it did."

"Food for thought. You should pursue that idea, Joe, in your post graduate studies."

"Think I will."

"Hmmmmm…does that cover 'Healthcare in the USA?'" Iris asked everyone?

VF, 18, looked around the table, "I'm ready to talk about what I'm doing to make this world a better place."

Jason, his father, said proudly, "Tell us, VF."

"Well, first, we made Bits leave."

Everyone laughed. Some yelled and clapped.

"And this year, I've registered to vote!" he continued.

"And so have I," his brother, LJ said.

"That will surely help the world," Mary said.

"I think making the world a better place begins within," Will said solemnly. "I've begun to practice meditation."

"Is that the mindfulness stuff you've been talking about?" asked his younger cousin Luke.

"Yep."

"So, is that the LaLa land mindful meditation?" Luke sniffed.

"Just because I live in LA does not mean it's any less significant than anywhere else Mr. 'Keep Austin Weird.'"

"Touché," Luke said, "but I now live in Houston."

"So, what's the Houston motto? Keep it butt ugly?"

Luke laughed, "I think the jury's still out on the Houston motto."

Vicki wanted the last word.

"To make this world a better place, I'm planting more wildflowers. More cultivars."

"In your garden at the ranch?" Joe asked.

"Uh huh. I think we should all plant something in the New Year—whether it's in an outdoor garden or an indoor garden. Let's all use the land wherever we can to grow something beautiful and/or delicious."

And so, they did. Iris provided each family member with packets of seeds from her and Vicki's gardens as a Christmas present to them.

Written on each packet's flip side was this reminder: *Remember that some day you too will have your own land—whether it is Silvercreek Ranch land or Thunder Valley farmland. The land, and its history, will always be part of you. Treasure it, and pass it on.*

There were wildflower seeds, herb seeds, and vegetable seeds. Some of the seeds came from Vicki's wildflower business, and some from Iris' herbs and vegetables. Each packet included instructions for the area in which they lived.

Each person took the seeds and planted them in the New Year, some with their parents' help, and watched them grow.

There were varieties of bluebonnets, Indian paintbrush, cornflowers, buttercups, cherry tomatoes, zucchini, poblaño peppers, rosemary, basil and chives grown in different US planting zones.

The following spring, the wildflowers, herbs, and vegetables flourished in each garden. Whenever one of the Landry tribe looked at or smelled the fruits of their labor, it made them feel a deep connection to their land and to Colonel Landry. His dream come true.

# Glossary of Texas Names and Terms

| | |
|---|---|
| Ann Richards | Governor of Texas 1991-1995, mother of Cecile Richards, former president of Planned Parenthood Federation. |
| Barbed Wire | A type of galvanized steel wire fencing with sharp barbs 6" apart used to divide property. |
| Bless Her Heart | What a bitch. |
| Bluebonnets | Texas state flower (see cover), from the lupine plant family, which bloom prodigiously along the highways in early spring and are used as a backdrop for family photos. |
| Buttercups | Texas wildflower from the Acanthus plant family, also known as pink evening primrose. |
| Caliche | A kind of sedimentary rock with calcium carbonate used for roads in Texas. |
| Carpetgrass | Ground cover on most Texas lawns. Very coarse, heavy grass that covers nicely, and looks like a flat-top haircut when mowed. |
| Covered dish | Potluck supper. |
| Dewberries | Texas Blackberries. |
| Dinner | Lunch. |

| | |
|---|---|
| Drippin' | Short for Dripping Springs, Texas. |
| Eddie Chiles | Texas oilman who ran for governor in the '80's; owned the Texas Rangers. |
| Fire ants | Or *solenopsis invicta*, Texas fire ants are large red ants that leave pustules when they sting. They have been known to kill small animals. |
| Flying roaches | Texas-size cockroaches that fly. |
| Freestone | White stone used for its impermeability. |
| H-E-B | One of the largest grocery story chains in Texas. Owned by the Butt family. |
| Huisache | A ground cover. Nearly impossible to kill. |
| Jeez ah Peat | Good God! |
| Kolache | Pronounced koh-lah-chee. A Czech roll made of sweet bread usually with fruit or nut filling. |
| Mesquite | An invasive, pervasive thorny bush. |
| Mockingbird | Texas State bird. |
| Molly Ivins | Writer, humorist, political commentator, newspaper columnist, born in California, raised in Texas, graduated Smith College and Columbia University Graduate College of Journalism. |
| Mush | Romance. |
| Nekkid | Naked. |
| Norther | A Texas cold front. |
| Ranchette | A faux ranch. Usually, 1-6 acres of land from a former ranch. |
| Rattlers | Diamondback rattlesnakes. Poisonous, deadly Texas snakes. Also, the tail end portion of the snake that makes a rattling noise to alert an intruder. |

| | |
|---|---|
| Seersucker | A cotton fabric worn in Texas mostly in the summer, characterized by its embossed stripes. |
| Shugah | Usually hugs and kisses. |
| Sticker burrs | Thorny, pea-size, solid pod that penetrates skin and clothes. |
| Sugar Daddy | Someone, usually a man, who provides money for sex. |
| Texas Gold | Oil, also referred to as black gold. |
| Ticks | Larger than most ticks, Texas ticks suck blood of humans and animals alike and bloat. One must remove their sucker to stop the itch. |
| Water moccasin | Texas water snake, very prevalent and poisonous. |
| Ya'll | You all, or just you. |
| Yew | Texan for you. |

# Acknowledgements

Thank you Vince and Virginia Taylor, my late father and mother, for giving me so much to write about, and to Polly Pridgeon, my sixth grade teacher, who was convinced I could and should write.

Thank you Murray Cantor for putting up with my ups and downs over twenty-five years of writing this book and forty years of marriage.

I am so appreciative of Vanessa Diffenbaugh, my Harvard Extension creative writing teacher and author of best selling novels including *The Language of Flowers*, and of the class members who encouraged me to publish this book, especially Janet C. Daniels. Thank you to Jan Lehman, who shockingly told me three decades ago that I was one among many rich white trash Austinites.

Thank you Jenn Gilpatrick, Diane McClosky, and Ilene Hawk for taking this trip with me as you cater to my vanity and my aches and pains.

My consulting editors David Groff, Emily Murdock Baker, Terry Schexnayder and Nancy Nicholas helped bring this to life.

Thank you to my sisters Mary E. Taylor Henderson and Vicki Taylor, and to my Acadia hiking buddy and oldest son John Williams who heard, read parts of, and suggested ideas for this book. I also thank my sons Jeff Williams and Michael Cantor and their wives Dr. Elisabeth Morray and Saroj Fleming, M.D. for their encouragement.

My love for my sister Veronika Taylor together with my grandchildren Leo Orion Cantor, Maxim Alexander Cantor, Alec Parker Williams, Isabelle Grace Williams, Julien Taylor Williams, Nicholas Connor Williams, Heather

Williams, John Matthew Williams, Reagan Elizabeth Williams, Shannon Williams, and Josh Williams is boundless.

Thank you so much to friends who encouraged me: Holly Hale, Steven Biondilillo, Donald Hannan III, Chris Sizemore, Anne Hubbard, and Karen Schwartz.

I am particularly grateful to Jaye Smith, who challenged me to self publish, and for the widow of my brother Hap who allowed me to play with his lyrics.